Praise for the No
Caitlín R. Kier

The Drowning

"With *The Drowning Girl*, Caitlín R. Kiernan moves firmly into the new vanguard, still being formed, of our best and most artful authors of the gothic and fantastic—those capable of writing fiction of deep moral and artistic seriousness. This subtle, dark, in-folded novel, through which flickers a weird insistent genius, is like nothing I've ever read before. *The Drowning Girl* is a stunning work of literature, and if I may be so blunt, Caitlín R. Kiernan's masterpiece."

—Peter Straub

"In this novel, Caitlín R. Kiernan turns the ghost story inside out and transforms it. This is a story about how stories are told, about what they reveal and what they hide, but is no less intense or suspenseful because of that. It's a tale of real and unreal hauntings that quickly takes you down deep and only slowly brings you up for air."

—Brian Evanson, author of *Immobility*

"*The Drowning Girl* features all those elements of Caitlín R. Kiernan's writing that readers have come to expect—a prose style of wondrous luminosity, an atmosphere of languorous melancholy, and an inexplicable mixture of aching beauty and clutching terror. It is one of those very few novels that one wishes would never end."

—S. T. Joshi, author of *I Am Providence: The Life and Times of H. P. Lovecraft*

"This is a masterpiece. It deserves to be read in and out of genre for a long, long time." —Elizabeth Bear, author of *Range of Ghosts*

"Kiernan pins out the traditional memoir on her worktable and metamorphoses it into something wholly different and achingly familiar, more alien, more difficult, more beautiful, and more true."

—Catherynne M. Valente, *New York Times* bestselling author of *The Girl Who Circumnavigated Fairyland in a Ship of Her Own Making*

continued . . .

"Caitlín Keirnan is a master of dark fantasy and this may be her finest work. Incisive, beautiful, and as perfectly crafted as a puzzle box, *The Drowning Girl* took my breath away."

—Holly Black, *New York Times* bestselling author of *Black Heart*

"A beautifully written, startlingly original novel that rings the changes upon classics by the likes of Shirley Jackson, H. P. Lovecraft, and Peter Straub, *The Drowning Girl* brings Caitlín Kiernan to the front ranks of contemporary dark fiction. Chilling and unforgettable, with a narrator whose voice will linger in your head long after midnight."

—Elizabeth Hand, author of *Available Dark*

The Red Tree

NOMINATED FOR THE SHIRLEY JACKSON AWARD

NOMINATED FOR THE WORLD FANTASY AWARD

"You may find your mind returning frequently to this tale, attempting to reconcile the irreconcilable, and you may find yourself, like me, bowing to Kiernan's artistry, and her ability to create Mystery. This is her most personal, ambitious, and accomplished work yet." —*Locus*

"Kiernan's chiller provides a strange and vastly compelling take on a New England haunting, and captures its spirit unnervingly well. Kiernan's still-developing talent makes this gloriously atmospheric tale a fabulous piece of work." —*Booklist*

Daughter of Hounds

"Kiernan's handling of underworld figures is impressive, and this book proves she's as adept at writing crime as she is dark fantasy . . . a thrilling page-turner that also features the depth, complexity, and unflinching willingness to contemplate the dark that we've come to expect from her books." —*Locus*

"A hell-raising dark fantasy replete with ghouls, changelings, and eerie intimations of a macabre otherworld. . . . The complex plot springs abundant surprises . . . on its juggernaut roll to a memorable finale . . . an effective mix of atmosphere and action."

—*Publishers Weekly*

Murder of Angels

"I love a book like this that happily blends genres, highlighting the best from each, but delivering them in new configurations. . . . Lyrical and earthy, *Murder of Angels* is that rare book that gets everything right."
—Charles de Lint

"[Kiernan's] punk-rock prose, and the brutally realistic portrayal of addiction and mental illness, makes *Angels* fly."
—*Entertainment Weekly* (A-)

Low Red Moon

"*Low Red Moon* fully unleashes the hounds of horror, and the read is eerie and breathtaking. . . . The familiar caveat 'not for the faint of heart' is appropriate here—the novel is one of sustained dread punctuated by explosions of unmitigated terror." —*Irish Literary Review*

Threshold

WINNER OF THE INTERNATIONAL HORROR GUILD AWARD FOR BEST NOVEL

"*Threshold* is a bonfire proclaiming Caitlín Kiernan's elevated position in the annals of contemporary literature. It is an exceptional novel you mustn't miss. Highly recommended." —*Cemetery Dance*

Silk

WINNER OF THE INTERNATIONAL HORROR GUILD AWARD FOR BEST FIRST NOVEL

FINALIST FOR THE BRAM STOKER AWARD FOR BEST FIRST NOVEL

NOMINATED FOR THE BRITISH FANTASY AWARD

"A remarkable novel." —Neil Gaiman

"A daring vision and an extraordinary achievement." —Clive Barker

"Caitlín R. Kiernan writes like a Gothic cathedral on fire."
—Poppy Z. Brite

BOOKS BY CAITLÍN R. KIERNAN

Novels

Silk
Threshold
Low Red Moon
Murder of Angels
Daughter of Hounds
The Red Tree
The Drowning Girl: A Memoir

Writing as Kathleen Tierney

Blood Oranges

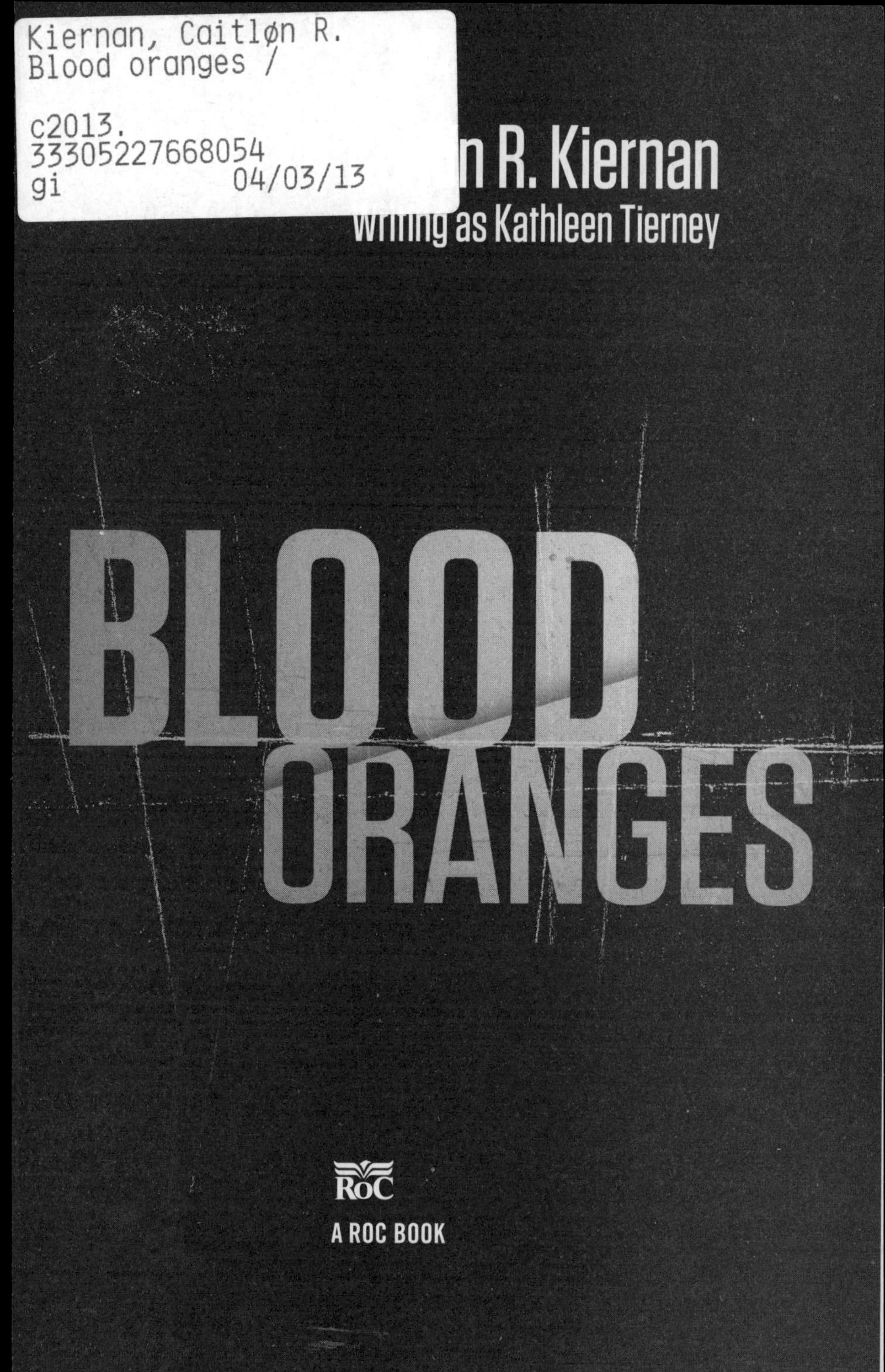
Kiernan, Caitløn R.
Blood oranges /
c2013.
33305227668054
gi 04/03/13
n R. Kiernan
Writing as Kathleen Tierney
BLOOD
ORANGES
RoC
A ROC BOOK

ROC
Published by New American Library, a division of
Penguin Group (USA) Inc., 375 Hudson Street,
New York, New York 10014, USA
Penguin Group (Canada), 90 Eglinton Avenue East, Suite 700, Toronto,
Ontario M4P 2Y3, Canada (a division of Pearson Penguin Canada Inc.)
Penguin Books Ltd., 80 Strand, London WC2R 0RL, England
Penguin Ireland, 25 St. Stephen's Green, Dublin 2,
Ireland (a division of Penguin Books Ltd.)
Penguin Group (Australia), 250 Camberwell Road, Camberwell, Victoria 3124,
Australia (a division of Pearson Australia Group Pty. Ltd.)
Penguin Books India Pvt. Ltd., 11 Community Centre, Panchsheel Park,
New Delhi - 110 017, India
Penguin Group (NZ), 67 Apollo Drive, Rosedale, Auckland 0632,
New Zealand (a division of Pearson New Zealand Ltd.)
Penguin Books (South Africa) (Pty.) Ltd., 24 Sturdee Avenue,
Rosebank, Johannesburg 2196, South Africa

Penguin Books Ltd., Registered Offices:
80 Strand, London WC2R 0RL, England

First published by Roc, an imprint of New American Library,
a division of Penguin Group (USA) Inc.

First Printing, February 2013
10 9 8 7 6 5 4 3 2 1

LIBRARY OF CONGRESS CATALOGING-IN-PUBLICATION DATA
Kiernan, Caitlín R.
Blood oranges / Caitlín R. Kiernan.
p. cm.
ISBN 978-0-451-46501-6 (pbk.)
I. Title.
PS3561.I358B58 2013
813'.54—dc23 2012032442

Set in ITC Galliard
Designed by Sabrina Bowers

Printed in the United States of America

PUBLISHER'S NOTE

This is a work of fiction. Names, characters, places, and incidents either are the product of the author's imagination or are used fictitiously, and any resemblance to actual persons, living or dead, business establishments, events, or locales is entirely coincidental.

The publisher does not have any control over and does not assume any responsibility for author or third-party Web sites or their content.

If your ears, eyes, and sensibilities are easily offended, this book is not for you. If you want a romance novel, this book is not for you. And if it strikes you odd that vampires, werewolves, demons, ghouls, and the people who spend time in their company would be a foulmouthed, unpleasant, unhappy lot, this book is not for you. In fact, if you're the sort who believes books should come with warning labels, this book's not for you. Also, please note: Siobhan Quinn is not a very good writer. Fair notice.

To paraphrase Ursula K. LeGuin, this is me taking back the language of the night. If only for myself.

The Author

You know what the definition of a hero is? It's someone who gets other people killed. You can look it up later.

—ZOË WASHBURNE

Revenge is never a straight line. It's a forest. And like a forest, it's easy to lose your way. . . .

—HATTORI HANZÔ

BLOOD
ORANGES

CHAPTER ONE

THE MATTRESS

First off, taking out monsters absolutely doesn't come with a how-to manual. Fuck that shit you see on *Buffy the Vampire Slayer*. The only "watchers" I've ever had are the cops and such, people who might wonder what the hell I'm up to in the middle of the night, wandering about in various unsavory places. People who might ask inconvenient questions, or see shit they're not supposed to see. So, yeah. No helpful mentor. What I've learned, I taught myself. It's all trial and error in the trenches. And another thing, I've never met anyone else who does this. Not even one. If there's some worldwide network of girls and guys who off demons, they've never bothered to contact me. Near as I know, I'm it. The one and only. Likely, that's not true. Surely other people are crazy enough to do this. Surely other people have idiotic, suicidal vendettas of their own. But I figure none of us lives very long, once we set to work. I sure as hell didn't.

Then again, I'm probably not a model of excellence. That is, if I were going to imagine the ideal monster hunter, she wouldn't have dropped out of school and run away from home at age twelve, and she sure as hell wouldn't be a junky. Yes, I'm a junky. Well, I was. Heroin. I like to tell myself I only started shooting up because of the monsters and the insanity and all, but I'm pretty good at lying to myself, and that's probably just another lie. The truth is, junk feels good. Way better than sex. You hear that, but it's not just hyperbole from the drug dealers. That's the god's honest fuck-you sideways truth. Never yet had an orgasm that could compare to a fix. Want to know about junkies without going to the trouble to become one yourself? Just read William Burroughs, because that shit's gospel.

Okay, so you know I kill monsters, and I'm an addict, and I figure that sets things up for the story of how my life went from being screwed up to being royally fucking *fucked up* in the space of a few hours. Well, to be truthful, in the space of about five minutes, though it did get worse as the night wore on (as you'll see).

If there were a how-to book, *Demon Slaying for Dummies*, or *The Complete Idiot's Guide to Vampire Hunting*, or a Wikipedia entry, or whatever, I think Rule No. 1

would be something like: Do not, under any circumstances, stop in the woods on the night of a full fucking moon and shoot up, when you know the rogue werewolf you've been tracking for a week is probably pretty close by.

That's another thing, okay? In monster movies, people do dumb things, and oftentimes, those dumb things get them killed. Or worse. And I've heard people bitch about it. "Hey, nobody's *that* stupid. He wouldn't do that. She wouldn't do that. I don't buy it." But all those naysayers are wrong, and they're wrong with a big ol' capital W. Wrong. Let's forget my little indiscretion I mentioned above. I've lost count of the people I've seen die at the hands of the nasties because they did something that was just plain stupid. The sort of shit we all like to tell ourselves we're too smart to do. But we ain't. Not you, not me, not anyone. The nasties bank on that, and it pays off.

Some dude hears a thud on the roof of his parked car? He doesn't drive like hell without once looking back. No. He gets out to see what made the thud. Some chick hears the proverbial thump in the night from a dark room? Nine times out of ten, she doesn't go straight to the phone and call 911. Nine times out of ten, she reaches into the room, switches on the light, and gets the last surprise of her life. Or (and this one always gets me) she stands at the threshold and calls out, "Anyone there?" Or . . . let's say you got a couple of inebriated young assholes from Tau Kappa Epsilon out on a dark road, hoping to get some something-something from a couple of drunken little sisters. Let's say they're pulled into a boneyard, because college boys, they have this notion cemeteries make girls all snuggly and easy. So, here they are, copping a feel, sporting hard-ons, and thinking they're about to get lucky when the air starts stinking of rotten meat. And I don't mean just a whiff. I mean *stinking* of the flesh of the dead. So, what do they do? They roll up the windows and get back to business.

You don't believe me?

I don't care.

Point is, the way you *think* folks behave, and the way they really *do*, those two things frequently have very little in common with one another. The prey has a tendency to imagine itself smart enough to outwit the predators. No. Strike that. The prey rarely even bothers to believe there *are* predators. Also, I'm not talking about rapists, murderers, and thieves. I'm talking about *predators.* I'm talking about the creatures lurking around out there with appetites most human beings can't begin to imagine, the ghoulies intent on making a meal of you and yours, or, hell, just intent on torturing someone until they grow bored enough to contrive some especially messy way to finish the job. Ever seen a cat play with a mouse? That's what I mean, only not with cats and not with mice. What I mean makes cats look pretty damn merciful.

Anyway, let's set aside for now how and why it was I started in killing monsters (and *continue* to do so). There will be plenty of time for that later. Let's get back to that warm night two Augusts ago, stalking that werewolf in the woods off the Hartford Pike, just a few miles outside Providence. Just back from the Scituate Reservoir. There's a turnoff for a dirt road, and that's where I cut the engine and left the car. A few days earlier, there'd been a murder about two hundred yards back from the highway. Was in all the local papers and on Channel 6, everywhere. The corpse was discovered nine feet up a white pine, gutted, decapitated, and tucked neatly into the limbs. The cops were on beyond clueless (I have someone on the inside, but that's another story, which gets back to me being a junky), though there was talk of animal tracks at the scene of the murder, and talk of bears, because, you know, Rhode Island is crawling with nine-foot-tall man-eating bears. Everyone knows that, right? But I digress.

It had been a good summer. I had a couple of pretty spectacular takedowns under my belt from June and July alone. Which means I was getting cocky, and sloppy, and, besides, I was either high or strung out about half the time. These are the unfortunate combinations that make for wicked outrageous calamity. The stuff that can turn the hunter into the hunted in the blink of an eye. Blink. You're a hundred and twenty pounds of fucking hamburger. So, there I was, the moon so bright you could have read a newspaper by it. The farther I walked, the harder it was to hear the cars out on Hartford Pike. Now, I'd planned to shoot up when I was done for the night. That's usually how it went back then. I liked to think of it as my just *reward* for fighting the good fight, etc. and etc. But my rig and a dime bag of China White was right there in my army-surplus shoulder bag, buried under the various grisly tools of my trade.

And I stood there a moment, not far from where they'd found the dead woman. There were strips of yellow crime-scene tape lying on the road, and I figured the wind had ripped them loose from somewhere else. There was a sort of hot breeze, and the yellow tape fluttered. I listened to the woods for, I don't know, five or ten minutes, and made one of those stupid scary-movie decisions no one likes to think *real* people make. I *didn't* smell a dog (though the kill had all that trademark werewolf style), and, believe me, the bastards stink. I told myself the perpetrator was probably miles away, and that night I wouldn't be settling any scores, full moon or no full moon. Possibly I was upwind. Whatever. I left the dirt road, went maybe twenty feet into the underbrush, crouched down behind a big oak, and fixed. Simple as that. I was just feeling the rush and untying the rubber hose from around my left bicep when I heard it coming for me through the trees. Coming at me fast and hard, and I knew exactly what I was hearing. Nothing else in the woods of New England makes that sort of noise. That *much* noise. Oh, and, belatedly, I smelled it. And I knew I was absolutely and utterly fucked.

Now, up on the big screen, this is the moment when Our Plucky Young Heroine would do something amazing. She'd grab her crossbow (loaded with silver-tipped bolts, blessed by Father O'Malley), pull off some kung fu moves so slick they'd make Jackie Chan wet himself, and drop the Big Bad Wolf in that *very last second* before the beast can rip out her throat. Then she'd say something witty.

Yeah, right.

Me, I blinked a couple of times, squinting through the haze of junk muddying my head. The werewolf was rushing towards me on all fours, quadrupedal-like—you know, one thing I always wondered about, ever since I set eyes on my first werewolf, is why the hell they're called were*wolves.* Because, trust me, they look about as much like a wolf as Benjamin Franklin looked like Paris Hilton.

Anyway . . . where was I?

Yeah, right. Big silverback werewolf rushing *at* me and the dope rushing *through* me. That moment was, indeed, a dizzying mixture of opiate joy and sheer fucking terror. All I really remember is, in this order, dropping the syringe, stumbling back against the oak, tangling my feet in the shoulder strap of my bag, and managing to scream just once before it was on top of me. That's an awful lot, really, all things considered. Thinking back on it, I don't know what astounds me more, that I remember those details, or that I did anything at all but scream.

Just my douche bag luck, this wasn't one of the scrawny mutts. Lots of them are, the weres, all ribs and mange and that dazzled cast to their eyes that comes from too much moonlight and empty bellies. This was one of the huge sons of bitches, maybe three hundred pounds of slobbering lycanthropic sinew and shiny white teeth barreling nonstop boogie towards me through the trees. Truth is, even if I'd *not* been high, and even if I'd had a couple minutes warning, and even if, say, I'd been holding, say, a Remington 870 12-gauge pump-action mounted on an M16 assault rifle with that sweet underbarrel configuration, even if I'd had that much firepower right there in my hands, all loaded, safety off, and my finger on the trigger, my ass would still have been grass. Sometimes, there's just no sidestepping your well-earned impending doom.

I remember its breath. Pretty much ripe summer roadkill, crossed with whatever you'd find in the Dumpster out behind a Korean restaurant. Then I remember the pain when it tore into me, pain like the holy hand of God grabbing hold, hanging on tight, and sinking "His" grimy, omnipotent fingernails straight into (of all places) my ass.

And then I remember the hissing thing dropping out of the tree onto the werewolf's back and dragging it off me.

After that, the events of that unfortunate August evening by the Scituate Reservoir get more than just a little fuzzy. I don't know whether it was the blinding pain, the very excellent heroin, or acute stress reaction (what you laypersons call "shock")—probably it was the combination of all three—but I fainted. First time ever in my whole life, I fainted dead away.

Okay, not *dead* away, because I do have a scant few hazy memories of being carried from somewhere to somewhere else, and of being in the backseat of an automobile that had that new-car upholstery fragrance. I remember music, too. Roy Orbison singing "Only the Lonely," like maybe when I'd fallen by that oak I'd landed in the second reel of a David Lynch film. After that, nothing, *nada*, *niente*, until I woke up on a filthy mattress in the corner of a filthy basement. I was lying facedown in a cooling puddle of my own drool, and the air around me was dank and smelled just about as bad as a steamy face full of werewolf breath. Not quite exactly, but very almost. More eau de mold, less roadkill, but still. It was plenty enough to make me gag a couple of times. I tried to sit up, but that didn't work out so well, at which point I groaned and lay right back down again. In that same cold pool of my own saliva. At least it wasn't puke. If I had a muscle that didn't hurt, I was unaware of its existence. Cramps, runny nose, sweating buckets, the chills straight to my bones—so it didn't take me long to figure I'd been out six, twelve, maybe as long as twenty-four hours, long enough since my last fix for withdrawal to set in. Oh, and my butt was burning like I'd taken a double barrel of rock salt down there.

"You're awake," someone said. The voice was unmistakably female, but only just barely. Yeah, that doesn't make much sense, *unmistakably* and *only just barely*; you had to be there. The voice was, in fact, only just barely even human. It came from the other end of the mattress, down past my Chucks, and a bit off to my right. With shaking hands, I fumbled for the coffin-handled Bowie knife I kept strapped to my belt pretty much anytime I was wearing pants, but it wasn't there. Big damn surprise. I know.

"If I were you," said that voice, "I'd worry more about saving my strength. You're going to need it." I shot back something brilliant, maybe "Fuck you." Or "Get bent." Then I thought for sure I was going to throw up, and she said, "There's a pail to your left," like she'd read my mind. She hadn't. It doesn't take supernatural powers to see when a junky in the agonies of cold turkey withdrawal—what German junkies call weltschmerz, and don't ask how I know this shit—is about to toss her cookies. I expect my face had gone green as a head of cabbage on Saint Patrick's Day right about then.

"I'm not gonna fucking puke," I barked at her. Okay, yeah. That was just dumb bravado and wishful thinking.

"Yes, you are," she assured me.

"Fine," I muttered. "Let me get there in my own time."

"You're hurting."

Another astute observation.

"Where's my bag?" I asked. "Give me my bag, and I promise you, lady, I won't be hurting anymore."

She didn't answer right away, and I lay there on the mattress shivering and wanting very sincerely not to vomit.

"Perhaps you lost it when you were attacked," she finally said. "Or, perhaps, when I found you, I didn't bother retrieving it, and you'll never see it again."

"Perhaps you could make up your mind and stop jerking me around. There's shit in there I need."

"Drugs. Your needle," she said, just cool as a moose. No, forget that. Ice fucking cold, that voice was so cool. "The spoon, the tourniquet. Why would I give you any of that? Assuming I didn't leave the bag lying there where you dropped it by the tree?"

I gagged again, caught my breath, and managed to whisper, "Because maybe you're not a *total* cunt."

"But maybe I am," she said, and the way she said it, I knew she was grinning ear to ear. "Maybe I'm the worst sort of cunt you've ever had the misfortune to cross paths with, Miss Siobhan Quinn."

Okay, an aside here. Yeah, that's my name, the name my third generation Irish-American, Roman Catholic mom and pop bestowed upon me in a spastic fit of Gaelic pride or whatever. And yeah, it sounds like one of those Young Plucky Vampire Hunters or, worse yet, like the women who write those trashy ParaRom paperbacks you see on the racks at the Stop & Shop or Shaw's. No one, and I mean *no one*, calls me Siobhan. You call me Quinn, which is my last name, or you keep your fucking trap shut.

"So, at least you hung on to my wallet," I said.

"At least I did that, yes. Though, I confess, I knew your name a long time before I read your driver's license and library card."

"Oh, yeah?" I asked. "And how's that?"

"People know your name. You haven't exactly been discreet. We are a fairly close-knit community, but then you might already know that. Yes?"

Which cleared up a few of my just-how-much-shit-am-I-in questions right then and there. I needed to review my options, even though I knew I had diddle jack in that department. Out of the frying pan, into the fire, so you clutch at straws. I tried to relax, willed my limbs to go limp and the ache in my chest and guts to back off a smidge, but I might as well have been hoping for divine intervention or a squad of heavily armed Jesuits to come storming into the basement with fire hoses that spewed holy water. I lay there, panting into the filthy mattress, wondering how long until the vampire grew bored enough and hungry enough to finish me off. I didn't bother to inquire why she'd taken on a werewolf to "save" me. These fuckers, they got their own unfathomable reasons, and most times trying to make sense of it just gives me a headache. Which I already had, thank you very much.

"You killed the werewolf?" I asked, because there was clearly nothing to be gained from more questions about the fate of my bag and the life-giving stash therein. "You took it out."

"It's dead," she replied, only those two words and no more, as if that said everything there was worth saying.

"Something personal?" I pressed.

"I hate dogs," she said.

I laughed. Must have been the shittiest excuse for a laugh in the whole history of the whole wide world, and I gagged a few more times before I could speak again. "So, least we got that in common."

"Do we? Are you certain of that?"

"Maybe not." I sighed and started thinking about the whereabouts of my rig again. I belched, tasted bitter, scalding bile and swallowed. "Can I ask a question?"

"I don't see why not," the vampire replied. (I know I haven't explained just how I knew she was a vampire, but I'm betting people never pause to meditate on how it is a stone-cold Pink Floyd fan knows the first few chords of "Wish You Were Here." Okay, never mind. Lousy analogy.)

"And you'll answer it?"

"If the mood strikes me," she said. "Ask me, Siobhan, and we'll see how it goes."

I wiped at the sweat on my forehead. "You're a fucking tease, but you know that."

"What's the question?"

"Why the fuck am I still alive?"

There was a long moment of silence—in books, it's called the "pregnant pause"—and then she said, "Because I haven't yet killed you."

I tried to laugh again, but almost threw up again. Then the cramps hit hard, and I don't know how long it was before either of us said anything else. Maybe five minutes, or maybe less.

"Would you like me to elaborate?" she asked, once the pain in my guts temporarily retreated to merely an excruciating throb.

"You have me on pins and needles," I wheezed.

"There's no single reason, Siobhan—"

"Stop *calling* me that. No one fucking calls me that."

There was a contemplative *snick-snick-snicking* sound then, and I tried not to think what the vampire was doing to make such a sound or what it might mean.

"As you wish, Quinn. There's no single reason. There is, rather, a tapestry of reasons."

"Reason number one?"

"Some time ago, back in the winter, you murdered my lover, and my daughter. Her name was Alice, but I doubt you bothered with introductions. You tracked her to Swan Point Cemetery, cut off her head, then sliced out her heart, which you burned. You filled her belly with bricks, sewed it shut again, and sunk her body in the Seekonk River."

"Yeah, well . . . floaters make people suspicious. Reason number two?"

"I delight in irony, and here I have before me a killer of killers, God's butcher, an executioner of monsters, who's just been bitten by a werewolf. And I want to watch."

I told her I was trying not to think too hard about that part. The being bitten on the ass part, and what it meant.

"But, you have to admit, it's ironic."

"Occupational hazard," I replied, eyeing the pail

she'd provided, because it was only a matter of time. And the time would be sooner, rather than later. "Is there a reason number three?"

"There is, as it happens. I need a weapon. There are worse things out there than you, or me, or that dog you had the run-in with last night. There are things you've never even glimpsed."

I shut my eyes a moment, wishing I had the strength to brush my sweaty, straggly hair out of my face. "Always sort of suspected that," I whispered. It's okay to whisper with vampires. Fuckers can hear a pin drop in a hurricane. "This has what to do with keeping me alive?"

I'm not going to lie. I'd been bitten by a werewolf, and you know how that goes. The old wives' tales and movies don't get everything wrong, and I'd rather the vampire finish me off than have to do the job myself. If this made me a coward, so be it. No one gets to be the brave girl all the goddamn time.

"I need a weapon," she said.

I laughed again, hard. A deep and wholehearted sort of laugh, which finally cost me whatever was in my stomach. For the next few minutes, the rusty pail by the filthy mattress was my dearest companion. When the hurling subsided and there was only the bliss of dry heaves, she said, for the third time, "I need a weapon."

And I replied hoarsely, "Then you've got the wrong little black duck. Maybe you haven't noticed—"

"I know your history, Quinn," she interrupted. Vampires love to interrupt, by the way, because they never doubt that whatever they have to say is vastly more important and/or interesting than whatever you were in the process of saying. Anyway, she continued. "Your childhood, your parents, the guilt, all those years on the street, what you've learned since then . . ." She trailed off, letting the thought go unfinished, and this seems like as good a time as any to insert what comic-book nerds would refer to as my "origin story." You know, like how Superman was born on Krypton, but his parents bundled him into a rocket and blasted him into space right before the whole planet went kablooey. Or how Peter Parker was bitten by a radioactive spider. Like that, only I didn't exactly get the cool superpowers, and, I'll tell you up front, mine's probably gonna come off like a plea for sympathy, reading as much like a sob story as an origin story. But—and this is as good as scripture—I've never wanted anyone's sympathy, and I'm not about to start in now. So, it's just a *story*. It is what it is, take it or leave it.

So, fade to black, and we'll get back to the vampire's moldy basement in due course. Fade in to me at age twelve and those third-generation Irish Catholic parents I mentioned earlier.

Pop was a deadbeat alcoholic, and Mom was the sort who thought all the world's ills could be solved by praying the rosary and never missing midnight mass. How's that for perpetuating the stereotype? The first twelve years or so, we had a fairly stable routine that involved his drunken rampages, and her beads, and my doing my best to keep my head down. Sadly, that last part didn't usually work so well. Pop would get a bellyful of Murphy's and whiskey, and I'd get a shiner or a busted lip because there were dirty dishes, or the litter box stunk, or my left shoe was untied, or anything else inconsequential he could latch on to as an excuse to beat the living daylights out of his child.

Oh, and I should add he was absolutely fucking obsessed with the notion that Mom was a slut who'd slept around on him, and that I was *not*, in fact, his kid. It really didn't make much difference to me, one way or the other. Though I did sometimes like to pretend that Pop was right, and my real father was some decent, straight-laced sort of guy with a good job and nice house, who loved his wife and kids, and maybe played golf every now and then. The golf part always seemed very important to me. I watched a lot of old sitcoms on Nick at Nite's TV Land, and I pictured that imaginary real dad as Fred MacMurray or Gomez Addams, or maybe Ozzie Nelson. Regardless, it was a clean life, my imaginary real father's life, and he'd never even seen the likes of that roach-infested Cranston shithole where we were living, because Dad hadn't paid the rent and we'd been evicted from our sumptuous Pawtucket shithole.

Finally, not long after my twelfth birthday (nope, no pony), Pop laid into Mom like he'd never laid into her before. She was late with supper. He beat her with a bar of soap wrapped in a dish towel until she was unconscious, and then he used his fists. I watched the whole thing from the kitchen cupboard. When he was done, he left, and I'm the one who called the paramedics. I hid outside, keeping vigil until the ambulance showed up, and then I turned tail and ran. And, in one sense or another, I kept running for years, even if I never went any farther than the abandoned warehouses and squats in North Providence and Olneyville.

I met other kids, and they all had stories of their own, right? On the street, *everyone* has a story. Jesus, Joseph, and Mary, that sounds like a line from a Dashiell Hammett novel. Well, to my knowledge, it's not. If I've plagiarized anyone, I've done so unwittingly. Anyway, like I was saying, North Providence, where I found a tribe of other runaways, a loose confederacy of street urchins that would have made Charles Dickens proud. Sometimes we looked out for each other. Other times, it was every urchin for him- or herself. I drifted from tribe to tribe.

Sometimes, I made it on my own. Other times, I found men—and women—who enjoyed the company and/or carnal services of someone my age, and it would keep me off the street for a few nights. I never really felt especially exploited by the peds, though I suppose I ought to have. But after my father, shit, that was Heaven and they were almost good as guardian angels. They fed me, and let me bathe, and sometimes bought me clothes, a winter coat, a new pair of shoes. The sex seemed a small enough price to pay. Most of us kids turned tricks, whether in back alleys, parked cars, in motel rooms, or bedrooms. It was a good way to supplement the Dumpster diving, panhandling, and shoplifting. You did what you did to get by, and, more often than not, dignity was just something that got in the way of staying alive. The way we saw it, and the way I still do, dignity's not a right, it's a privilege.

There was sour coffee from Cumberland Farms (sometimes the clerks let us have that for free), loads of Sweet'N Low, and those packets of salsa from Taco Bell. No one cared how much of that shit you stuffed into your pockets. There was vodka and beer when we got lucky. There were a hell of a lot of stale Dunkin' Donuts.

Later on, the vampire would remark that I seemed awfully literate for a street-junky dropout. Truth is, it's usually pretty dull out there for Providence's wretched refuse. There's a whole lot of time on your hands between foraging and dodging the police and the gangs who want to fuck with you. A whole lot of boredom. You deal with it best you can: sex, drugs, conversation, walking the tracks. I knew two girls who decided they'd be hobos, both of them all full of Depression-Era romance of life of the rails. They jumped a boxcar headed for Manhattan, and we never heard from them again, so maybe they found something better. I can't even remember their names. I like to think the two of them, they're still out there somewhere and they're okay.

But me, for the first couple of years I dealt with the boredom by hanging out in the Providence Athenaeum on Benefit Street. The librarians didn't mind, just so long as they didn't catch me sleeping. They knew me by name, and every now and then, this one particular librarian, she'd recommend a book she thought I might like; usually, she was right. I couldn't have a library card, of course, since I didn't have a permanent address (never mind it cost a hundred bucks). Anyhow, there you have it, the mystery of my literacy solved. Also, the Athenaeum's restroom was a good place to wash up every now and then.

The heroin didn't come along until three years after I took to the streets. Not a long story there, and I won't try to make it one. It was a snowy day in November, and I was camped out in an old textile mill, wrapped in stolen U-Haul moving blankets and a sleeping bag I'd found somewhere. And Jim, this mostly Portuguese dude, with a green Mohawk and duct tape on his boots, he told me he could keep me warm. He cooked my first dose over his shiny silver Zippo, and shot it into my arm. Next day, he came back to the mill and taught me how to do the deed for myself, and sometimes he'd even get generous and slip me a free Baggie, if I'd blow him or jerk him off. He knew there was no turning back for me, and I knew it, too. Jim, he gave me wings (that was, by the way, drug slang a long time before Red Bull came along). He showed me how to fly.

I stopped going to the library. I almost stopped eating. Whatever money I could scrounge went to smack. The days blurred together. But it was good. Or at least it was better. Lots of times I thought I'd get lucky and OD, or get a bad batch—a ten-cent pistol, in junk-speak. I never scored from anyone but Jim, and his junk was always clean. I took up with this chick from Wickford who was also a junky. We were both always too fucked up for sex, but it was good to be close to someone on the freezing nights. Her name wasn't Lily, but that's what she liked to be called, so that's all I ever called her.

And now, at long fucking last, I'm coming to what the vampire referred to as the "interesting portion" of my sad, sad tale of woe and misfortune. The night one of the nasties came creeping up from the sewers and the subbasement and the basement of our abandoned mill by the Woonasquatucket River. We'd both shot up, and were cuddled together in our grimy blankets. There was a smoky barrel fire stoked with pilfered plywood and two-by-fours crackling and burning brightly, so we had a little heat, a little light. The redbrick and mortar walls were washed with dancing shadows, and watching them caper and prance about made for an entertaining diversion. Near as we ever got to the movies or television. Point is, neither of us saw it coming. The ghoul, I mean. Didn't even hear its hooves on the concrete floor. One moment, Lily was there in the blanket with me, next moment she just fucking wasn't.

I turned my head, slo-mo like, because everything's slow motion when you're that fucked up. And there it was, crouched over her. I knew she was already dead, considering it had bitten off the top of her skull and was making short fucking work of her brain. There was blood everywhere. I'd never seen so much blood, and I'd seen a fair bit of bleeding in my sixteen years on earth. Far as I could tell, the bastard hadn't noticed me. Or it just didn't care, was just saving me for dessert. Oh, by the way, I call them ghouls after a story by H. P. Lovecraft, "Pickman's Model," because they sort of look like the corpse-eating, subterranean creatures he described—shaggy, gangly, hunchbacked beasts with vaguely canine faces, wicked overbites, and the sort of hooves that horses have. Not cloven, that other sort. I have no idea what they call themselves, if they call themselves anything at all. Maybe the demonologists have a name for them, but I ain't no demonologist and never will be.

I pulled one of the burning boards from the barrel and beat the thing to death. Shouldn't have been that easy, but I think maybe the ghoul was too dumbfounded to fight back. Five minutes later, it was sprawled there by Lily's corpse. I held her all night, and the next morning I burned both the bodies on a rubbish heap out behind the mill. I don't think anyone else saw any of this shit. No one even asked where Lily had gone. It was like that. My compatriots came and went, and the disappeared were just a fact of life.

And that's how it began. Suddenly, I knew there were monsters in the world. *Real* monsters, straight out of the storybooks. And one of them had come along and killed Lily, whom I might have loved, if I hadn't always been so wired up on the Judas. After that night, everything changed. Well, except I stayed on the streets and was still a junky. So, strike that. Everything didn't change, but suddenly I found I had a murky sort of purpose. The night after I burned Lily and the ghoul, I went down into the basement of the mill and found another one of the ugly sons of bitches. It was sleeping in a corner, huddled in an oily heap of rags and burlap. I cut its throat with a broken whiskey bottle and left it there. I wrote Lily's name in blood on the wall above it. And I signed *my* name. So, that was the night I started the war. I suspect all I wanted was for them to get pissed and kill me, too. I certainly didn't have anything to live for, except the rush from shooting up. But that's not what happened. Oh, they came after me. But I kept killing them. It was the first thing I'd ever been good at, and the more I killed, the better I got. At first, I killed to get even. I killed and called it payback. But after a while, I was just killing because it felt good.

Pretty soon, no one wanted to be around me, and I

didn't see much of anyone but Jim. I don't think the others knew about the monsters. I just figure they all saw something spooky in my eyes that made them uneasy, and some of us were more interested in staying alive than others. I didn't hold it against them. I did, however, do a pretty respectable job of making sure the nasties stopped snacking on street kids and bums and winos.

And that's how it started.

I know. Not as cool as Wolverine or the Incredible Hulk's origin stories. But it's all I have. The vampire already knew most of it the night she dragged me back to that moldy basement and dumped me on the dirty mattress. Though, while I lay there hurting, vomiting, wishing she'd be done with it and do me, there was this *one* incident she insisted on coming back to again and again. I'll get to that shortly.

"You're not going to bleed to death," she said. "I took care of the stitches myself. You're fortunate it didn't hit an artery."

"Yeah. Lucky me."

By this time, seemed like she'd been yammering at me forever, and I asked, "Isn't it dawn yet? Aren't you up past your bedtime?"

"You still haven't looked at me, Quinn."

I wiped at my mouth and muttered something else about sunrise, which I prayed to that Big Daddy in the Sky Catholic God—in whom I do not actually believe—that sunrise truly was imminent.

"Why haven't you looked at me?" she asked.

"I've seen more than my share of vampires, lady," I told her. "So, you're just going to have to forgive my lack of enthusiasm on that count." But that's another thing about the undead, and I've always figured it was because they don't cast reflections: They love to be looked at, and they get positively fucking gaga if you tell them what you see. Even if you're honest, and the best you've got to say is that you've seen much worse. Or much better. Either way makes them happy. I think they just want to be reassured they still have faces.

"I did save your life," she reminded me, and now her voice was all silk, all peaches and cream.

"That remains open to debate," I replied, just then realizing some of the mold stains on the mattress were actually bloodstains. I also saw a cluster of fleshy white mushrooms sprouting from a crack in the floor, and they seemed to glow faintly in the gloom.

"Please," she said. "Look at me."

"Do you say please very often?" I asked her, then rolled over onto my right side, turning my back to her. I'd rather stare at the puke pail than give her—give *it*—the glance it so desperately desired.

"No," she replied, though I hadn't expected an answer to what I'd considered a rhetorical question. And I especially hadn't expected the detached sort of resignation in her voice, resignation and maybe a hint of melancholy, too. Like a child who's finally realized it's not getting what it wants. I admit I felt the tiniest, most useless twinge of satisfaction, that even in the sorry state I'd found myself, I still was able to cause the creature discomfort.

"Fortunately, I'd not expected gratitude from the likes of you, Miss Quinn."

"Miss Quinn? Thought we were on a first-name basis," I muttered, "you having saved my life and all." She didn't take the bait, and for a moment I squinted silently at the pail and the shitty gray wall beyond it. I spotted more of the tiny white luminescent mushrooms. Now that I'd noticed them, they seemed to be everywhere.

"Appears you'd have it otherwise," she said, and then she changed the subject. "Aren't you wondering what the beast was doing so far south?"

And now that she mentioned it, yeah, I was. I'd been wondering that since I first got word of the attack over the police broadband. "Never saw a loup this far south," I told her. "Or so near Providence, for that matter."

See, the local dogs, they tend to stick close to Woonsocket, or what's left of Woonsocket, a rundown strip of factories and crumbling mills hugging the polluted waters of the Blackstone River in the northwest corner of the state. Woonsocket has been loup-garou turf since way back in the seventeenth century, when they arrived with the French-Canadians who first settled the area. And, usually, they keep to themselves. The dogs, that is. They're not the sort to mingle.

"Any thoughts on that?" I asked.

"None. Unless it was fate," she replied.

This being a fairly cryptic statement, and the vampire having set my mind to chewing at the problem despite the pain and chills and nausea, I raised my head and looked at her. Immediately, she smiled and glanced shyly at the floor, the floor or her bare feet.

"What do you mean by that? Fate."

Now, that's what I said, and I did want to know, but mostly I was thinking how she wasn't in the least what I'd expected. You don't see many vampire children, like maybe there's some sort of prohibition against them or something. But she didn't look much older than eight or nine. I knew better, how looks can be deceiving and all. She was an old one, at least two, two hundred and fifty years. Only a few strands of pale, gossamer hair remained on her scalp, and her skin was getting that jaundiced look that afflicts the more venerable of the bloodsuckers. Her canines and incisors, the color of old ivory, protruded very slightly over her cyan lower lip, and her nails were long and brown, two other signs of advancing age.

Oh, there's another myth. Forget all that crap you might have read about immortality and vampires who are thousands of years old, who saw medieval Europe and ancient Egypt and Rome, the Hanging Gardens of Babylon and whatever the fuck. Not true. Sure, they get more time than living, breathing people, but not *that* much more. Three or four centuries tops. Then, well, I'm not sure. They just seem to fade away. Maybe there's only so much walking around a reanimated cadaver can endure before it finally comes apart at the seams. Even now, I really don't know, and if I've ever met anything that does, it hasn't bothered telling me.

I gawked at her, marveling—even through the agonies—at how something could simultaneously be so loathsome and so beautiful. She could have been cast from porcelain. She sat on a tall wooden stool, a strange doll wrapped in an antique gown of threadbare, moth-gnawed lace and

crinoline. I thought she might shatter if she tumbled off the stool and landed on the floor. I didn't even blink until my eyes began to water.

"A first-name basis," she said, "that would require your knowing *my* name."

"I suppose it would," I replied, and I wiped at my eyes, but I didn't look away.

"Mercy," she said. "My name's Mercy Brown."

When I laughed, she raised her head and fixed me with those inky black eyes. Vampires, they've got eyes like a shark's, black and nothing but black. Eyes you can fall into, and never find your way out again, eyes like a labyrinth, and you just fucking know there's a minotaur waiting in there. "No you're not," I said. "To start with, you're too old. For another, they dug up Mercy Brown and burned her heart."

Another aside. Though lots of people don't know about it, New England has its own vampire legends—Rhode Island, in particular—just like Hungary and Transylvania and places like that. Mostly, these tales date back to the 1890s, and mostly they're just stories superstitious Swamp Yankees hauled over from the "Old Country." Mostly, these so-called vamps were nothing more than tuberculosis victims. Sometimes, the disease would wipe out a whole family, as was the case with a girl named Mercy Brown. But there were stories of specters rising from their graves and stealing away the health of those they'd once loved. Finally, after Mercy's sister and mother died, her father and some of the townsfolk in Exeter, where this all went down, they exhumed Mercy's body, found the corpse suspicious, cut out her heart and

liver, and burned them on a stone not far from her grave. The doctor who'd attended Mercy during her illness, and who was also present during the exhumation, correctly diagnosed her condition as "galloping consumption," but no one much listened to him. Supposedly, the Mercy Brown affair was one of the things that inspired Bram Stoker to write *Dracula*. Anyway, you can still see her grave in the Chestnut Hill Cemetery. You can even see the stone where the organs were burned to ash. But if you believe Mercy was a vampire, you might as well start believing in Bigfoot and the Headless Horseman of Sleepy Hollow.

"You ain't her," I told the vampire.

"I'm fond of the name," she responded, very quietly, so quietly I almost missed the words.

"You could have said that."

"Does it make any difference? Call me the Bride of Quiet, if you prefer. Others do."

And no, I suppose she had a point. It didn't make much difference what I called her or what she wanted me to call her. At that particular and miserable juncture I couldn't imagine myself going around calling her the "Bride of Quiet." I'd like to think I have my limits (all evidence to the fucking contrary).

"It's rude to stare," she said, and I forced myself to turn away and lie down again. I was honestly surprised she'd not asked me to offer my opinion of her appearance. It makes me nervous when the nasties deviate from the script. My heart was thudding like a jackhammer in my chest, and I stunk of flop sweat, and I knew there was more to it than the withdrawal. I've heard stories of people dropping dead at their first sight of a vampire. It's an exaggeration I can almost buy into.

"Sorry," I muttered. I actually did. I actually fucking apologized to a vampire.

"No such mea culpa necessary," she said, delivering the words with an excruciating primness.

"Also, that's my bag, right there by your feet."

"Yes, it is, Quinn," and she glanced down at it.

"But you're not going to toss it over here," I said, and it goes without saying I was much too weak to try for it myself.

"No. Not yet. Maybe later."

"Well, you ought to know I don't feel like I have a whole lot of later left."

"You won't die," she said, sounding awfully goddamn sure of herself. "At least, you won't die from the heroin, or from the dog bite."

Which brought us back around to why she'd taken on a monster six times her weight, then brought me back to this dump, why I was still talking and drawing breath and hurting like I'd never hurt before. I didn't say that, but I knew *she* knew that's what was going through my head.

"Quinn, you stole the one thing left that was precious to me. You hunted her down, and you murdered her."

"That's what I do." Probably not the smartest reply, but it's what I said.

"In my eyes, Quinn, this makes mere death a kindness you don't deserve. Even the curse in the werewolf's bite, that doesn't make us even by half."

"So, why don't you tell me what that's going to take?" But before she could answer, I was hugging the pail again. My guts didn't seem to care there was nothing left in me to come back up. When I was done, she resumed.

"Dear," she said, "long ago I made a wager and lost, and with you I may be able to settle that debt."

"You told me you needed a weapon," I replied and coughed, my throat raw and burning.

"It's complicated."

"Maybe you just want to get even. With me, I mean, not with whoever you lost this bet to."

"Yes, Quinn. Maybe I want that, too. It would be reasonable, would it not? After your crimes against me and mine. Fair *is* fair."

I turned my head towards her, and her black eyes were still trained on the floor. She was smiling now, thin blue lips pulled back to reveal those fangs that reminded me of netsuke carvings yellowed by the passage of time. I got a glimpse at her tongue, even bluer than her lips. There are snakes and lizards with tongues that color.

"I haven't seen much fair in my lifetime," I told her.

"But your lifetime has been so very short, Quinn. And it's true, I will admit, some of us are more prone to misfortune than are others."

I made myself stare at my green canvas bag instead of staring at her. She terrified me, even after all I'd seen. Worse yet, she made me want her, which is one of those things vampires excel at, forcing desire on anyone unlucky enough to get a glimpse of them. I don't even think they do it on purpose, not most times. They radiate this fucked up sexual magnetism, no matter how monstrous she or he—it—might be, and the creature on the stool was one of the most monstrous I'd ever come across. She turned my stomach, and filled me with fear, and with awe, and made me want her, never mind how perverse the urge might be. But, I will say, not nearly as much as I wanted that bag, the *contents* of that bag. Right then, I'd never wanted anything more.

"How about this, Mercy. You toss me my kit, I'll retire from the demon-slaying business for good. That sound fair enough to you?"

"No," she said flatly, and I told her to go fuck herself. Not that she could have, not literally, anyway. Another fun fact about vamps: as they age, their genitals quickly atrophy, and after fifty years or so, they're as smooth down there as Barbie and Ken.

"Then why don't we stop playing games, and you tell me what I got coming?"

"It isn't a game, Miss Quinn. Nothing of the sort. It's only me taking delight in your dread of the unknown."

I called her a sadistic bitch then, which was even sillier than telling her to go fuck herself. Hello, Captain Obvious.

"But if you insist," she added, and stood up. Her feet made no sound on the cement. I'm not even sure they were touching the floor. Maybe she was able to float along an inch or so above it. I've seen that sort of shit before. So, I gave up on the bag, once and for all, and somehow succeeded in sitting up enough to scoot a foot or so across the mattress until my back was pressed against the clammy basement wall.

That's when she began to sing. It was the high, sweet voice of a child, and the sandpaper voice of a very old woman, maybe the oldest woman in the entire stinking universe. It was the voice of the void, and, if Death has a voice, it was the voice of Death, as well.

Where are you going, my pretty fair maid? Where are you going, my honey?

She answered me right cheerfully, I've an errand for my mummy.

My shaking hands scrambled about for anything that might serve as a weapon, but there was nothing within reach, and I was pretty sure tossing a pail of puke at her wasn't going to help.

How old are you, my pretty fair maid? How old are you, my honey?

She answered me right cheerfully, I'm seventeen come Sunday.

Since my days on the streets, I'd gotten the notion I was tough as they come, one hardcore bitch who didn't flinch at anything. Killing those first two ghouls, the one killed Lily and the one I found asleep, well, that only made me believe it that much more. And over the years, facing down the shit I'd faced down, my little crusade against what Mercy called the Rakshasas, I'd finally been left with no doubt that I could stand up against the worst Hell had to sling my way (maybe I didn't believe in God, but I sure as fuck believed in Hell) and stand my ground. But here was this one vampire, who'd been a child centuries before I was born, and who'd been trapped in that child's body forever, here was her and her creepy-ass voice singing that creepy-ass song, coming nearer and nearer. And here I was losing my cool. Here I was flinching. Here I was, hiding in the closet while my drunken asswipe of a father did his best to beat my mother to death.

"Stop! Please, just fucking stop!" I pleaded, and then I screamed. Yeah, you bet your life I did. I screamed, as loudly and shrilly and as pathetically as any victim in any slasher flick ever screamed. And it made no difference whatsoever. Whatever dignity might have remained, after the werewolf and after coming to *a la canona* in the doll's dungeon of horrors, feeling like my innards were being scraped out with a grapefruit spoon, that smidgen of dignity was gone now. Everything was gone but the fear, and the noises the fear could make.

But if you come round to my mummy's house, when the moon shines bright and clearly,

I will come down and let you in, and my mummy shall not hear me.

By the time she reached me (and that seemed to take forever), I'd stopped screaming, and was sobbing and begging. I'd have gotten on my knees if I'd been strong enough. She reached out with her right hand, her razor-blade nails and palm cold as marble, and she ran her fingers through the blonde snarl of my sweat-drenched hair.

So I went down to her mummy's house, when the moon shone bright and clearly,

She did come down and let me in, and I lay in her arms till morning.

Finally, she stopped singing, and kneeled beside the mattress. She was so small, and seemed so impossibly frail. But she'd dropped out of the limbs of that tree onto the back of the biggest, meanest loup I'd ever seen. She'd killed it, and there wasn't a scratch on her anywhere. I thought these thoughts, and gazed into her eyes, and knew I'd never really seen evil before I'd seen her. Here was a whole new ballgame. Here was the end of me.

Words squeaked out of my mouth—tiny, ruined shards to pass for words. "What are you going to do?" I asked her. "Please, just say it. What are you going to do?"

Those claws brushed my cheek as gently as they were able, but still cutting me, drawing blood. Compared to the freezing air coming off the vampire, my own blood felt hot as molten steel. It ran down my face and chin and neck and pooled wetly at the collar of my T-shirt. She leaned close then, and a wintry gust of breath washed over me.

"Alchemy," she whispered. "I like to think of it that way, Quinn, as an act of alchemy. The birth of a new being, transmutation from one state to another. My gift to you."

"I don't know what you're talking about," I said, though maybe by then I did.

"When I'm done, you'll be something marvelous. You'll be something held so taboo by my race, you may even be the first of its kind we've ever seen."

There wasn't so much as a hint of malice in her voice. She could have been any little girl, describing nothing more wicked than a tea party.

"And you'll be my pet," she said, and a few seconds later, I felt her teeth against my throat. I didn't struggle. I made no sound whatsoever.

Bride of Quiet.

Yeah, okay. Maybe that's not so far from the mark after all.

CHAPTER TWO

SONGS FOR MY FUNERAL

I came to in a weedy ditch. Specifically, I came to in the weedy, garbage-filled ditch on the south side of the abandoned train tracks that lead out over the Seekonk River to the old drawbridge. You know the one. Everybody in Providence does. Been stuck in the up position since, like, 1976, I think. A hundred feet high, if it's an inch, and there's nothing much left of it these days but rust. Tons of rust defying gravity. Anyway, fuck the bridge. Who cares about the drawbridge. There I lay in the stinking, wet ditch, dreaming about puking until I woke up and did exactly that.

When I was done, I wiped my mouth on my T-shirt and climbed out of the ditch. I sat curled up on an old sofa someone had left sprawled across the tracks. Knees drawn up beneath my chin. The sun was starting to set, and I wondered how long it had been since that business with the loup, and how long it had been since the mattress, and the basement, and the rotten old china doll calling itself Mercy Brown. Reluctantly, my fingers went to my throat, and right there on the left side, just below the line of my chin, there was a seeping welt. Felt like the bull-bitch of all wasp stings. So I knew, right? Pieces, meet falling into place. First, I'd gotten myself bitten in the ass by a werewolf, and then I'd been bitten in the neck by a bloodsucker. Lucky as lucky gets, that's me—damned, and damned again. I sat there on that reeking, mildewed sofa, and I shivered and cramped and watched the sky fading from blue to indigo. Mostly, I was trying to figure out what I was supposed to do next, only I was sort of *also* trying not to think about the very same thing, what was gonna happen next. One thing I knew for sure, it was gonna suck (hahahahaha, I know, wicked funny).

Now, let us pause right here for a moment of quiet reflection. Let's pause here, me and whoever's reading this, and I'll try to come clean on a few of the lies I've been telling you. (Come clean. Yeah, the puns, they're flowing outta my pen like Biblical rivers of milk and honey, like shit from a dog's behind.) Firstly, junkies lie. No exceptions. Show me a junky that doesn't lie, and I'll show you a lobster doesn't turn bright and shiny red when you drop it in a pot of boiling water. Junkies lie, and they'll rob you blind given half the chance, and about all that matters to them is the next fix. But let's stay with that first point for now, junkies being liars. Sometimes I think we don't even mean to; we just can't help ourselves. We open our mouths, and lies come out.

So, to start with, you might be wondering how this chick with a monkey on her back about the size of King Kong is running about staking nasties and whatnot. Well, truth be told, I've been stretching the truth like it was a big handful of raspberry-flavored saltwater taffy. Let's start at the beginning. That ghoul back in the warehouse, the one killed Lily when I was sixteen. I didn't beat it to death with a two-by-four I pulled from that burning barrel. It saw me, dropped Lily, and lunged. I screamed and tried to crawl away. Actually, I scream a lot. I'm a pretty good screamer. The ghoul (get this) tripped over Lily's corpse and landed headfirst in the barrel. That is, the beast set *itself* on fire. I didn't do the deed. I just ran. And then the nasty's death throes must have involved quite a lot a flailing about, because the whole place went up like a Roman candle, and by the time the fire department arrived, there wasn't much left to save. If anyone found Lily's body, or the ghoul's, I never heard about it. Oh, and that second ghoul I supposedly sought out and killed, that was a lie, too. Oh, what a tangled web we weave. Did you know it wasn't Shakespeare said that? Lots of folks think it was, but it was really Sir Walter Scott, some other fancy-pants English playwright. Read that one day when I was camped out in the Athenaeum. Anyway, here's my tangled web, me having practiced plenty to deceive in the first chapter. Forget my purported heroics. The ghoul fucked up, and everything that came after was a cut-and-dried, open-and-shut case of self-immolation. Let's call that lie Numero Uno.

Now, moving along to Numero Dos: In the months leading up to the night I drove out to the Scituate Reservoir, you'll remember I'd killed exactly *two* vampires, and the first was an accident. Of course, that was after I met Mean Mr. B (and you'll meet him shortly) and after he'd put all these bullshit ideas in my head (which kinda—but not quite—means I lied about the mentor thing, too). But, back to that vampire, that first vampire. I think it (she) might have heard about the thing with the ghoul, because this wasn't long after. I'd taken to carrying around a plastic crucifix and this pocket-sized copy of the New Testament some Hispanic woman over on the West Side had given me, just for listening to her spiel about la Virgen de Guadalupe. The vamp jumped me in an alley next to the Starbucks on Thayer Street, sometime after midnight. I was picking through the Dumpsters for whatever pastries and muffins and shit might have been thrown out that day when the fucker came at me. She was tall, and naked, and smelled worse than the trash I'd been rummaging through. I screamed (I bet you saw that coming) and, like the best horror movie cliché, I tore that cruddy plastic crucifix from around my neck and thrust it at her. The string snapped and cheap pink plastic beads went bouncing everywhere. The vampire wasn't the least bit taken aback by suffering Jesus and INRI and the crown of thorns. No, really. The motherfucker laughed. I threw the crucifix at it, she ducked, slipped on the beads, and fell backwards, impaling herself on a two-foot section of PVC pipe jutting from the side of the building.

Oh, and she didn't go poof like in some of the movies, and she didn't burst into flames, and she didn't dissolve into a green puddle of goo. She just looked surprised, then died. Well, died again, or died the rest of the way. Whatever.

I didn't stick around. I spent the night in a squat down by the river (the Providence River, not the Seekonk River). Next day, bright and early, Mr. B found me. Someone offs a vamp, even without meaning to, and she's the same someone inadvertently offed a ghoul, that has a tendency to attract attention, most of it from distinctly unsavory circles. That's just how you might describe Mean Mr. B—distinctly unsavory. Short little sawed-off son of a bitch, faintly effete Brit accent, looks like the far end of fifty, greasy black hair, and he wears these suits might have been in style back in the 1940s. Don't know where he gets them. Maybe he has a tailor, because they always look brand spanking new. Also, he's a total faggot, which is neither here nor there, except he's usually got a pretty young chicken or two with him. He has this manner about him, like the Big Bad Wolf, all dainty, fucking manners and smooth talker, right. Real suave, with his voice like melted butter. Always a white handkerchief folded tidy in his breast pocket. Shoes shiny enough to blind you. But, make no mistake, he'd slit your throat in half a second and not think twice, would Mean Mr. B (I don't call him that to his face, not ever, but we'll get to the matter of his "name" in just a minute).

So, stupid clumsy vampire up and stakes herself, and this dude comes around telling me how I've set tongues to wagging, tongues in certain unwholesome circles, and maybe I'd benefit from a long talk with him. That is, if I wanted to stay alive. Sure, I said, why the hell not. Nothing better to do, right? Only, I told him I had to score and shoot up first, and that's when he produced a Baggie seemingly out of nowhere, abracadabra, and smiled that slick, ugly smile of his.

I stared at the smack, and said something like, "You've done your homework, mister."

And he said something like, "You'll find I usually do, Siobhan."

I told him straight off not to call me that, not ever again. I told him he could call me Quinn, and so that's what he calls me. Usually. Except when he's trying to piss me off, which, come to think of it, is quite often. Anyway, since then he's been my sole supplier (or *pusher*, if you must, but you spend five minutes with the dude, meet him, and you'd never call him a pusher). Most times, he doesn't even charge me for the dope. Not so long as I eat at least one meal a day, and listen when he talks. I slip and mouth off, though, and it's street price for a week.

God almighty, how about I stop reminiscing and get back to that evening I woke up in a ditch sick as a dog?

By the time the sun was down, I'd managed to crawl off the sofa and get my wobbly legs working. There was ground glass between every joint, and my stomach was Narragansett Bay on a stormy day. I knew full well it wasn't the tail end of withdrawal. By then, denial was a luxury I couldn't afford, and, unless I was going to take the easy way out, there was just the one person I knew might have some inkling of a clue what I was supposed to do next. So, on beyond miserable, I dragged my sorry self the mile and a half from the old tracks by the river, north and west across Fox Point, to the dive on Wickenden Street where Mean Mr. B hangs out most nights. Babe's on the Sunnyside, total fucking dump where blue-collar sorts gather after work. Precisely the opposite of the sort of place you'd expect a latter-day fop like him to plant his ass every evening, but he claims it has "an undeniable je ne sais quoi." Right. Anyway, I stuck to the sidewalks, hoping I only looked suspicious and not like some sort of rabid coyote slinking through the shadows. I did my best not to meet the eyes of anyone I passed along the way. It's pretty much all residential through there, Monopoly houses from the 1800s and 1900s lined up in neat rows with huge oaks and manicured lawns out front. The sort of places I've never seen the inside of and figured I likely never would. Anyway, my belly rumbled whenever I *did* pass someone, rumbled loudly enough I imagine they heard, and my mouth watered so much I caught myself drooling a time or two. They all smelled like dinner, and the most delicious dinners I'd ever smelled. By the time I made it to the bar, it was almost impossible to think about much else but food. Except food didn't mean what it once had. Now, food meant killing. I have to admit, the thought of killing hardly seemed to bother me as much as it once had, and did nothing whatsoever to dint my appetite. I stumbled into Babe's on the Sunnyside, and then stumbled some more, all the way to the booth in the very back, where Mr. B sat in a pinstripe suit, nursing a Cape Cod.

"Well," he grinned, "looky what the cat dragged in. You're terribly mimsy tonight, Miss Quinn."

Right off, I knew he knew, because he didn't seem

the least surprised. Then again, Mr. B doesn't really do surprised, so never mind. I sat down across from him and told him to fuck off.

"Sweating like the axiomatic pig of yore," he said, then took a sip of his drink.

My stomach lurched. I groaned, then growled, "Last I heard, 'fuck you' ain't exactly an ambiguous statement."

"Touché," he replied, and set his glass down. In the dim light, every bead of condensation sparkled like a diamond, and I could smell the cranberry juice and cheap vodka, and when the base of that glass met wood, it made a sound like a goddamn hammer. See, that's one thing some of the books and movies get right. A vampire's senses are off the scale, which I suppose comes with being a predator. And right then, I was carrying the weight of enough noises, sights, tastes, and smells, I kept expecting the pressure of it all to crush me flat. I put my hands on the table in front of me, folded them, and tried to stop shaking, which, of course, was worse than pointless.

"So, would you be more consoled were I to simply say you look like shit?" he asked and stirred at his drink with a swizzle stick.

"I'm in trouble, Bayard," I said through gritted teeth, then realized I was drooling on the table. He saw, too, and passed me a cocktail napkin.

"So I've noticed. And it isn't Bayard. Not tonight. Tonight, it's Barlow."

Well, at least that was better than the last time we'd talked, when he'd insisted I call him Baptiste. But Jesus H. Christ. Barlow? He might as well have called himself Barnabas Collins.

"Shit," I hissed. And, by the way, when I use words like *growl* and *hiss* here, I mean them in their purest animal meaning. Or close enough. I hissed that word, and it came out sounding a lot more like an angry snake than it did like me. "I don't care *what* you call yourself." More saliva dripped from my lips, and I wiped at my chin with the napkin, which was already too soggy to do much good.

"Does this mean I get to call you Siobhan tonight?"

I didn't answer the question.

"Fuck you," I said again.

"Not my type, but thanks for the offer all the same. So, Quinn, I heard about your tête-à-tête with the Bride, and also that run-in with Monsieur Jack Grumet."

He pronounced the name "GROO-may."

"Mr. Who?" I grunted.

"Jack Grumet, dear. The departed lycanthrope, lately of Woonsocket."

I lay my head down in a cooling puddle of slobber (flashback to the Bride's basement), and shut my eyes. Even then, it wasn't dark enough by half, and my head throbbed.

"How'd you hear?"

"Small town, dear, and people talk whenever something as curious as your recent misadventure comes to pass. Let's just say a little bird told me."

"I am so screwed."

"So it seems."

"What am I gonna do?" I asked, and there was a cramp then that probably would have put me on my knees if I hadn't already been sitting.

When it passed, Mean Mr. Barlow said, "Well, I've been wondering that very same thing myself."

"You're a bastard."

"Undoubtedly. But it's impolite to bring that up. Nor does it help with your current predicament. Right about now, you'd best be thinking about *not* pissing me off. I can always finish my cocktail, pay my tab, and leave you sitting here. And you know I will, Quinn."

I belched then. Nothing in my stomach, but I belched anyway and tasted, well, nothing.

"You're the sweetest guy I ever did meet," I whispered in the quiet that followed the belch. "You're one delightful dude."

"That's better. Now, first things first. I assume you're starving. Am I right?"

I nodded without sitting up, so I smacked my forehead against the wood several times and the table shook like it wasn't bolted to the floor (though I knew it was).

"Then I imagine you're going to have to find something to eat. And soon. That part's not optional. Anyway, even living people tend to think more clearly after a square meal. There you go. Step number one, advice for the asking, free of fucking charge."

"I'm not going to kill anyone. I'm not going to eat anyone."

"Sure you will, Quinn. Not that I don't respect your reverence for the sanctity of human life and whatever other high-minded morals you may yet harbor. I do, cross my heart. But you are going to kill, and I'd wager you'll do it before sunrise. Then, once that's out of the way, we may proceed to step number two."

"I'm *not* going to kill anyone."

"I'll put down green folding money to the contrary."

"I'll find a rat," I said. "Or a cat, or a stray dog."

He was silent for a moment, sipping his red drink. Then Mr. Barlow laughed and said, "Kiddo, you know as well as I do that won't work."

He was right, of course. It's not like Louis de Pointe du Lac or Angelus or one of those guys. Vampires can't get by on rodents, pigs, poodles, and such. Not even monkeys will do. Vampires need human blood. Accept no substitute. It's the real McCoy, actual and factual hemoglobin from some unfortunate Homo sapiens, or it might as well be nothing at all. Might as well be a mouthful of air.

"Fuck me."

"If you can stomach it, I suggest one of our local homeless denizens," Mean Mr. B(arlow) suggested with utmost seriousness. "Or you could try Brown, but college kids go missing, it never fails to attract attention. There are tourists, of course, but the Chamber of Commerce frowns on that sort of shit. Go for the homeless. A transient if possible. Fortune might even smile on you, and you'll find someone who's bathed this year."

"I'm not going to kill anyone, *Barlow*," I told him, trying hard as I could to make the name sound like the bad joke it was. Guess it's safe to assume he'd read *'Salem's Lot*, or at least seen the movie. But maybe not, which makes it even funnier.

"You keep saying that. I might as well say I'm a lace doily, or pinch of lint. It's just about that ridiculous, you know."

"You could always kill me," I mumbled, my words

muffled by all the slobber and the wood I was speaking into. The ground glass had spread from my joints to my guts and throat.

"I could," he said in a thoughtful, contemplative sort of way. "I considered that, because I can be merciful when the mood strikes me. But I'm not going to. Better for my health if I don't start crossing the Bride. Isn't she a pip, by the way?"

"The Bride?" I asked.

"Well, you don't truly think she's Mercy Brown," he said. "Perfectly fucking ridiculous, the way she goes about calling herself that."

"I told her that."

"Good for you. Best we stick to calling her the Bride of Quiet. I think she acquired that nom de guerre in the winter of '42 and '43, during the Battle of Stalingrad. Must have been a feast. Oh, she's Russian, as it happens, from some horrid village on the banks of the Volga. Anyway, I've always thought it had a nice ring to it—Bride of Quiet. The German soldiers started calling her that, *Braut der Stille*, and they got in their heads she was some sort of angel or—"

"I'm *not* killing anyone," I said again (for—what?—the half-dozenth time?). I said that, then gagged on hunger pangs and at the cloying smell of the air trapped inside Babe's. It stank of my sweat, of Budweiser and Jäger shots, of the ghost of cigarettes, from back when smoking was still legal in Rhode Island bars. It stank of piss from the toilets and the cakes of deodorant that are supposed to cover up the stink of piss. Unless you're a vampire. A vampire who's also a werewolf.

"As you wish," he sighed. "Either way, I'll be here until last call. Try not to do anything else outrageously stupid."

I have no idea how I got to my feet again and made it back to the front door of Babe's, but I did. And, one teensy-weensy step at a goddamn time, I made it to the other side of I-95 and found a woman sleeping off a quart bottle of Thunderbird. She was my first. When it was over, I dumped the husk of her into the Providence River, and made my way back to Wickenden Street. As they used to say (and maybe some people still do), I felt like a million bucks.

I was back at Babe's on the Sunnyside half an hour before closing. You live in Providence, you know that's one a.m., as mandated by state law. Mr. B—Bayard, Baptiste, Barlow, whoever—was still in his booth at the back, finishing off what would be his last Cape Cod of the evening. He saw me coming in, and the motherfucker totally looked like the cat that swallowed the canary. He knew right off what I'd done, though I'd washed in the river. Washed as best I could. I knew there were still bloodstains on my jeans and T-shirt, but I was trying to pretend there weren't. No one at the bar seemed to notice. Anyway, there he sat, all smug and pleased with himself. Probably, I hated him more then than I ever had or ever would (which is saying quite a lot).

"Brava," he said, and slowly clapped his hands. "The gourmand returns victorious from her banquet, cherry popped."

I sat down, and ran my fingers through my wet hair. I realized there was still blood caked under my nails and wondered if I was going to have to get used to that sort of thing. Speaking generally, you see two sorts of vampires in novels and the movies. You see clean, fastidious vampires, and you see filthy wretches that can't be bothered with the likes of hygiene. In the real world, they come in both those varieties, though it's been my experience most are perfectly content with the "can't be bothered" category. Truth is, all the primping and perfume in the world only does a half-assed job of covering up the facts. There's only so many ways you can beautify a corpse.

"I trust your repast won't be missed? I trust it certainly won't be found?"

I didn't answer either question. I said, "You trust an awful lot, Mr. B." Then, well, I just sat there staring at the blood under my nails. I realized there was a Patti Smith song playing on the bar's stereo. Not just any Patti Smith song, but "Land." I closed my eyes and listened. See, there's a story here. That song's not just any song. There was this game me and Lily used to play, when we were too cold or hungry or strung out to sleep. At some point, she started calling it Songs for My Funeral, and that's all we ever called it. She'd say, "At my funeral, I want them to play 'Black Star' by Radiohead." Then it would be my turn, okay, so I'd say something like, "At my funeral, I want them (*them*, whoever *them* was gonna be) to play 'Hate My Way' by Throwing Muses." Or, instead, I'd say I wanted the song to be something by Tom Waits, or the Rolling Stones, or Elvis

Costello. See, it didn't matter what the song was, only that there *were* songs. But the song I named more times than any other was "Land" by Patti Smith, and I sat there with my eyes shut, the lyrics and drums and guitar chords spilling over me, mocking me, reminding me of shit I didn't want to be reminded of. But also washing me lots cleaner than the river ever could. Back then, fuck, we'd both been so innocent, and here I was never gonna be innocent again.

Songs for my funeral.

And I opened my eyes and stared into the steely eyes of Mean Mr. B in his razor-sharp pinstripes, wondering if any vampire had ever gotten a funeral. I wondered that, and Patti Smith sang about rape and horses and dances from the 1950s and *la mer*.

"Step number two," I said.

"I always appreciate an eager student. Now, what shall step number two be?"

I thought about it a minute before answering him. "Mercy, she believes I killed her lover. Her daughter. Some bitch named Alice. I've been assuming she was talking about another vamp, one she made."

"Good call. That would be one Alice Cregan, who was, as it happens, a young lady our Miss Brown dragged out of her mortal coil about four decades back. I'm going to take a stab in the dark and guess that name doesn't ring a bell?"

"Alice Cregan?"

"Yes. That very name."

"Doesn't mean a goddamn thing to me," I replied, wishing the song would end and another would come along to take its place, one that had never been part of me and Lily's stupid, fucking, morbid game.

"Well, it ought to," said Mean Mr. B, Mr. Barlow, Mr. Whatever He Pleases, Mr. Whim. "Not too long after we met, you and her tangled one night amid the gravestones and mausoleums of—"

"—Swan Point," I interrupted, finishing his sentence, knowing how much he hates being interrupted. So, my second vampire, whom I had indeed offed at Swan Point Cemetery, now I knew her name.

He sipped his drink and nodded coolly, like someone who didn't mind being interrupted. "That's her. Seems like the Bride took it personally. Also, seems like she's the sort holds a grudge. Not that you can necessarily blame her."

"Yeah, okay. But . . . that was like six months ago."

Mr. B, he leaned back in the booth and grinned. "The undead, they don't think of time the way you and I think of time. Six months. Six weeks. Not much difference to them. But then, you'll eventually figure that out for yourself. Hell, might be the old lady didn't even miss Alice Cregan until a few days ago. But when she finally *did* miss her . . . daughter . . . she found you and delivered unto our fair maiden her proper comeuppance." He raised his glass, which was mostly empty, like I had a drink of my own and we were supposed to toast.

"You must put a lot of effort into being an asshole," I said.

"No I do not. I assure you, it just comes naturally."

"It's not that simple. There was more. I mean, she talked about more than me having killed this Alice Cregan."

"Ah, so the plot thickens."

"She said what she did to me, before she did it, she said she was paying off a debt, something about a bet she lost a long time ago. And she went on about me being something she was forbidden to create. Taboo, she said."

"Obviously. A vampire that's also werewolf, or, conversely, vice versa," he said and thumped the rim of his cocktail glass. It emitted a painful, high-pitched ring I felt in my teeth.

"Jesus," I hissed. "Don't you fucking do that again."

"Je suis désolée," he smiled, without so much as half a scrap of contrition in his voice. "All apologies."

I rubbed at my temples and gritted my sharp teeth.

"But yes, that's a no-no from the long ago, bygone days. As for the debt, that's between her and her creditor. Unless, of course, she was speaking metaphorically."

"She called me her pet."

"How very fucking sweet of her. She should know you're not exactly housebroken."

I ignored him. Finally, the music wasn't Patti Smith anymore. It was another song. I don't remember what. And just now I almost wrote "but at least it was easier to breathe" again. Only it wasn't, but I hadn't noticed until "Land" ended that I wasn't breathing, that I hadn't *been* breathing since I woke up in the ditch by the railroad tracks. I put my right hand over my chest. Nope, nothing there, either. No reassuring cardiovascular thump, thump, thump. Not a peep. Naturally, Mr. B was watching me like a hawk.

"Do you know, Quinn, the meaning of the word *apocalypse*?"

"End of the world."

"Wrong. It's from the Greek *apokalypsis*, and it means a revelation, a disclosure. Hence, the Book of Revelation of Saint John the Divine, or, alternately and more concisely, the Apocalypse of John. The book isn't named that because it talks about the end times—if you approach it as a futurist and not a symbolist—but because of the revelatory visions experienced by John while on the isle of Patmos."

I think it fair to say I glared at him. I think I was wishing becoming a vampire had given me the power to make people's heads explode just by *thinking* about their heads exploding, like in that old movie, *Scanners.*

"Are we done with the fucking history lesson now?" I asked him, and Mean Mr. B shrugged.

"If you wish. Still, I believe you've just had your own personal apocalypse."

I rubbed at my face and ran my hands through my hair again. It was sticky, my hair, so I knew I probably hadn't gotten all the blood out.

"That shit at Swan Point, I didn't even start that. It was that fuckwit Bobby Ng."

"But, dear, it was *you* who finished it, and that's all that really matters to the Bride."

"I should have let the son of a bitch die. I should have let her eat him."

"I do believe that's exactly what I said at the time."

"Don't do that."

"Don't do what?" he asked and straightened his lapels.

"Don't fucking say I fucking told you so."

"I didn't."

"Yes you did."

"Not in so many words. Anyway, we're in agreement, kitten. You should have left that fuckwit Bobby Ng to his fate, the one he'd brought upon himself. Let's not argue, not when we so obviously agree."

By now, I was trying so hard to make Mr. B's head split open in a steaming burst of brains and bone and gore, my own head was beginning to ache. Maybe I did have skull-rupturing superpowers, but they were about to backfire.

"I heard he's down in Cranston these days," Mr. B said. "Delivers pizzas on the side. Didn't that used to be your neck of the woods, Cranston?"

Okay. Stop. Right about here I should probably explain a little bit about Bobby Ng, Demon Hunter. That's what the asshole called himself. He even had these embossed business cards printed up, and that's what they said. Bobby Ng was half Chinese, half Portuguese, and generally he used to run around stirring shit up that needed to be left alone. He was aces at not letting sleeping dogs lie. Styled himself all things dark and spooky—an exorcist (he was even ordained by some church or another), parapsychologist, occultist, palm reader, practitioner of witchcraft and voodoo, UFOlogist, a magician with ties to the Illuminati, an escape artist, a Rosicrucian, clairvoyant, and all-around psychic, but was, at best, a sort of cut-rate Van Helsing. Oh, he also claimed to have a fourth-degree black belt in tae kwon do and to be the Worshipful Master of a super-secret Masonic Lodge somewhere in Massachusetts. Fall River, I think he said.

Mostly, though, I think he'd just spent too much time watching *Scooby-Doo* and Peter Cushing films. If there's a douche bag hall of fame, I hope to hell Bobby Ng has a bronze plaque front and center.

And *everyone*—the nasties included—had a Bobby Ng story or three. Mr. B, he had about thirty of them. I'm pretty sure the only reason Ng was still alive back then was that he was either too goddamn funny to kill, or not worth the trouble. This isn't to say he was exactly harmless, mind you, because lots of times an inconvenience can turn into a shitstorm—as was the case with Alice Cregan—but still he lived. Maybe some people are too stupid to die, or maybe it's just that even the damned need comic relief.

Once, and this was a year or so after the whole mess with the Bride was over and done with, Mean Mr. B dragged me to a local demon brothel and bookie joint (with which I was already familiar, as you shall see) over on Federal Hill. Neither of us was there to get our freak on with Hell's outcasts or place a bet on the next Red Sox game. Mr. B, he had some business or another with the proprietor, this utter skank of a succubus who went by the moniker Madam Calamity. Her real name was Drusneth, but I'm not supposed to know that. You know how demons are about their real names. The walls of her parlor were upholstered with a gaudy combination of human skin and orange crushed velvet, and the legs of all the furniture were made of shin bones and barbed wire. You can't make this stuff up. Well, no . . . I guess you can. Bunches of people get paid to make this kind of shit up. So, strike that.

Point is, Madam Calamity had this great Bobby Ng story, which she told us right after her and Mr. B had concluded whatever eldritch transaction had brought us to that house of exceptionally ill repute and he'd called me into her office, because he was of the opinion that I just *had* to meet old Drusneth. Seems holier-than-thou Bobby Ng wasn't as pure as he let on, and he suffered from a horn fetish. Seriously, to hear this mistress of the night tell it, antelopes gave the guy a hard-on. She said he'd once gone to jail and had to do a month of community service for whacking off in front of the gazelles at the Roger Williams Park Zoo. Anyway, he'd had this crazy-ass plan to storm the brothel and banish the whores back down to Hades or Sheol or wherever (and the bookies too, I guess). Then, he was gonna torch the place, bless the whole block, and sow the scorched ground with salt. Bobby's plans can get pretty elaborate.

But *then* he got a look at one of the girls, and to hear Drusneth tell it, no demoness was ever possessed of a better rack. Of horns, I mean. Nothing was said of her tits. Not that I recall. So, Bobby Ng falls for her—or at least he fell for her pointy parts. Which leads to him trying to sneak in and buy an hour of her time, only nobody south of Boston or north of Brooklyn hasn't heard about the jerk. His face is pretty much seared into the minds (or analogous organs) of everyone in the lower half of New England. At least, anyone who runs in these particular circles.

So, the guys at the door, they make him right off, but Drusneth, she wants to see how this scene's gonna play out. The goat-headed kid (sorry, pun unintended) named Agoston, he's told to go ahead and lead Bobby upstairs same as any other trick. Ng gets naked, and the whore lets him feel her horns up for ten or fifteen minutes, then they get around to the fucking part and hilarity ensues when he discovers what she has between her legs. I'm not gonna go there. No need for the gory details. But, by the time all was said and done, he needed twenty fucking stitches. Madam Calamity said one of the bouncers drove him to the emergency room, after she placed a geas on him, preventing Bobby from ever telling a living soul what had happened. She said "living soul," so I'm guessing he was free to tell all the vampires and ghosts he wanted, fat lot of good *that* would do him.

Back to Babe's on the Sunnyside and Mr. B.

"Yeah," I said. "I spent some time in Cranston."

"You have my sympathies," he replied and reached into his jacket. He pulled out a blood orange and began peeling it. Anytime he was drinking—and that was almost every time I saw him—he'd finish up with citrus. Claimed it protected him from hangovers, the big dose of vitamin C and all. Might be a tangerine or a lime or, if he'd really tied one on, even a whole pink grapefruit. But that night in the bar it was a blood orange.

"Very fucking funny," I said.

"What?" he asked, trying to sound innocent and probably failing on purpose. He continued to peel the fruit, exposing the wet crimson flesh.

"The orange, that's what."

"You want half?" he asked, tearing it in two. "I'll share, if you do."

"Creep."

"One day, Miss Quinn, we're going to have a talk about your manners. A polite 'No thank you, Barlow. I'm not in the mood for half of your delicious orange' would have sufficed."

"Never saw you eating a blood orange before," I said, and glanced back at the bar. The place was emptying out.

"There was a special at Whole Foods. The world doesn't revolve around you, dear, not even after the Bride's spot of mischief at your expense."

I tried not to watch as he ate the orange, and I tried even harder not to think how much the juice reminded me of the woman's throat I'd torn open a couple of hours earlier.

"Okay, so I save Bobby Ng's ass six months ago by killing Mercy Brown's special lady friend. Only Mercy can't tell time, what with being dead and all, so out of the blue she saves me from a werewolf—sort of, but not really—and then, exacting her revenge, she turns me. But it's not *only* about vengeance. It also has something to do with a debt she owes—fuck only knows to who or to what—and by making me a vampire—"

"—who's also a werewolf—" Mr. B interjected, then popped another section of orange into his mouth.

"Yeah—fuck you—who's also a werewolf, by doing that, she's breaking some unspeakable bloodsucker taboo, and this matters how?"

"Oh. I haven't a goddamn clue. Not the foggiest. But don't forget she also called you her *pet*."

"When she said that, I half expected I was about to wind up in a cage or boarded at a kennel or something."

"She didn't even have the decency to give you a collar and tags, or see to it you were vaccinated for rabies."

"You are so not funny," I said, picked up a strip of orange peel, and threw it at him. He didn't even flinch, just brushed it off his right shoulder.

"Really? I think I'm a scream," he said and bit off the last bloodred section.

Not much else to say about that night at the bar. He finished his orange right as Jack the Bartender was shooing people out the front door. The bartenders, they never shoo Mean Mr. B. But he never keeps them waiting, either. So, a minute past two a.m., we're standing on the sidewalk outside Babe's on the Sunnyside. I'm watching Jack wipe down the bar and tables with a soppy gray rag. Mr. B, he lights a cigarette, the Nat Shermans he smokes, cigarettes in all the colors of the rainbow. He offers me one, and then lights it for me. There's a chill in the air, and I wonder for the first time if vampires are supposed to feel the cold.

"So, dear," he says, smoke leaking from his nostrils, "here's where we part company for the evening."

"Wait. There's something else she told me."

"Who?"

"Mercy Brown. The goddamn Bride. Who do you think?"

"I wouldn't want to be presumptuous." Mr. B takes another drag off his cigarette; then he asks me, "So, what, pray tell, was this something else she said, this something else that has me standing on the sidewalk outside a closed bar instead of walking home to the comfort of my bed?"

"Can you stop being a jerk for like two minutes?"

"Not bloody likely."

I tapped ash onto the cement at my feet and watched Jack, still busy with his bar rag.

"She said I was a weapon. That she was making me to be a weapon."

Mr. B seemed to consider this a moment. I only *say* considered, because who the hell ever knows what's going through his head. But he chewed at his lip in a thoughtful way, so I figured it was a safe enough bet that he was considering what I'd said.

"So, you're her vengeance for the death of Cregan, and also you're the breaking of a taboo, *and* you're her pet, but you're also a weapon that she's fashioning. That's quite a bit of multitasking, wouldn't you say? The all-purpose werepire."

"Werepire?"

"Would you prefer vampwolf, dear? By the way, there's blood in your hair. You should really do something about that."

"You're not even going to *try* to give me advice?"

He chewed his lip some more, smoked his Nat Sherman, and finally said, "Lay low. Keep your head down. You'll need to feed every couple of nights, but, of course, you already know that. Don't make messes you can't clean up. I'll ask around, hit up the usual suspects, see if I can find out what machinations the Bride might recently have set in motion. How's that?"

"Shitty," I muttered.

"Best I can do, kiddo. At least for the time being."

"And the loup thing?"

"I have heard it said that a devotion to Saint Hubertus has been known to keep the symptoms in check. Patron saint of hunters or some such. Did you know . . . no, I bet you don't . . . did you know that the Jägermeister logo—the stag with the cross above its antlers—is a reference to Saint Hubertus? Also, don't eat the neighbors' cat, or any of the neighbors, for that matter. Draws attention."

I sighed, dropped the rest of my cigarette to the sidewalk, and ground it out beneath the heel of my sneaker.

"I'm going home," I said, with as much disgust as I could muster.

"As well you should. Ta. I'll be in touch."

So, he left me standing there, and I watched Jack until he noticed me watching him, then headed back to my own place. Which, by the way, was an apartment down on the south end of Gano Street (coincidentally, not too far from the rusty bridge and the ditch I woke up in that night). First floor of an old house, and it must have been nice once upon a time, before the fifty years of frat boys and other assorted college students. It had shag carpet the color of vomit, and the paint was peeling off the walls like scaly patches off a shedding reptile. Still, better than abandoned warehouses and couch-surfing, right? Sometimes, the hot water was even hot. And it was easy enough to avoid the hole in the kitchen floor. The rats, I just thought of them as roommates.

It occurs to me I haven't explained *why* Mr. B showed up that day, bearing gifts of heroin and a free apartment. It's not all that complicated, but it did take me about a month to get him to confess his motives. You live on the streets a few years, you learn to be suspicious of any act of goodwill. There are almost always strings attached, so it's a question of weighing the pros against the cons. Just how badly are those strings gonna cut you? Actually, sometimes the strings, they're more like piano wire than strings, if we're talking string in the twine sense. Anyway, I'd had my fingers sliced enough times that I was wary, but not so wary that I was about to turn down free smack and a cleanish place to live. So, dude sets me up, assures me he's on the level, and no, he's not looking for sex, not unless I decide to grow a dick.

But I knew there was more to it than a random act of kindness (to quote the bumper stickers), and one night at Babe's I popped the question. I'd already taken to meeting him there. It seemed to make him happy, and he'd buy me beer and talk about vamps and loups and ghouls and shit. And things I'd never even heard of. I learned there was this whole fucking underworld, and I don't mean the Mafia. I mean the things that hide *beneath* the Mafia, and would have the La Cosa Nostra bosses quaking in their shiny Italian croc-skin shoes. Where was I? Oh, right. Popping the question. So, what's in this for you? Or something of the sort.

Mean Mr. B, he stirred his Cape Cod and smiled, and at first I figured he'd find a perfectly good reason not to answer the question. Or maybe he'd act offended, knowing I'd apologize and drop it for fear of losing such a sacchariferous deal. But that's not how it went. He had one of his boys that night, a cross-dressing piece of arm candy whose name I've long since forgotten. Also, I should note, the aforementioned burly blue-collar types, who were Babe's bread and butter, never even blinked an eye at his boys. Not even at the drag queens and transvestites. Working guys, they drank their beers and watched the ballgames playing on the widescreen TV behind the bar and minded their own business. But, I was saying, I was thinking Mr. B's not about to come clean, when he sends the pretty boy off to powder his nose.

"You keep secrets from them?" I asked.

"Only the secrets that might get them hurt," he replied. "The sorts of secrets with which your query is concerned."

"Then maybe I'm better off not knowing, either."

"Possibly. Probably. Then again, not knowing, sooner or later, that might also mean your arse, yeah? Damned if you do, damned if you don't, getting yourself hemmed in between mademoiselles Scylla and Charybdis, eh?"

By this time, I'll admit, I'm sweating, and the bastard's starting to scare the hell out of me. I'm thinking, what in the devil's pajamas have I gotten myself into? Going back to the streets and whoring for dope was starting to seem like a good idea.

"What do you mean?" I asked. My mouth had gone bone dry, and I'm sure he could tell.

"Man like me, man in the sort of trade I'm in, he needs himself a spot of insurance now and again. And you surely don't think I'm going to that cocksucker Bobby Ng? Certainly not."

(I'd already been regaled with a few of Ng's misadventures and exploits.)

I managed to nod my head.

"See, that lot you call the nasties, time to time they need a job done that's best handled by us quotidian and mortal sorts. So as not to draw an undue degree of cognizance from the mundanes. Makes good business sense, yeah? Sure it does."

I nodded my head again and stared at my bottle of PBR.

"Right, so, returning to the matter of insurance, which is where you come in. I hear about this girl killing off a ghoul and a vamp. Bang, bang. Just like that. Nobody has any idea who she is or where she's come from, but everyone's talking about her. Suddenly, she's the *it* girl, if you know what I mean. Me, I know it's only a matter of time until the monsters take this girl out. They can't have that shit. Makes them look bad. But I'm thinking, knowing them like I do, they're at least a tad bit afraid of this chickadee. And, with a little PR, the right management, they could be a whole lot more scared of her. But, first, I gotta keep her alive and well."

"Insurance," I whispered.

"That's just what I said, isn't it? Insurance. Now and then, a deal goes south. I find myself in a tight squeeze, and I turn this over and over in my head, cogitate on it a while, and it seems worth a try. Small investment, potential for substantial returns."

"But you know they were both accidents."

"Didn't know that when I picked you up that day, and, what matters, Miss Quinn, no one else out *there* knows it. We play it smart and keep things that way, sure. And we build you up a bit more, arrange for another *accident* or two, and people won't be so quick to do me mischief if a transaction goes bad."

"I ain't no bodyguard," I told him. My heart was racing by then, pounding, and all I'm wondering is how I get out of this mess without getting myself killed. Or worse.

"Never said you were. But they don't know that."

"Jesus fuck."

"You're always free to return to your previous lifestyle, dear." And right then he takes a Baggie from a pocket of his blazer and lays it on the table between us.

"Is this blackmail?"

"Why don't you tell me?"

I started to reach for the heroin, then pulled my hand back.

"Whether it is or whether it isn't," he said, smiling that Cheshire Cat smile of his, "you best work through all the angles and consequences. For example, the nasties, they might not be too keen on the idea of me having backup, but they also know that if they clip you, I might not be so eager to run their little errands. You try going it on your own again, I fear for the duration of your life expectancy."

"Asshole," I said, and that was the first time I ever said a word against the bastard. It was the beginning of our long and tumultuous love-hate relationship.

He leaned back and held both his hands palms out. "You're a free agent, precious. Free to get up and walk out that door, return to the everlasting glamour of your previous existence, and never will we meet again. Just you remember, odds are good you had a price on your pretty head *before* I found you, and maybe the only thing keeping the wolves at bay—so to speak—is your affiliation with me. I'd bet my bottom dollar you'd be dead by now if I hadn't come along. Best the devil you know, isn't that the expression?"

Of course, Mr. B ain't no devil. He's just a two-bit lowlife ballsy enough to have cornered a niche market no other lowlife would go near. But what the fuck was I supposed to do? I knew he was right. I knew I'd been played, and there was no going back. Some vamp comes looking for me, was I really gonna say, "Oh, so sorry. Please excuse me. It was a terrible, terrible accident, really it was." Yeah, that would've saved my narrow white keister. A few seconds later, Mr. B's boy came back, all lipstick and purple patent-leather pumps, and I picked up the dope and slipped it into my jeans pocket. And the rest, as all the cold-blooded motherfuckers of the world are forever reminding us, is history.

But here's the kicker. No sooner had I pocketed the heroin, Patti Smith was singing "Land" through the speakers mounted on the walls. And all I could see was that beast crouching over Lily, and her blood spreading across a dusty warehouse floor. Songs for my funeral? You bet your life.

CHAPTER THREE

BOBBY NG, ALICE CREGAN, AND THE TROLL WHO LIVES UNDER THE BRIDGE

Okay, so somewhere back there I know I mentioned the apartment Mean Mr. B rented for me, down at the sketchy post-apocalyptic end of Gano Street. Just a block or two over from my place, you segue back to those spiffy Victorians with their tidy front yards and lawn gnomes. But my building, it's seen better days. Maybe back in the 1940s. The tendrils of gentrification haven't reached the corner of Gano and East Transit, and the way the economy's headed, it probably never will. I don't even know what he pays every month. Maybe he doesn't pay anything. Maybe he owns the place, and twenty bodies are buried in the basement.

That night—my first as a full-fledged lupine bloodsucking abomination in the eyes of all vampkind—I walked from Babe's on the Sunnyside back to the apartment. There were the usual guys on the sidewalk outside my place playing dominoes on a folding card table. Sometimes, they played all night long, dusk till dawn. Which was fine by me, just so long as they kept the Mexpop blaring from the stereos of their parked cars down low enough I couldn't feel the bass pulsing behind my eyes like a migraine. And as long as nobody got shot. Not that I much cared what people did with their firearms, but I hardly needed the police hanging about. Because, remember, this was after Bobby Ng and Swan Point, so, technically, I was already a bona-fide killer. Not sure whether or not it would have mattered to the cops that my victims had been dead a spell *before* I killed them, but I didn't want to go there.

That night, it was after my first *human* kill, so all the more reason to be cautious.

As I was unlocking the door, one of the domino players noticed the dried blood on my T-shirt and jeans. Maybe he saw it in my hair, too. I suppose there was enough illumination from the streetlights, it was probably hard to miss.

"Hey, chica. You been in a fight?" he shouted. I think that one's name was Hector. Or Hugo. Or . . . okay, so I don't remember. I do remember he had something Catholic tattooed on his left bicep, Mother Mary and a heart wrapped in thorns. Something generic, something cliché.

"You could say that," I replied.

"Hope you gave good as you got."

"Better," I replied, turning the key, hearing the tumblers roll loud as thunder. Since I'd awakened by the tracks, the whole damn world was loud—sound, sight, smell, touch—all of it LOUD.

"Your blood or theirs," he asked, and the others laughed. I almost told him to mind his own business.

"*Mostly* theirs," I lied, seeing how it was *all* theirs. Hugo (or Hector, whatever) nodded and gave me the thumbs up.

"Muy peleonera," he grinned. I had to ask him what that meant, which made the guys playing dominoes chuckle again. They laughed a lot, the guys who played dominoes on the sidewalk outside my apartment.

"Don't you worry," he said. "Means you did good."

Insert ironic laughter here.

Cut to me stepping into the apartment. It was stifling, the air stale and warm as any other summer night because Mr. B didn't spring for a window unit. Only, it had never seemed quite *as* stale and stifling as it did that night. Thank you, werevamp super-senses. And there was the smell. Sure, my housekeeping skills were nonexistent. Still are. But the mess in the kitchen sink, and the mold running rampant in the bathroom, and the fast-food bags strewn around the place had never stunk even half as bad as they did that night. I may have actually gagged. Look at me, all creature of the night and shit, ready to spew at the smell of a filthy apartment. But like I said, the stink was LOUD. I mean, you'd think some kind soul had left a dead elephant to rot in that dump. I took a few steps across the mustard-yellow shag and could hear the bodies of roaches—some dead, some not—crunching LOUD in the home they'd made between the carpet and the floor-boards. I could still hear every word the guys on the side-walk were saying, and the Mexpop was starting to make my head ring. I went straight to the bathroom—and I'll spare you further details of that *parfum*, except to say the gagging got worse before it got better. Last thing I wanted to do was vomit the belly full of blood, because, for all I knew, that meant I'd have to hit the streets again before sunup. Anyway, I found enough cotton (scavenged from an aspirin bottle and Q-tips) to stuff into my nose and ears, and that helped just a little. Okay, hardly at all, but give the girl an *E* for *Effort*, right?

I stalked around the place with a Hefty garbage bag (I found a box of them beneath the kitchen sink, though I have no memory of ever having bought such things), tossing everything into it that I could stand to touch and cursing my slovenly ways. Fuck you, Siobhan. Fuck you, too, Mr. Month-Old Mystery Thing from Taco Bell. Fuck you, Miss Ashtray I'd Not Emptied All Summer. Let my vengeance rain down upon thee. By the time the sky was growing light, I'd made a few craters in the clut-ter, but I'd also come to appreciate the futility of my ef-forts. Might as well have been trying to tidy up a landfill.

I couldn't take the reek any longer, so I went outside and sat on the steps and smoked as the streetlights winked out. The domino boys were gone and had taken the card table with them. I sat and stared at the used car lot across the street. A sign promised me the best deals in town. I wondered what had happened to my own car after the encounter with the werewolf and the china doll who wasn't Mercy Brown. Maybe it was still parked out by the reservoir. Maybe she'd pushed it into the water. You know, to cover her tracks, hide the evidence, whatever. Any bitch strong enough to take out a bull loup that size, she'd have no trouble rolling my beat-to-hell-and-back '99 Honda Accord into the Scituate Reservoir. Sure, my Honda wasn't as spiffy as the great deals to be had just across the street, lined-up safe behind chain link and razor wire, but it usually ran and was all I had. It tended to get me where I needed to go. Most times.

Must have been about six or seven ayem when I smoked my last cigarette, got bored, and decided to take a stroll down the street, to the shade below the cavernous I-195 overpass. It's not at all like most highway overpasses. It's more like, I don't know—like someone *had* to build an overpass when they actually *wanted* to design a Gothic cathedral. It's like that. Sort of. Oh, by the by, that crap you hear about vampires bursting into flame if they're caught out in the daylight? Utter nonsense. Just a lot of twaddle concocted sometime around 1922 by a German director named F. W. Murnau when he made *Nosferatu*, a loose adaptation of *Dracula* (which promptly got him sued by Bram Stoker's widow for copyright infringement; she won). You may recall, Stoker's count doesn't have too much trouble with the sun. And, take it from me, vampires sure as hell don't sparkle . . . or glitter . . . or twinkle, no matter what that silly Mormon twit may have written, no matter how many books she's sold, and no matter how many celibate high school girls have signed themselves up for Team Edward. Worst it ever gets, I might feel a prickle on the back of my neck round about noon. Oh, and naturally it's best to feed after dark, but mostly that's so you're less likely to be spotted. Common fucking sense. But that's it. No fiery conflagrations, and no fucking glitter.

It's not far, the walk from my apartment to the overpass, but far enough that along the way I had time to think about how I could have at least changed my clothes and maybe washed my hair. I suppose I'd been too distracted, what with all the retching and cleaning and retching and all. The stains had made the fabric stiff and had gone sort of the color of raisins. My dinners would get a little less messy later on, but that morning in August I was still too entirely stupefied by the curveball the universe had thrown my way to worry overly about hygiene. I just hoped no one noticed, like Hector (or Hugo or et al.), and walked faster. But not too fast, because I was feeling paranoid and thought maybe walking too fast might attract as much attention as the bloodstains. And the two together, doubt anything short of dragging a dead body behind me would be more conspicuous and likely to get me noticed, right?

It's actually pretty nice there under the interstate on hot summer days. You can sit on a plastic milk crate, say, or a cardboard box someone's mashed flat and spread out across a patch of gravel. The traffic roars and rattles by fifty feet or so overhead, but the roadway and those immense support arches of concrete and steel absorb and muffle the worst of the racket. Even after I got smacked with the double whammy of the loup and Mercy, after my senses went all cacophonous on me, it was peaceful enough. And sometimes there were other people to talk to, maybe a homeless woman or a couple of boys with their skateboards headed for the park at India Point. And, of course, Aloysius. He's a troll. Yes, I mean the sort that lives under bridges (and in culverts and beneath railroad trestles), just like you might have read about as a kid in the "Three Billy Goats Gruff."

Of course, Aloysius isn't his *real* name. Trolls are fairies, after all, and fairies ain't so free with their true names. Same as demons, they let that intel get out and they're screwed. You know a troll's name, he's your servant for life. Though, it's a risky business, binding a troll, and it rarely ends well for the one doing the binding. It occurred to me that morning, standing below the interstate and calling out for Aloysius, that an awful lot of folks (or what have you) were dumping pseudonyms on me. Even Bobby fucking Ng, I knew that wasn't his real name. Sure, with Aloysius, he had his reasons, but not so with "Mercy," Mr. B, and Bobby Ng. I considered chalking it all up to the sheer and perverse joy some assholes take in fucking with your head. Or maybe they were all too crazy to know better. From what I'd seen, Mercy Brown was certainly minus a fair share of her marbles. So maybe she and (this week) "Barlow" both had a bee buzzing in their bonnets, and maybe both had gotten the notion their true names were as dangerous . . . shit, wait, where was I?

Oh yeah, Aloysius.

I shouted for him, just like always, and, just like always, the brute came shambling out of the shadows. The special shadows that hadn't been there a few seconds before, and that went away again as soon as he'd appeared (oh, another myth: trolls don't turn to stone in the sun, but I don't know who made that one up). Aloysius, he spoke with this rolling brogue might have been Scots or Irish, possibly Welsh. Never bothered asking him, but figured maybe he'd immigrated to the States back in the 1800s when so many Irish came over. He was a good nine feet tall, with these long ears like those lop rabbits have. They sort of dragged along on the ground, his ears, and each one had so many piercings I never bothered trying to count them. Some held loops of bronze and copper, others elaborately carved wooden rings, and still others were threaded through with bones. Didn't take a professor of anatomy or anthropology to recognize most of those bones were human. Aloysius was a troll, and trolls eat people (and pigeons and rats and stray cats, pretty much anything else too slow to get away), simple as that. But, to his credit, he never tried to eat me. Oh, also, none of his piercings were steel, because that's another tale apparently gets it right. Fairies can't bear the touch of iron. Not even a little bitty bit. No idea why, but there you go.

Back then, Aloysius, he possibly was about as close as I came to having an actual friend-type friend. Someone I could talk to and whatnot. I brought him porn mags, 3 Musketeers bars, and pint bottles of Jacquin's ginger-flavored brandy (all of it shoplifted). And sometimes he paid me in peculiar gold coins that always turned into stones or bottle caps by the time I got home. But hey, nothing lost, nothing gained. It's not like I'd paid for the stuff.

That morning, he got a good look at me and cocked

one warty eyebrow. I'd never seen him look so surprised. In fact, I'd never seen him look surprised at all, and it took me a moment to realize that was the expression on his face. Surprise. Aloysius wrinkled his nose, obviously disgusted, like he could smell my apartment from two blocks away, and he took a step backwards. The special shadows reappeared behind him.

"What?" I asked, like I didn't already know.

He narrowed his orange eyes and glared at me.

"You're not you no more, Quinn girl, *that's* what," he snarled. "*They* been at you, ain't they?" And he pointed a four-jointed index finger at me, scratching at the air with a thick brown nail.

"Yeah, but . . . I'm still *me*."

"No, you're *not*," he declared. "You're what they made you. You're *dead*. You *smell* like death, the sort what don't know to lay down and *be dead*, 'cause they been at you."

Ever had a best friend stare at you like you'd just become a steaming heap of horse shit?

"It wasn't my fault," I said, even though that wasn't precisely true. But near as I knew, trolls didn't have magical lie-detecting abilities. Aloysius flared his wide, hairy nostrils again, snuffled, and looked about as revolted as I imagine a troll can look. Which is kind of ironic when you think about it, given trolls themselves are hardly easy on the eyes.

"You ain't only dead," he said despairingly. "You're gone dead *and* wolfish. You're twofold balled, you are, Quinn girl. Me, I can't even conjecture how that's practicable and likely."

"It's complicated," I replied, hardly speaking above a whisper. "Well, not so much complicated as . . ." and then I stammered something incoherent and trailed off.

Aloysius gritted his massive eyeteeth, sat down with a thud that raised a cloud of dust and grit, and buried his face in one huge hand. Those special shadows behind him evaporated again.

"They done plugged you," he moaned through his fingers. "Told you they would, now didn't I? Didn't I say 'Quinn girl, you go tumbling to that bastard B's angles and contrivances, sooner or later, you'll get plugged good and proper'? I told you that, eh, didn't I?"

"Yeah, you did," I admitted, wondering if trolls could eat people who were half vampire–half werewolf. "Sure, that's what you said, time and time again."

A couple of fingers parted, and he peered out at me from the space between them. His eyes were glowing. "This is fair awful," he said. "This is *worse* than awful. This is . . . odious. An odious crime, what this is."

I waved my hands about, coughing and trying to clear some of the dust from the air. Mostly, though, I just managed to stir it around. Also, I wondered why I was coughing, when I wasn't breathing.

"Jesus, Aloysius, you think I don't know that?" I said, wondering exactly what he meant by *crime*, if he meant the same thing the Bride and Mr. B had meant. "You think I need *you* to tell me it's awful?"

"And you were such a fine lass and all."

"I most certainly was not!" I all but shouted at him. Guess that takes some *cojones*, as Hugo (or Hector) might say, shouting at a bridge troll. "I was a goddamn junky so deluded I thought I could run around slaying nasties, *that's* what I was. Strung out and suicidally foolish, and I don't see how that makes a 'fine lass'!"

"No cause to yell," he said indignantly, still peering through his fingers.

"The hell it ain't. I came down here needing somebody to talk to about this mess, not to have you getting all up in my face with what I already know full well. Not to have you tell me how I brought it on myself."

"I sure enough didn't mean it like that."

I swatted at the dusty air again. "Well, that's *sure enough* the way it sounded."

"You bring me a pint?" he asked, trying to change the subject.

"No, Aloysius. I didn't bring you a pint. I've been sort of fucking preoccupied."

"Killed anyone yet?" he asked, lowering his hand and pointing at my bloodstained clothes, now also coated with a fine layer of dust.

"No, I cut myself shaving."

"No cause to be sarcastic," he muttered.

I wanted to ask him how many human beings he'd snacked on in the last few months, but I didn't. Wouldn't have gotten me anywhere, but I wasn't about to have a *troll* get all high-and-mighty on me for eating any*one* or any*thing*.

"Just one," I said instead.

"No one whose sudden adjournment gonna be noticed, I hope. No one with pals what might get—"

"Shut up," I snapped, and he did. I'd already answered that question for Mr. B, and I didn't see the need to answer it again. I was not yet so keen on the idea that killing people and sucking them dry was okay, just so long as it was some pathetic soul who'd sunk so far down the social ladder no one was likely to miss them. And even if their disappearance was reported to the cops, what the fuck would they care. Just one more scrap of street trash the Providence PD wouldn't have to worry about. A drunk, a bum, a vet who'd been cold shouldered to the gutter by the VA, a runaway teen, a whore, a schizo off his or her meds, and who gives a shit. Or a junky living from score to score, fix to fix, just like I'd been before Mr. B showed up. Just like Lily had been.

Sure, I'm a blood-drinking freak and a loup, but I only prey on the dregs of society, so I'm really just doing a public service, right? Bullshit. I called it bullshit then, and, two years later, I still call it bullshit, that attitude or mind-set or whatever it is. That belief that great swaths of humanity are disposable, just so long as no one gets wise to the fact they're being disposed of. We'll come back to this.

"Gotta learn to clean up after yourself," he said, and poked at my T-shirt. "Ain't nobody gonna buy that's from a nosebleed."

I turned away from Aloysius and rattled off my entire repertoire of profanities. Which is saying something. The troll waited until I was done, and then he poked me in the back almost hard enough to knock me over. Sure, I know he hadn't *meant* to poke me that hard, but I wasn't much in the mood to cut him any slack.

"Stop that!" I barked, whirling on him. I think if I'd had a pool cue or a lead pipe or anything else handy, I'd have smacked him upside his craggy, pockmarked face.

"Stop what?" he asked. And never had a troll sounded so goddamn innocent.

"Stop shoving me around, that's what."

"Weren't my intent." He was silent for a few seconds, then asked, "You brought me a candy bar, eh?"

I scowled. I stared icily. I gave him the dirtiest look I was capable of. "I came here, Aloysius, because I'm freaked out, and Mr. B's worse than useless, and I thought maybe—just maybe—you might be able to answer at least one of the questions that seems awfully important at the moment."

"Not even a dirty magazine?" he whispered hopefully, and I kicked him in the ankle. Hard. Hard as I could kick. He made a noise like . . . I don't know . . . a sheep caught in a wood chipper.

"I'm going home," I said, and turned my back on him a second time. "I was an idiot, coming down here. I can get more answers from comic books and monster movies than I'm ever gonna get outta you."

He reached out, seizing my left shoulder and yanking me roughly back. My feet got tangled up together, and I landed on my ass in the dirt. I just sat there, my tailbone aching like a motherfucker, sure I'd pushed my douchebag luck (think I mentioned that early on, the nature of my luck, or lack thereof) all the way into the red. I was pondering how many mouthfuls I'd make when Aloysius lifted me easy as you'd lift a ragdoll and set me on my feet again.

"You gonna ask me a question, Quinn girl, and you ain't got no sort of offering on hand, like you don't know the rules. As if, of a sudden, the rules don't apply no more, 'cause you gone and got yourself twofold plugged."

"I forgot, okay," I said and rubbed at my bruised tailbone. "Believe it or not, sort of had a lot on my mind lately. Did I mention that?"

Aloysius frowned and furrowed his gray-green brow. He shrugged. "Were it just me, Quinn lass, were that all there is to it . . . well, you versed sufficient in the ways of the fair folk to know . . . no exceptions and such . . ."

"I was hoping for a freebie," I told him. "Just this once. Maybe a favor for a friend."

"Ain't the way of my vocation, and I know you cognize that perfectly fine without me havin' to spell it out."

"I think you broke my ass," I mumbled.

"Your coccyx," he said.

"My what?"

"Your coccyx," he said again, but this time taking care to pronounce the word very slowly, drawing out the two syllables—*cahk-six*. "Almost indescribably tasty, marrow what a fella can dig from a coccyx. A bone I hold in highest esteem, it is."

"Well, I think you broke mine."

"No freebies," he said.

"I don't *have* anything on me, Aloysius. And I don't feel like petty theft today, all right?"

"No freebies," he said a third time.

And that's when it occurred to me, something that a troll might count as a gift, and I said, "Okay. How about Mr. B's phone number? And I mean his top-secret, utterly confidential, private fucking cell phone number. Sure. That's gotta be worth at least one of your riddles."

Aloysius made a sort of confused face. "Ain't never used no telephone," he said.

"Doesn't mean you can't learn. Hell, next time I make it down this way, I'll bring you a fucking phone, okay?"

"Irregular," he said and scratched his chin. "Prodigiously irregular, at that."

"Come on, dude. You can have a blast with prank calls, right? Better than a whole stack of nudie mags. I know you hate the cocksucker, and this would piss him off on beyond royally."

"Prank calls?"

"Yeah, you know. Call him up and . . . well, you'd think of something, I'm sure." Right about here, I was starting to believe this was actually going to work. Aloysius was getting that gleam in his eye, the one he had whenever his curiosity got the better of him.

"Might be," he said to himself. "Might be at that."

"And look, let's say it doesn't work out for you, fine. I'll owe you a whole *box* of 3 Musketeers."

Still scratching at his chin, the bridge troll narrowed his eyes at me again. "King size," he said. "Big on Chocolate, not on Fat."

"Right. Whole damn box."

"How many is that?" he asked and cocked an eyebrow.

Hell if I knew, so I said the first thing popped into my mind. "Two dozen, twenty-four."

"Deal," said Aloysius, so I told him Mr. B's phone number. I didn't have anything to write it on, but I figured Aloysius would remember. And if he didn't, well, I could worry about that later, when I came back to the underpass with a stolen cell phone and twenty-four candy bars (and yes, there's iron in chocolate, I know; don't ask). I looked at the troll's fingers, big around as sausages, and wondered how in hell he'd manage the buttons on a phone. Something else I could worry about later. Maybe I could snag a stylus somewhere. Or just a pencil. Maybe that would work for him. Anyway, Aloysius repeated the number back to me several times, and each time I told him, yep, that's precisely what I said. The seventh or eighth time through, I asked him if he was stalling, trying to welch. He looked hurt, and I apologized.

"Always so impatient, so hasty, always so hurry-me-up, Quinn girl. What's your question?"

I chewed my lip and drew circles in the dust with the toe of my tennis shoe. "Is there any way to control lycanthropy? I mean, to keep myself from changing?"

"Ahhhhhh, now that ain't no easy query. Riddle might take me a while, you know."

"Just spit it out, Aloysius. You ever stop to think I might not have all day to stand around here shooting the shit with you?"

"Gets fair lonely here under my bridge," he sighed, all but moping now. "Not even a proper bridge, at that. Now, if I had a proper bridge, ah. If I had a *proper* bridge—"

"The riddle, please," I interrupted, and Aloysius sighed again. (Oh, that's the catch with trolls—and all fairies, for that matter—they'll only answer a question with a riddle. They swear it's the best they can do; I have my doubts.)

"You know the rules," he said.

"Yeah, I know the goddamn rules. Just one riddle, that's all I get, and I can't ask for another for a fortnight, and blah blah fuckity blah. But, I *also* know you can't cheat. No riddles that don't have answers. No 'Why is a raven like a writing desk' nonsense."

"Ain't nonsense," he said. "Has an answer, it does, so can't be nonsense. A raven is like a writing desk because it can produce a few notes, though they are very flat. And it is *never* put with the wrong end in front."

I stopped drawing circles in the dust and seriously considered kicking him in the ankle again.

"I gave you B's number, now I want my riddle. Pretty please. With whipped cream and sprinkles and a cherry on top."

"Oh, and what's moreover," he continued, "a raven's like a writing desk since they both come with quills."

"Aloysius . . ."

"Likewise, Edgar Allan Poe wrote *on* both," he said, and I was silent a moment, making sure he had nothing further whatsoever to add on the similarities of ravens and writing desks.

Then I said, "That's another thing. The riddle has to have a single answer, right? And it has to be the answer that I need, the answer to the question I ask. See? I know the rules. Now, ask me the goddamn riddle."

He made a harrumphing sound and took a magnificently exasperated breath, a magnificently *deep* exasperated breath, and then let it out all at once. Standing there, it was briefly like being in a wind tunnel with something that had been decayed a long time. In fact, it might have smelled worse than my apartment.

"You ready?" he asked. "I only put forth the riddle once, and not twice, or thrice."

"I know that, and I'm ready."

"Fine," he said, and I realized I was going to have to memorize this, because, as I mentioned already, I didn't have anything to write on.

"A child of woman newly forged,
The pump what drives the rosies.
Round about, round about,
So Bloody Breast flies home again.
Soldiers come in single file,
Aphrodite's child tills loam."

When he was done, I don't think I stared. I think I gawked in utter indignation.

"What the hell sort of riddle is *that*? It doesn't even rhyme!"

"Rules don't say no-how that my riddles have to rhyme, now do they, Quinn lass?"

"No . . . but . . ." And then I reminded myself I needed to remember every single word. So, I stopped arguing with Aloysius and began repeating the six lines back to myself again and again and again. I've always been pretty good with rote memorization. In third grade, I was the first kid in my class who could recite the multiplication tables. For all the good it's ever done me.

"Okay . . . wait . . . so 'A child of woman freshly forged,' that's easy. A baby. It's a baby, isn't it?"

"Perchance."

"Oh, no. None of that *perchance* rubbish. You *have* to tell me if I'm right," I reminded the troll.

"I prefer suckling, is all," he said more than a little defensively.

"I'm sure you do. Turning on a spit, with an apple in its mouth."

Aloysius just grinned and gazed up at the roadway far overhead.

"So, the answer to the first line is 'an infant.' And the second line, a pump that drives roses."

"I said rosies."

"Same thing."

"Perchance."

I raised my voice and repeated the second line, "A pump that drives the roses. What's *that* supposed to be?"

"Can't say."

"I was asking myself, not you."

"Gotta go now, Quinn girl. Got to see a man about a horse. Gotta get a wiggle on."

I rubbed at my head, which was starting to ache, and I wondered if that was something to do with being a vampire, or with being a werewolf, or both, or if it was Aloysius' fault.

"You just claimed you were lonely."

"Was then, that was. Now I gotta go."

"Dude, *was then* was like thirty seconds ago."

"3 Musketeers," he said, almost growling. "That's what you promised, and that's what I get, elsewise . . ."

Those special shadows were beginning to slink back from wherever they hid when I couldn't see them. They began to creep over Aloysius' shoulders like a cloak.

"Jesus, I thought we were friends, and here you are threatening me."

"Not a threat," he said, his voice already beginning to sound distant. "Loves you dear as peaches, does I. Even now. But our rules are rules, and Good Lady Underhill, queen of us all, she don't suffer them what breaks 'em."

"Just give me five more minutes," I pleaded.

"Creamy nougat," he said. "Delicious milk chocolate. Five grams of saturated fat."

"I *know* what a 3 Musketeers bar is, you idiot!" I shouted at the vanishing troll.

And then he was gone. He was gone, and I was left there alone beneath the I-195 overpass, alone in my blood-stained jeans and T-shirt, with nothing much to my name but my unanswered questions, a filthy apartment, and the riddle. I sat down in a patch of ragweed, and began working at the five lines I'd not yet solved. I decided I might as well sit there until dark. I certainly had no desire to return to my apartment, and nowhere else to be.

Now, there are two versions of what happened that night in Swan Point Cemetery, the night I killed the vampire named Alice Cregan. There's the way I still thought it had come about and gone down, and then there's the second version, which is the truth. However, sitting there beneath the overpass, I didn't yet know the truth. I only knew that first version, what Mean Mr. B had a stake in me believing was the truth. So, for now, that's the version that I'm going to relate here. Just seems more honest that way. I'll get around to the facts a little later on. They can wait.

Swan Point Cemetery is the most stately and well-manicured boneyard in the city. Pretty much anyone who has any cause to think about Rhode Island cemeteries knows this. There are graves there dating back to 1732, I think (but don't quote me on that). Lots of famous folks got themselves buried out there: Revolutionary War soldiers, Civil War generals, congressmen, ambassadors, poets, political bosses, governors, painters, prominent industrialists, the man who invented the Corliss steam engine, and even the author H. P. Lovecraft. Some idiots actually tried to dig Lovecraft back up on October 13th, 1997. They only made it a few inches before giving up. Exhuming a corpse isn't anywhere as easy as people tend to think. Not unless you have a backhoe. But, for a time, it did lead to security getting very paranoid and viciously obnoxious about certain sorts of visitors showing up to pay their respects to the Old Gent, which led to ugly altercations with fans, a local writer, and even filmmakers. Fortunately, the whole brouhaha eventually quieted down. I think some of the pushier guards were sacked. You ask me, it was a case of security getting their panties in a twist over a whole lot of nothing. Lovecraft isn't even buried beneath his headstone, but, I think, below the adjacent Phillips family obelisk. Anyway . . .

Back in the day, Lily and me, along with a constantly revolving cast of other sleepwalkers and homeless ne'er-do-wells would show up at the cemetery after hours, scale the stone walls, and shoot up among the narrow houses. It was a peaceful place, as long as we avoided the zealous security guards, which, somehow, we always managed to do. Frankly, we worried a lot more about the quality of the smack, getting a ten-cent pistol, for instance, which would have been all she wrote. Hell, back then, I thought there was no safer place to be than a graveyard. Bill Burroughs once said, "Dead people are less frightening than live ones," and that was pretty much our reasoning. As for the zealous, lurking guards with their pickup trucks and spotlights and sidearms, that just added an edginess, though not one I think any of us took very seriously. Heroin addicts don't tend to make a whole lot of noise once they've fixed.

I'd lie there in the grass with Lily, spread out among the slate and marble headstones. Sometimes, we'd neck or sloppily, halfheartedly play at heavy petting. Other times, we'd just stare up through the tree limbs, at the light-polluted sky, wishing we could see the stars. We rode the dragon hard, and it rode us right back, and Swan Point was pretty close to Heaven in those not-so-long-lost days. Sometimes, two years and change seems like forever to me; other times, it's not much more than yesterday.

Now and then, one of us would pretend to spot a falling star or Venus or whatever. One night, Lily swore she saw a flying saucer, but we both knew it was only an airplane heading into T. F. Green International down in Warwick (by the way, that's *War-ick*, not *War-wick*, just like Greenwich is *Gren-itch*, not *Green-witch*, and so forth, unless you *want* to sound like a tourist. Maybe you do. None of my business, either way).

I've strayed a long way from what went down that night Alice Cregan bit the dust, chasing all these bittersweet reminiscences. It's hard not to linger on those happier days. And they *were* happier days, whatever the clean and sober might think, those self-righteous assholes who've never been out on the street, who've never fixed, and who think anyone who has is surely bound for that oft-rumored Lake of Fire and Brimstone. Well, fuck them. Ignorance ain't bliss, theirs or anyone else's; it's nothing but ignorance, plain and simple, and it rarely leads to anything good.

But I'll set those memories aside. Worrying at them doesn't do me any good, change public opinion, nor does it get this story told.

It was a night in February. There'd been a heavy snowfall a couple of days before, nine or ten inches, and Swan Point is always beautiful in the snow. The moon was a few nights before full, and everything was bright and glorious. I'd scored my Baggie from Mr. B, and decided to head out to the cemetery, despite the cold, just for old times' sake, right? That night in February—I remember it was a Sunday night, not long after sunset, so maybe sometime around six or six thirty. I stuck to familiar paths, and finally huddled in the lee of a mausoleum. I had my army-surplus messenger bag I'd taken to carrying, and my kit was tucked safe inside. I wrestled with the bag's buckles and snaps, dug about inside, and finally opened up the leather case that held all the precious accoutrements of my addiction. I cinched the rubber tubing around my left bicep, and started cooking with my spoon and Zippo lighter (the latter was a gift from B). I was just about to do the deed—I mean, the needle was loaded up and maybe a millimeter from piercing a bulging vein—when I heard someone talking, talking loudly and not very far away from the place I was crouched. First thought, fucking security, and I was getting ready to pack up and scoot. But then, a second or two later, I recognized that voice.

Bobby fucking Ng.

I cursed and slumped back against the wall of the crypt, then slipped the full needle into my kit again. I sat still and listened. Near as I could tell, he was tromping around helter-skelter, making about as much noise as you might expect from a rampaging bull moose. The snow did nothing whatsoever to stifle the commotion. I couldn't begin to guess what the hell he was up to out there, and, frankly, I didn't care. I was just pissed at having been interrupted in that split second before the junk flooded my veins and let me forget for a few hours everything I wanted or needed to forget. Right about then is when he started hollering at the top of his lungs.

"I *know* you're here, foul daughter of Lilith! Show yourself, you unholy *strigoi* fiend! Rise from the putridity and foul matter of your undead sleep and face your final earthly judgment!"

Now, this probably isn't exactly what he said, but you get the gist. It was pure and classic Bobby Ng, and I giggled quietly to myself and figured I'd at least have a funny story to relate to Mr. B and Aloysius and whoever else wanted to hear it. Bobby continued shouting.

"Wamphyri! You hear me? I *know* you hear me! I also know you've already feasted on the sanguine juices of some innocent soul this very night! And now I mean to put an end to your depredations, once and for all!"

Right about here, I was in danger of giggling so loudly he'd hear me. He actually fucking said "sanguine juices," with dog as my witness. Oh, and later on I'd find out he'd snagged "wamphyri" from a series of books by some hack of an English writer whose name I can't presently recall. Probably, that's for the best.

"Show yourself, Alice Cregan!" he screamed, and by now, I'm just waiting for the guards to show up and haul him away. No such luck. Maybe it was too damn cold that night for them to give a shit about some loon calling out a vamp in their cemetery. Maybe they all had something better to do. Whatever. Bobby Ng continued to stomp about, making such a ruckus I was sure he *had* to be doing it on purpose. Clearly, stealth was the last thing on his mind.

"Show yourself, you coward of Hell! Suffer the wrath of Bobby Ng, Demon Slayer!"

Okay, so this is when I cracked up, and clearly he heard me, because he stopped stomping about. All at once, the cemetery was quiet, except for my laughter, and I clamped my hand over my mouth. The last thing I wanted was a face-to-face with Infamous Ng.

And right then, that's when I heard another sound. It was a sound I'd never heard before, but straightaway I knew what it was, and I reached for my bag. My kit wasn't the only thing in there. There was the self-cocking, pistol-grip mini-crossbow Mr. B had given me. Lightweight aluminum frame, a 50-pound draw, and it was loaded with silver-tipped bolts carved from an ash tree, supposedly blessed by some priest or another. B had assured me there wasn't a vamp or loup in all the world those bolts wouldn't bring down. I pulled it from the bag and stood, my cheek pressed to the freezing stone of the mausoleum, my ears trained on that awful sound, familiar as waves against the shore or wind in the trees . . . or the opening guitar riff of Nirvana's "Smells Like Teen Spirit." It was a leathery sort of sound, the flutter of enormous wings.

Bobby Ng had come looking for a nasty, and this time he'd found one.

There was a woman's voice then, colder than the snow and ice, colder than any February's ever been. Sharp as a goddamn machete.

"You *woke* me," she said, that keen and icy voice choked with a mixture of disbelief and pique. I think she was near to sputtering. "I was sleeping, and you dare to come here and wake me?"

"I dare more than *that*, succubus," Bobby said, though he didn't sound so much a quarter full of himself as he had only a few moments before. "I *dare* to send you back to the pits of Hell!"

The vampire started laughing at him then, just like I'd been laughing at him. And I knew how this was going to turn out. Any second now, Bobby Ng would be dead as a doorknob, and sure, I hated the ridiculous little weasel. But, I remember standing there thinking how our lives would be a lot less interesting without the continuing antics of Bobby Ng. Still, that was hardly cause to do what I did next. I stepped out from behind the cover of the mausoleum.

The pair of them couldn't have been more than ten yards from me. Bobby was standing in a knee-deep snowdrift clutching something that looked like an antique blunderbuss in one hand (I shit you not) and a crucifix in the other. The vamp was perched atop an especially tall headstone, right in front of him. Fuck me, but she hardly even looked real. I'd only seen that one vampire in the alley outside the Starbucks on Thayer, but *this* nasty, she was a whole different ball game. The air around her swirled, the snow whipped up into a silvery whirlwind, and her skin was dark as pitch. And yeah, she did, in fact, have wings, like a goddamn prehistoric reptile and at least fifteen or twenty feet across. I couldn't see her face, thank fuck. I didn't want to see her face. But I could tell by Bobby's expression that he saw it, plain as day.

What happened next, it happened so fast there wasn't time to wonder if I was doing the right thing. There wasn't time to consider that, just maybe, ol' Mr. B was full of shit about that crossbow, which, by the way, I'd only ever had occasion to fire at soda cans lined up on a brick wall. And I'd missed every single one of them. What happened next, well . . . you hear people talk about shit going all slo-mo in the split second before a car crash, right? It wasn't like that at all. If anything, time seemed to rev its engine and speed the hell up.

The vampire leapt from the headstone, and it moved the way a lion with wings would move. If lions had wings. If griffons were real (and for all I know, they are). Part pounce, part glide. Its hands were talons. It was stark naked and almost thin enough for me to make out every rib and vertebra, every bone in its skeleton. In the moonlight, its skin looked like velveteen, and that snowy whirlwind trailed out behind it. Bobby, he screamed like a girl in a slasher flick, which is to say, like me, tried to back away, and fell on his butt. The blunderbuss, pointing skyward now, went off and blew a couple of branches off a poplar tree. They landed on him.

I aimed the crossbow like I'd been born with it in my hand, like it was maybe a natural extension of my arm. I leveled it at the nasty, and I squeezed the trigger. I squeezed the trigger twice. And the vamp crumpled in an ebony heap mere inches from Bobby Ng. Me, I just stood there, shivering, suddenly freezing, my heart pounding hard enough it made me dizzy. My arm drifted a foot or so to the left, and I squeezed the trigger again. A third bolt whizzed from the crossbow and hit Bobby Ng just above his right knee. He screamed even louder than he'd screamed when the vamp rushed him. He called me a bitch and a few other things I won't waste time repeating. He rolled around in the snow, caught beneath the branches, clutching his leg and bleeding all over the place.

My pulse was normal again, and the dizziness passed as quickly as it had come.

"You really are a fucking moron," I said, the February night making a puff of fog from each and every word. "I ought to put another of these right between your legs."

I noticed he was trying to pull the bolt out, and I told him it would only bleed worse if he did, and he called me a bitch again. I lowered the bow, and stared at the dead vampire. It's not like in stories (she said, again). They don't turn into a steaming pile of goo, or quickly decompose as decades or centuries of decay catch up with them all at once. They sure as hell don't go up in a nice clean puff of dust. They just lie there, like any corpse. In this case, a corpse that only looked vaguely human, and that I knew Mr. B didn't want one of the Swan Point rent-a-cops stumbling across, a monstrosity he wouldn't be at all happy to see splashed across the front page of the *Providence Journal.* Me, I didn't give a shit. But, back then, I wasn't working for me.

"Fuck," I muttered. "Guess I shouldn't have shot you

after all, Bobby. Now I have to clean this mess up all on my own."

"She was *mine*," he whined. "They *promised*. She was supposed to be mine. You fucking cheated, Quinn. They swore Cregan was mine."

At the time, I had no idea what he meant by that. Later, though, it would all be crystal clear.

"Yeah, well," I told him, "now she's no one's. Now, she's just meat. Shut up, before someone hears you."

I went back for my bag, dug out the huge hunting knife stashed there (*another* gift from B, cause he's such a generous soul and all), then walked back to the remains of Alice Cregan. While Bobby rolled around in the snow, managing to push away the branches that had fallen on him, whimpering and begging me to call an ambulance, I cut open the vampire's chest and sliced out its heart. It was the shade of red that comes just before black. I don't know a word for that color and don't feel like reaching for the thesaurus, but that's the color it was, and it was still beating. Weakly. I probably wouldn't have noticed if I hadn't been holding the thing.

"I've half a mind to make you eat this," I told Bobby, and he stopped rolling in the snow just long enough to give me the middle finger.

"Raw," I added.

There's not much left to tell. It went pretty much like the Bride said the night she turned me. I decapitated her, burned the heart to ashes (which is a lot harder, and takes a lot longer, than you might think, by the way), gutted the vamp's velvety black cadaver, stuffed it with stones (not bricks, as the Bride had claimed; where was I gonna get bricks?), then dragged it through the snowy cemetery, following one of the lanes leading down to the Seekonk River. Fortunately, it wasn't frozen solid. I pushed the body into the water, dark as slate. I was relieved that she had the decency to sink.

I wanted to wash my hands, but I'd probably have gotten frostbite. Instead, I followed my footprints (and the gory furrow the dead vampire had made) in the snow back to the mausoleum. By then, of course, the smack in the needle was ice. Oh, and Bobby was gone. There was a bloody trail where he'd limped off to lick his wounds. Maybe he'd wandered away to look for the conspicuously absent security guys. I slung the bag over my shoulder and hiked back to the place where I'd climbed over the wall. It had started snowing again, hard. In another couple of hours the sun would be up, and all I wanted was to get back home, fix, and sleep about twenty hours. I headed south down Blackstone Boulevard, hoping I didn't encounter any unduly curious policemen along the way.

And that's the night I killed Alice Cregan. At least, that's pretty much all I knew about it six months later, sitting there in the weeds beneath the interstate.

About two p.m., maybe two thirty, I was pretty damn sure I'd puzzled out the answer to Aloysius' riddle. Also, I needed a cigarette so bad it hurt. Maybe Mercy had cured me of the need for junk, but my body still craved nicotine. Just something else that doesn't make much sense, right? Anyway, I called the number I'd given the troll, and after six rings, Mr. B answered. I told him I needed fifty bucks. He said no problem, and I was instructed to meet one of his mollies at the corner of Gano and Pitman. Which worked for me. Boy arrived in a candy-apple red C6 Corvette coupe. The top was down, and when he gave me the fifty, I almost asked for a ride. But I knew *he* knew what I'd become. I could tell by the way he flinched when he handed me the bill that he was scared shitless of me. I let him off the hook. I just didn't feel like bothering with the spooked kid.

I had the presence of mind to head back to my place, shower, and change out of the bloodstained clothes. I found a tank top and a pair of jeans that were merely dirty, then headed off in the direction of a shopping plaza just north of the rusty old drawbridge I mentioned earlier. Just north of where I'd awakened the day before. I ducked inside a grocery store and bought a pack of Camel Wides and twenty-four king-sized 3 Musketeers bars (and did my best to ignore the smell of blood wafting from the meat department). There's a liquor store next door, so I picked up a bottle of the ginger brandy Aloysius loved so much. I probably could have gotten a cheap prepaid cell phone at the Rite Aid across the parking lot, but I most likely didn't have enough money. I doubt he *wanted* the damn phone, anyway, and if it turned out he did, I could get it later. Instead, I headed down Gano again, stopping at a convenience store where I grabbed the latest copies of *Hustler* and *Juggs* (and that killed the fifty). The clerk made a joke about dykes. Then I lugged this veritable cornucopia of earthly delights back to the overpass.

The domino guys were out, and they shouted at me as I passed.

"Where you headed in such a hurry, *chica*?"

"Gotta see a man about a horse," I shouted back, and they hooted and returned to their game.

I was beginning to feel hungry, a faint gnawing in the pit of my belly, even though vamps usually only need to feed every couple of nights. Maybe it was the loup bite throwing the schedule off, I thought, and tried not to dwell on my nagging stomach. The day was hot as fuck, the sun a white-hot bastard in the sky, and I'd started to feel that peculiar tingle on the back of my neck. I found myself grateful for the cover of the overpass. There was no one around, so I set the three plastic bags on the ground and shouted for Aloysius. The special shadows appeared, and, just like always, he trundled forth, those long ears dragging along, his elephantine feet raising dust as he came.

"Already?" he asked, cocking an eyebrow and frowning. "Already has my answer, Quinn lass?"

"I thought I wasn't me anymore."

"Easier than making up some other name," he said and shrugged his wide bony shoulders.

"Yeah, already. I figured it out, and I come bearing presents. So, don't look so glum."

Aloysius peered in each of the three bags, then looked up at me. "Where's the phone?" he asked. "That was the deal, yes? What good's the number I got without the phone?"

I groaned and stared up at the steel and concrete overhead, towards all those unseen cars racing to and fro. "I was in a hurry. I'll get you the phone later." I wasn't about to give him mine.

"But that was the deal, it was."

"Jesus, dude. Look at all this shit," and I motioned towards the candy, the booze, and the porn. "With all this shit, you can eat and drink and jerk off until you're half comatose."

"But that wasn't the deal," he protested, still frowning, picking at a huge mole on the end of his nose.

"It's gonna have to do for now. I think I know the answer, and I need to be sure I got it right."

"You *think*? You call when you only think, not *know* for sure and unequivocal? I was fair busy, I was."

Aloysius had never not been glad to see me. But I got it. I wasn't me anymore. I was a facsimile, a cheap imitation. I was this thing the Bride had made of me.

"I'll have the phone to you by tomorrow evening," I said. He stopped picking at the mole and licked his lips thoughtfully, indecisively.

"Just tell me if I'm right, okay?"

"Fine. Can't expect someone dead and wolfish to play by the rules. Quinn girl always played by the rules, didn't she? Quinn lass, she never tried to cheat me."

"I'm not trying to—"

"No more wasting of my time," he grumbled, waving a hand at me. "You so smart, lass. What's my answer?" He pulled a candy bar from the bag, not bothering to remove the wrapper before he popped it into his mouth.

"The child of woman newly forged, that's an infant. And the pump that drives the roses—"

"Rosies," he mumbled around the 3 Musketeers.

"Fucking *rosies*, that's a heart. The whole round about, round about business, that one was hard, but you were talking about the moon."

He chewed and watched me.

"Bloody Breast, that was almost too easy. That was a gimme. It's a robin."

"Soldiers come in single file?" he asked, reaching for the brandy.

"March. Specifically, the *month* of March."

Aloysius nodded, then broke the paper and plastic seals on the bottle. He tossed the cap aside.

"The last line, that was the kicker. 'Aphrodite's child tills loam.' Took me two hours, that one line, cause she had like a hundred children. But the one you meant was Hermaphroditus. And the line, that refers to earthworms."

The troll belched. "Fine and true, one by one. But now you gotta add it all up, yes? Add it one to one to one and one, and tell me the sum."

I crossed my arms, so fucking sure of myself I wanted to smirk. But I didn't. "A full moon, and specifically, the Full Worm Moon, the full moon in March. I can break the spell if I sacrifice an infant who was born on the night of the Full Worm Moon, and remove its heart."

Now, knowing the answer to the riddle, like I thought I did, don't get it in your head that means I was too keen on the idea of murdering a baby. But I figured I'd cross that bridge when I came to it.

Aloysius took another swig from the bottle, then shook his shaggy head, all that lichen-colored hair whipping back and forth. "Nope. Wrong. Don't bother me again until you got the solution not for maybe, but for certain." And the special shadows reappeared and began to slither towards him like a living oil spill.

"Bullshit! That's the answer."

"Can't lie to you. Not on a riddle. You said yourself. You have intimate knowledge of Lady Underhill's rules. Gotta go now." And he snatched up the bag of candy and the bag with the two magazines.

"Don't you fucking dare!" I shouted and seized his arm. He shook me off as easy as I'd flick a mosquito away, and I was left sprawling in the dirt.

"When you know. Not before," he growled, his eyes burning like embers in his skull. The shadows swallowed him, and there I was, alone again.

And what do you say?

What do you do?

Me, I went back to my stinking, roach-infested apartment. I realized I was sleepy, maybe sleepier than I'd ever been in my whole life. Sure, I'd been up since twilight the day before. But I knew it wasn't just that. Maybe I'd gotten the riddle wrong, but I understood the sudden grogginess perfectly well. I went home, crawled onto the bare mattress lying in a corner of one room, and—like any good vampire—I slept the sleep of the dead.

CHAPTER FOUR

LIMBO AND CLEMENCY

Just read back over the first three chapters of this thing, and seeing everything that's been left out and told the wrong way round (never mind the bald-faced lies), I feel it's necessary to call attention to the fact that I'm not a writer. In fact, I am most *emphatically* not a writer. An actual writer, he or she probably wouldn't be making all these stupid mistakes right and left, the omissions and continuity errors and whatnot. For example, I didn't mention how B slipped me a pair of sunglasses when I showed up at Babe's on the Sunnyside (before the first kill, not after). They were a pair of Ray-Ban Wayfarers with fancy tortoiseshell frames, and I'm thinking maybe he'd had them since the 1980s. Don't know why I got that impression. They just had this 1980s vibe about them.

"Don't want anyone getting a good look at those peepers, kitten," he'd said. "You're going to need to be as inconspicuous as possible, and those new eyes of yours just scream bad news."

So, yeah. If you want a point A to point Z narrative, you're sure as hell not gonna get it here.

As for the lies, I'm guessing writers lie at least as much as junkies, and maybe more, so I'm gonna cut myself some slack in that department. Oh, and if you're thinking, "But wait, Quinn, she ain't a junky anymore. She's a vampire." To which I would reply, only difference between the me of now and the me of those days before the Bride is that now it's blood, not heroin. As William Burroughs (yeah, I quote him a lot) wrote, "Once a junky always a junky. You can stop using junk, but you are never off after the first habit." So, there you go, constant reader. Straight from the horse's mouth. Anyway, just remember this is a book being written by someone who dropped out of school when she was twelve, and after that whatever she learned about grammar and composition was cribbed from library books.

Jesus, why do I even feel the need to explain such a thing. It ought to be obvious, right? And who do I think will ever read this?

Okay, so now it's the day after all that business with Aloysius. And I tried to call Mr. B, but all I got was this message telling me the number I'd called was no longer in service. Sitting on my filthy mattress in my filthy apartment, I must have tried the number twenty or thirty times in two hours. The sun was getting low, and I was starving half to fucking death, and I still had a boatload of questions no one had bothered to answer. I started to wonder if maybe Aloysius had gotten his paws on a phone after all. Maybe he found a pay phone somewhere (though I doubt any of those still exist), or maybe he'd eaten someone and, later on, found their mobile while picking his teeth. Maybe he'd been ringing Mr. B the whole time I was sleeping, and finally B had the number disconnected. Bought a new phone. Whatever.

I haven't really taken the time to say a whole lot about just how messed up Miss Mercy Brown had left me. I suppose I take it for granted people know this shit, when obviously they don't. They know the shit they read in books and see in movies, and that's about it. And, as I have been pointing out all along, most of that pop-culture lore is nonsense. Of course, you gotta take my word for that, and—don't forget—junkies are, by definition, liars. So you believe whichever parts you wanna believe and chuck the rest. Won't be no skin off my nose.

In between trying to get B on the phone, I'd go to the cruddy bathroom and stare at my face in the cruddy bathroom mirror. I kept hoping that I wouldn't be so shocked the next time I looked, but every time I went back to that mirror, same . . . ah, what would a shrink say? Maybe that I was experiencing intense dissociative disruptions triggered by a traumatic situation. Me, I'd say I was freaked out as freaked out gets, but I guess that's a case of six of one, half dozen of the other. All semantics. Anyway, my skin was already sickly pale, and those eyes Mean Mr. B was worried about, yeah, full-on vamp. Some of the identifying characteristics of bloodsuckers take years, or even centuries, to manifest. But not the eyes. The Quinn staring back at me from the medicine cabinet looking glass had eyes robbed of even the least trace of their former humanity. Only, there was a twist. These were not the shiny black eyes of just any vampire, devoid of pupil, iris, and sclera—shark eyes, like I said earlier on. No, these were *almost* those eyes, but shot through with amber threads. So, I guessed that was the loup part of me showing through. The sight of them made me dizzy, and did nothing good for the mounting nausea from the hunger. From the need to eat, or fix, or whatever you wanna call it.

Oh, and my teeth. We're not talking normal human teeth, only with elongated canines or incisors. Not Barnabas Collins or Christopher Lee. Oh, sure, the canines were longer than normal, but have you ever seen a piranha's teeth? Those tiny sharp-as-fuck triangles? Well, that's what the Bride had left me with. You can chew through bone with those teeth. Hell, you can chew through wood and linoleum and leather and lots of other stuff with teeth like that. White as milk, those teeth. Not a trace of the coffee and nicotine stains I'd had before she turned me. I wondered if my old teeth had maybe fallen out while I dozed there beside the railroad tracks, and then these had popped in. But I would have noticed a pile of shed teeth, wouldn't I? Maybe so, maybe not. Also, my gums were tender and would bleed a bit whenever I touched them. But that stopped after the first week.

So, there I am, alternately gazing at the monster in my mirror and trying to call Mr. B, and also beginning to think maybe I should crawl through that hole in my kitchen floor and stay there for a long, long time. Pretty sure that's exactly what I was thinking when someone started knocking at the front door. No one ever knocked on my door. That might have been the first time, and I'd have jumped even if I hadn't just joined the ranks of the walking, talking dead. I seriously considered not answering it, but the knocking continued, and after maybe five or ten minutes, I slipped the Wayfarers on and went to the door. I peeked out through the curtains first, and saw it was one of B's boys. Not the one who'd brought me the money. It was the kid with his hair dyed blue, blue with turquoise streaks. Most times, he was in drag, but maybe he'd been warned about the neighborhood, 'cause that day all he was wearing was a White Stripes T-shirt and an expensive-looking pair of jeans. When I unlocked the deadbolt and opened the door a crack, he didn't even say anything, just handed me a small paper bag.

"What this?" I asked.

"Contact lenses," he said. He pointed two fingers at his eyes and wrinkled his nose, more likely at the smell wafting from my apartment than the sight of me. Mr. B's boys, they see lots of weird shit and so get pretty jaded pretty fast. "A pair a contacts and a bottle of saline. Benedict said you'd find them useful, if you get tired of those sunglasses."

"Benedict?"

"*Le nom du jour*, dead girl," he said and smiled. I wanted to punch him.

Instead, I said, "That's gotta be one of the worst he's come up with yet."

"Ours is not to wonder why—"

"Speaking of whys, why isn't he answering his phone?" I asked, interrupting the boy (like I said before, vamps love to interrupt people). "I've been trying to catch him all day, and I keep getting a recording telling me the number's no longer in service."

"Oh, that," the boy said. "Yeah, Benedict is presently incommunicado. He was getting these weird calls, lots of heavy breathing and a bunch of other awful noises, so . . ."

So, I was right about Aloysius.

The blue-haired boy was still talking. ". . . he'll be out of touch until he's got a new phone. Said be cool, hang tight, and he'll call soon as he can."

I told the kid to fuck off and slammed the door in his face. I knew damned well Mr. B had gone to ground, that it was more than the phone, even if I didn't know why. He does that, if the need arises. Rarely bothers to tell anyone why. Just *poof*, and he might as well be Jimmy Hoffa until he decides to resurface. I took the paper bag to the bathroom and looked inside. Sure as shit, there was one of those glass vials with a rubber cap, the lenses floating inside, along with a plastic case for whenever I wasn't wearing them. Right side blue, left side pink, as if the lenses should be separated on the basis of their gender. They were hazel green, never mind my own eyes had been blue before Mercy got at me. I don't suppose it made much difference. Obviously, it didn't to Mr. B.

I opened the vial and put in the contacts. They were the scleral sort, like you see used in films sometimes, so they covered over all the black (and hurt like fuck, by the way, but eventually I got used to that). They didn't exactly make me look normal, but I figured I could pass, long as I didn't smile, and I never was much the smiling type. If I picked up some makeup—a good concealer, for example, and some base and powder—maybe no one would stare.

So, I knew I wasn't gonna be talking with Mr. B any time soonish, and my guts felt worse by the minute. Or so it seemed. The nausea was being replaced by cramps. Didn't matter how badly I didn't want to kill anyone else, no way I could take the pain much longer. Still, I lay on the mattress and held out until dusk. Then I called a cab, guessing I wasn't in any shape for a stroll. The driver showed up in a silver minivan a couple of hours before sunset. Yeah, a goddamn minivan, like he'd come for half the block. He asked where to and I told him Federal Hill. First thing that came to mind. Anyway, we were on the Point Street Bridge, crossing the Providence River, when I realized I didn't have enough cash to pay the fare. I had maybe three or four bucks left from the fifty the day before. I told him to take Atwells Avenue, buying time to think through the money situation, and we passed all those restaurants: mostly Italian, with a few Chinese and Mediterranean places dropped in here and there. Used to, the cooking smells from those places would make my mouth water, and I'd long for pizzas and big plates of spaghetti and meatballs, lasagna, whatever. But *that* night, it all smelled about as palatable as dog shit. I rolled the window up and tried not to think about it.

The driver asked for a specific address. Third or fourth time he'd asked, and I told him to turn right, onto one of the shitty little side streets. Fancy restaurants give way to slums real damn fast along that stretch of Atwells. By sheer stinking happenstance, I'd told him to turn onto Lily Street, and no, the coincidence wasn't lost on me. Anyway, it's only one block from Atwells to Spruce, and then you have to turn left or right. I said left, and then had him pull over in front of a deserted garage, between the yellow-white pools cast by the mercury-vapor streetlights.

I'd solved the money problem, as well as the need to hunt down a meal. Two birds, one stone. I killed the cab driver—tore out his throat and drank my fill—and the pain in my belly went away pretty as you please, just like a good shot of H after a few hours of withdrawal. I broke his neck, like Mr. B had told me to (don't think I mentioned that), tossed the corpse in the back, then drove around while I mulled over the best place to ditch the car. Oh, by the way, I'd brought a clean shirt, so I could change after eating. Or drinking. Whatever. Point is, you live and learn, right. Finally, I left the van in an alley. I was so high off my *new* H—hemoglobin, that is—I hardly even worried what the police were gonna think when they came across an exsanguinated cabbie. I walked home, wishing all the way I had wings like Alice Cregan's, wishing like hell that sensation of flying wasn't only in my head.

I have never been, by nature, a paranoid individual. And I haven't ever been one of those people who claims they're just being "realistic" in an effort to cover up the fact that they're actually paranoid. Cautious, sure. I've always been as cautious as I could afford to be, and certainly after running away from home at the age of twelve. Oh, it just occurs to me that it might seem strange that a twelve-year-old kid runs away and her parents never come after her.

My first few weeks out on the street, I was shit-sure they would, that it was only a matter of time, right. I fully expected that the cops would snatch me up at any moment and deliver me back into my mom and pop's loving arms. So maybe that was being realistic, but it *wasn't* paranoia. For a while, maybe I even *wanted* to go home, that first year or so. Maybe I missed my mom and my warm bed and just being as close to a normal fucking person as I'd ever been allowed to be. Possibly, I forgot there were worse things than being a homeless girl. Regardless, no one ever came. Not the cops. Not a private detective. No one from child protective services. No one. And, eventually, I stopped expecting to be retrieved, which is good, because, obviously, I never was. I know my mother still lives in Cranston, and that she and Pop split a few months after the night I left. Isn't it illegal to let your twelve-year-old run off like that and not at least *try* to bring them home? Wouldn't my school have . . . hell, whatever. You get the gist of it. Or not. Hardly matters.

I woke late in the afternoon after the night I ate the cabbie, and, as the events of the previous evening went from murky half memories to crystal clear recollection, I sort of panicked. Plainly, I was an idiot. I'd left the minivan where anyone could find it. If it wasn't the police, whoever it was would *call* the police. The police would call the cab company (who might have already reported the driver missing), and they'd learn that no one had heard a peep from him after he was dispatched to my address. And so on and so forth, and I had no doubt whatso-fucking-ever that folks in uniform would be banging on my door any minute. Only question in my mind was why that hadn't already happened. It was almost four thirty in the p.m., and I was still scot-free. I got dressed and headed for the front door, suspecting I was safer just about anywhere but home. I thought maybe I could even count on the domino guys on the sidewalk to keep their mouths shut about seeing me leave. They certainly had no love of the law (not gonna get into all the whys of that). There were places I could hide. If there was one thing I'd learned in my time on the streets, it was how to hide.

Okay, so I headed towards the front door (in retrospect, a smarter woman would probably have headed for the back door), and there, on the fugly yellow carpet was a white envelope. While I slept, apparently someone had come along and slid it underneath the door. I stood staring at it—I don't know how long; longer than I should have. When I finally did pick it up, the envelope was heavier than I'd expected. Also, it stunk of cologne. Maybe that was just my preternatural vamp-loup senses kicking in, but the smell was so strong it briefly managed to mask the reek of the apartment.

"Well," I heard Mr. B say from inside my skull, "are you just going to stand there gawking, or are you going to look inside?" This wasn't unusual. I often imagined Mr. B's voice in my head. It's like, after he scooped me up and made me his own personal junky (because who doesn't need one of those?), the voice of my own conscience or common sense or whatever was subsumed by that purling, snide way he had with words.

"Are you going to look inside?"

I ripped the envelope open, and, lo and behold, there was five hundred dollars. Five hundred fucking dollars, and a handwritten note. I recognized B's handwriting straightaway. There's this thing he does, so all the letters lean back to the left, and the way the dots on his j's and i's lean right. Anyway. The note from the envelope read:

Dearest Siobhan,

Don't worry about the fellow in the taxi, but know that I'll not wipe your ass a second time. One more bit of mayhem like that, and, I can assure you, you'll have much worse than the police about which to worry your pretty head. Also, do not attempt to contact me. When I can do so safely, I'll find you. But not before. Meanwhile, here's a little spending money. Use it wisely. Must go now. Ta.

Affectionately,

Bartholomew

"Fuck you, Bartholomew," I said, and sat down on the carpet. I think maybe I just sat there counting the money over and over. Don't know how long, but it finally occurred to me the first thing I ought to use the money for was to do something about the way I looked. My face. The countenance of the Beast and all. The blue-haired boy had brought the means with which to hide those black-and-amber eyes. Short of a good cosmetic dentist (and a lot more cash than five hundred dollars), I was just going to have to deal with my newfangled piranha teeth. But, my complexion, that was something I *could* address.

I made myself as presentable as possible (which included a shower and washing my hair, though I didn't have any shampoo and had to make do with Ivory soap). I changed my T-shirt again, but the jeans I'd slept in had to suffice, as I only had the two pairs (the ones from two nights back were still caked with the "sanguine juices" of my first victim). My pink converse sneakers looked like a train had run over them, and, besides, I noticed there were bloodstains on them. So, I pulled on my battered old Chucks, pocketed the money, and headed for the mall. Which felt utterly fucking ridiculous, by the way. And now, fresh from her latest slaughter, the undead, lycanthropic fiend goes shopping, like any other good American girl.

There's a MAC counter in the Nordstrom's at the Providence Place Mall, and the walk only took me about half an hour. You can't get winded when you don't have to breathe. Oh, but you do have to *pretend* to breathe in order to talk, and also . . . it's amazing how people pick up on something as subtle as the person sitting next to them on the bus not breathing. Anyway, at the mall, I went directly to the MAC counter. I told the woman who waited on me I had a very rare skin disease, a nasty case of cutaneous porphyria (from time to time, all that reading at the Athenaeum pays off), which is why my skin was so pale, and why you could see the veins so clearly here and there. She looked alarmed until I assured her my condition wasn't contagious (at least that part was true), but then she noticed my teeth and wanted to know if the disease had caused that as well. I told her it had.

"I am so, so sorry," she said, doing a halfway decent job of actually looking so, so sorry while still maintaining her original expression of revulsion. Since things were going so well, I figured why not fuck with her. Her name was Allison. She looked about my age.

"My boyfriend left when he found out," I told her. "But you can hardly blame him, can you?"

So, I earned myself another round of "Oh, that's just awfuls" and "Oh, I'm so sorries" and "poor dears."

"We'd just gotten engaged," I added, no longer trying to hide the teeth. "The wedding would have been next June, once he returned from Guatemala."

"Guatemala?" she asked.

"He's a Presbyterian missionary," I replied. How I got through this without laughing, I'm still not entirely sure.

Fast forward past my lies about losing my Presbyterian missionary fiancé, though it went on awhile longer. She sat me down in a chair and proceeded to demonstrate how she could have me looking good as new, quick as a flash. Mostly, I remember her whipping out a concealer that she claimed was so good the Mafia used it to cover up bullet holes. I assumed she was joking, though she dropped her voice to just above a conspiratorial whisper when she said it. After that, I sat still while she smeared this on my face and brushed that on my cheeks and talked incessantly about how sad it all was, my diseased situation.

"Maybe, when he sees you now," she said, obviously pleased with both the quality of her artistry and the product she was selling, "perhaps then he'll have a change of heart."

"I seriously doubt it," I said. "After all, cutaneous porphyria is hereditary. Think of the children." I'm pretty sure I had her close to tears.

"Dear," she said, as her knuckles and fingertips lightly brushed across my skin while she worked, "you're so cold." Never mind that the AC in the department store must have been cranked down to subzero, and it's a wonder the place wasn't crawling with hypothermia cases.

"Yeah," I told her. "Lower body temperature. The megadoses of vitamin B12 do that," at which point I was no longer even trying to make sense. Still, it sounded good, and near as I could tell, she bought it.

When she was finished, she handed me a mirror. And right then's when I realized something I should have fucking realized the day before, if not sooner. I cast a reflection. I was a vampire, but *I cast a reflection.* There I was in the mirror, gazing back at myself with eyes of phony hazel green, and I could see that Allison had done a fine, fine job.

About three seconds later I dropped the mirror, and it shattered loudly on the floor between us.

"Oh," she said. "Oh my goodness." No, really. That's what she said. Not "shit" or "damn it" or a good ol' "what the fuck." Allison the MAC consultant, she said, "Oh my goodness."

"Sorry," I all but squeaked. "Sporadic momentary paralysis. Never know when it's going to happen."

She stared at the shards of glass and sighed. "Well, don't you worry. I'll have someone sweep it up right away."

So, I bought from Allison a compact of Studio Tech NW20 foundation ("a tri-system of water, emollients, and powder"), a small container of Studio Finish NW20 concealer and another of matte buff-colored blush. She even threw in a special bonus pity gift, a black suppository-shaped tube of lipstick (a shade called "hug me," and, again, I shit you not). Exiting Nordstrom's, seventy dollars the poorer, I made a mental note not to forget the porphyria story, as it might come in handy in the future.

So, another day goes by. I sit in my apartment and stew. I walk the streets. Another night passes, then another day, and I have to feed again. This time it's a street crazy, the sort who ought to be in a mental institution, but he's not, because Mr. Ronald Reagan ruined that safety net before I was even born. I rationalized his murder by telling myself he was better off dead. I did a decent enough job of disposing of the body, but I see no good reason to go into the lurid details. Another day. Another night. Another day. Another night. Another victim. And it went on like this for a week. A week became two weeks, and August was about to become September. Still no sign of Mr. B. No sign of Aloysius, either, and no more envelopes pushed under my door. The latter's of no particular concern, as I still had a third (give or take) of the five hundred. After the visit to the MAC counter, I bought some clothes at a secondhand shop on Thayer Street and picked up a few things from a hardware store to assist in the disposal of my meals. I worried just a little about what was going to happen when the rent came due at the end of the month, but I was so busy fretting over other shit *and* staying well fed *and* ditching the bodies, there wasn't a whole hell of a lot of time left over to worry about things like rent. I'd been homeless before, I could do it again, especially now that I'd been relieved of my mortality (though, to be honest, fleecing my victims of green, folding money was helping out; I steered clear of credit and ATM cards). I kept an eye on the papers and local television newscasts (I had a tiny color TV with a built in DVD player, which was in the apartment when I'd moved in, placed there by B, I always assumed) for any news of the spoils of my appetite, but there was nothing.

It did occur to me that if police *were* finding the bodies, and maybe they had gotten it in their heads there was a serial killer on the loose whose modus operandi was bleeding out his quarry, they might be keeping a lid on it for any number of reasons. By the way, here's another by the way. I never have yet seen any reason to distinguish vamps from serial killers. Same damn thing, near as I can tell. Sure, vamps *need* the blood. But then, seems like an awful lot of mortal serial killers are driven by their own needs, impulses, compulsions, whatever, and that those compulsions can be as maddening as a bloodsucker's need to feed. Which, of course, makes *me* a serial killer. We call this avoiding denial and self-delusion. We call this keeping myself honest. I simply see no reason to lie, not in this instance. Way I see it, I'm not a predator, not like a grizzly bear or a lion or a great white shark, I'm just a killer, and me being dead and still walking about might make me a different sort of killer, but if we believe Ted Bundy and John Wayne Gacy had a choice, I sure as hell do. Questions of the existence of Evil—capital E—arise. Anyway. You believe the nineteen-year-old murderess who, last count, has chewed her way through some three hundred (yeah, I keep score) human beings, or you don't. Not my problem.

Back to our story, already in progress.

Two weeks come and go. On the one hand, I was getting the hang of the vampire thing. On the other, I was waiting to get fuzzy with no warning whatsoever, wondering how that would go, and also wondering where the fuck Mr. B was holed up. Finally, last week of August, I decided it was high time that I at least tried to get a few answers from someone who wasn't a troll who preferred to speak in unsolvable riddles.

Now, my first trip to a demon whorehouse (or bordello, or bawdyhouse, or house of ill repute, or whatever strikes your fancy) was not that night B dragged me down to meet Drusneth, a.k.a. Madam Calamity, the night we all had a laugh at Bobby Ng's expense. A couple of months before the disaster by the Scituate Reservoir, B had me tag along with him to this dump over in the Armory District. If you're not from Providence, I know that means fuck all to you, which is why Rand McNally sells maps; find one, if you actually care. This place was in an old Victorian, about as rundown as they come. The ladies were mostly, as you'd guess, demons of various stripes, while the clientele consisted not only of other demons, but also a motley assortment of human mystics, warlocks, and necromancers. They even tolerated the occasional vamp. Oh, but all these joints have a very strict, zero-tolerance no-loup policy. Anyway, while I was waiting for B to finish up whatever dubious transaction had brought us there, I got to talking to one of the girls. Turns out, she wasn't such a bad sort, despite her pedigree and her specialty, which was taking the souls of mortal customers in exchange for a single night of unspeakable pleasure of the carnal variety. She went by the ironic anonym Clemency Hate-evill. I've already pointed out how demons don't use their real names, and a doozy like that, you know she cadged it off a Puritan headstone somewhere like the Old North Burial Ground (ca. 1700). Before we left, I was on friendly enough terms with Clemency, she'd even offered me a freebie should I ever find myself in the mood. She kindly pointed out (as if I didn't know) that the age of consent in Rhode Island is sixteen, so whether or not there might be a law somewhere governing transplanar prostitution, at least no one could cry statutory rape.

Since that night, I actually had visited her a few times. Though, for one reason and another, I'd never taken her up on that generous offer (mostly because I suspected there was a loophole that would land me in whichever realm of eternal torment she called home). So, maybe Aloysius *wasn't* my only friend-type-friend in those days. Maybe Clemency Hate-evill was, too. Which, as you'll soon see, was enough to get her killed (or banished to another dimension, or whatever it is happens to demons when they "die" here on Earth).

It was a Thursday, and I knew the whorehouse was closed on Thursdays. So I called her. Clemency said she was "relieved" to hear from me. I didn't ask why, though it did nothing good for my nerves. I figured I could ask her face-to-face. I took the bus cross town, got off on

Westminster, and walked the rest of the way, past the green swath of Dexter Training Ground and the bizarre towers and turrets of the Armory itself. The sun was setting by the time I reached the rundown house on Cranston Street. I went around to the rear entrance (only customers are permitted to use the front, and no one uses it on Thursdays, no exceptions). There were the usual wards to keep just anyone from strolling in, but Clemency had given me the incantation that would grant me access. Then I got a thorough patting down by the *se'irim* bouncer. Once I was pronounced clean, I was led through three parlors, their walls plastered with velvet wallpaper, each room a different garish color, and each decorated with a confusion of threadbare antique furniture. Clemency was waiting for me in the foyer, at the bottom of the staircase.

As demonesses go, she was a looker, no denying that. Hell, as human women go, she was a hottie (pun unintended). Clemency was about a foot taller than me, and I'm five seven, so, to say the least, she was an imposing presence. Her skin was a faintly pearlescent hue of very pale blue. Let's say sky blue, because I've always liked the way "sky blue" rolls off the tongue. I've always liked blue skies. Anyway, Lady Clemency Hate-evill, with her spiraling ram's horns, her stormy gray eyes, and those carefully braided fetlocks that all but hid her hooves from view—it wasn't hard to see why she was a house favorite, despite her admittedly exorbitant fee. Also, I'm pretty sure she was immune to even the concept of clothing.

"Hello you," she said when she saw me. She was smiling, but it was a nervous smile. "You're a sight for sore eyes. Let's go to my room." I hugged her, hugged her hard, because at that point it was good to see anyone familiar. Anyone at all. Any*thing* at all.

Then I followed her up to the third floor, trailing one hand along the polished oak banister as we went. We passed a few others. I smiled and made no more eye contact than necessary. To them, I was just another mark, another bit of candy with a chewy center. The sort of acquaintance I had with Clemency, it wasn't so much frowned upon as it was deemed extraordinarily peculiar and unprofitable. Demons are all about profit; they make great madams, and even better CEOs.

Her room was the same brand of tawdry as the rest of the house. She shut the door, locked it, and pointed to a wide récamier. The cranberry upholstery looked like several very determined cats had taken exceptional joy using it as a scratching post. I knew plenty better. She sat down next to me, and slipped an arm around my shoulders. She stared intently at me for . . . I have no idea how long. But I couldn't turn away from those eyes until she was done.

"So, *this* is the new Quinn," she said, seeming to relax now that we were in her room. "Must admit, I'd prefer you without the phony headlights and all that war paint. A crying shame, hiding whatever's under there." She ran a finger beneath my chin, and I told her I'd wash my face and remove the contacts before I left, if she wanted, and she said she did, very, very much please.

"The word going round," she sighed and sat back, "it isn't of the good sort, my lamby darling."

"I didn't expect it to be. So, you've heard?"

"Enough to put the pieces together. Likely more than

you, and I'm guessing that's why you're here. Knowing you, it isn't small talk and chitchat. And I know you're not here for a good belly-bumping."

"Yeah," I said, my throat gone dry. Until then, I hadn't realized vamps throats *could* go dry. "Wish it were." I didn't precisely mean that, but I said it, anyway.

"Lucky they even let you through that silly maze of phylacteries. I hate to say, and no offense, but you stink of dog. And you know how that goes."

"No offense taken." I'd been thinking the same thing myself.

"I asked for a favor," she said. "Old Wormlash, she owes me a few." Wormlash was Clemency's madam, and she had a rep as a hellion among hellions.

"You probably shouldn't have wasted it on me."

She leaned close again, flaring her nostrils and curling her lip to expose teeth that made mine look like nubs. "I do so loathe the smell of dog," she said.

"Then maybe you should stop sniffing at me," I said, trying not to sound annoyed. Never, ever fucking pays to get annoyed with demons, not even the ones who, inexplicably, have a soft spot for you. "I need to know whatever *you* know. Anything at all."

She sat back again, frowned, and propped those hooves up on a crooked footstool. Her arm remained around my shoulders, and I tried to ignore how horny it was making me, her touch, just being so close to her.

"You went after a loup named Grumet. Ugly bastard had the butcher's trade cornered up in the Blackstone River Valley. No idea why he was down here. He took a chunk out of you before the Bride of Quiet put him down."

"Maybe tell me something I *don't* know?" I suggested as politely as possible. She stared up at the water-stained ceiling for a moment.

"See, that's where I have to be careful, dumpling. That's where a girl can get herself arseholed seven ways from sundown. So, what I tell you, I need to know it won't leave this room. And even then . . ."

"I fucking swear."

"Of course you do, sugarplum. You're scared, and scared human beings—well, in your case, former human beings—will swear to almost anything if they think it'll save their backsides."

I fished my Zippo and a crumpled pack of Camel Wides from my jeans pocket, then asked if she minded if I smoked.

"Of course not, pumpkin."

I lit a cigarette, and held that first drag until my ears started to buzz. I exhaled, and the smoke curled into a vaporous serpent. That was Clemency's doing, and I complimented her on it.

"Don't think it's so much about what I can tell you, Quinn, as much as it is about the questions I doubt you've started asking yourself."

"I'm asking quite a few," I replied.

"Not the right ones, or you wouldn't be sitting here. Not the genuinely unnerving ones."

I took another puff. This time I blew smoke rings that she shaped into a pentagram. "And what, pray tell, are the right and unnerving questions I'm not asking?"

She hesitated a couple of seconds, then chewed at the ebony talon at the end of her right thumb for a bit.

"Look," I said, "I didn't come here to get you in Dutch with anyone. I'm not here to fuck up your shit."

"Yes, you are," she softly growled. "Mayhap you don't understand that's how it is. But, nonetheless, that's how it is, dumpling."

"Then don't say another word. I'll leave right now."

The arm about my shoulder tightened enough there was no chance of my standing up.

"Just for starters, ask yourself this. What was the Bride doing there? How did she know you were tracking Grumet, and yes, I'm assuming you and the loup, that wasn't a chance encounter. You were calling him out."

"He was hanging bodies in goddamn trees."

"He was a dog. Dogs like their sport."

I frowned and watched the smoldering tip of my cigarette. "As it happens, that question's already been asked."

"But has it been *answered*?"

"No," I admitted.

"Well, that's a step in the right direction, plumbing the depths of that particular mystery. Someone had to have tipped her off you'd be up that way that particular night, and you need to start asking yourself who that someone might have been."

"I killed her twat of a daughter. She could have been stalking me for who knows how long."

"Maybe," said Clemency, "and maybe not. Where's that son of a bitch B run away to, and why?"

"Hell if I know," I said, and then (lightbulb) I saw what she was getting at. "No fucking way he set me up. I'm his prize pit bull . . . or something like that."

She shrugged. "Here's another news flash, darling.

The grapevine leads one to believe Mr. Bobby Ng isn't long for the world."

"Who the hell would bother killing Ng?"

"He's the reason you killed Alice Cregan, yes?"

"Well, sure. Yeah, but . . . he's worse than harmless."

Her skin darkened a shade or three, the way it did whenever she was holding back.

"Nevertheless . . ."

"Nevertheless nothing. You came wanting answers."

"And mostly I'm getting more questions, or answers that might as well be questions."

"Better than the troll gave," she said, and went back to chewing at the claw. She pulled a sliver loose, then spat it at the floor.

"You know about Aloysius? His dumb-ass riddle?"

She nodded. "Ears everywhere. Quinn, you ought to understand that by now. Want the answer?"

I chewed at my lip, then told her sure, of course I did.

"Death," she said. "Think about it later on. The answer is death, not a sacrifice. Your death, Quinn. Only cure for going wolfish."

"But I'm already dead."

"This does present a conundrum. Though I'm guessing you'd find it an unsatisfactory antidote, if you weren't."

She was right, but I didn't tell her so.

"B absolutely did not set me up."

"Never said he did. I only asked a question."

"You implied."

"No, sweetheart. You heard what, possibly, you were already thinking."

I finished the Camel, and she pointed towards an ashtray that had once been the top of a human skull, balanced on the arm of the récamier. I crushed the butt out. The ashtray wasn't there before I needed it, which hardly came as a shock. It immediately vanished.

"At any rate," Clemency said. "Lots of people looking for B these days. Lots of loose ends, business he didn't see fit to conclude before this disappearing act. Money he took from the powers that be, the high on high, and then failed to deliver the goods. He's slipping from the kindly graces of the Dukes and Duchesses. Must have been terribly afraid to let it come to that, wouldn't you think?"

I admitted it wasn't like him, and you don't screw around with the sorts that hire Mean Mr. B. You take a job, you see it straight through to the bitter end, or it's your ass. No way I couldn't admit that much.

"How'd you know to go looking after Mr. Grumet?" she asked, and the nervousness I'd heard downstairs was returning to her voice. "What put you on the dog's trail?"

"It was in the papers."

"Darling, you don't strike me as a news junky."

"B, he said I should pay attention to the newspapers. That sometimes the nasties slip up. No offense."

"None taken," she said very softly, her voice growing brittle. "So, B, he started you reading the papers, looking for the doings of the unholy and carnivorous, that's what you're telling me?"

I furrowed my brow and lit another cigarette.

"You smoke too much," she said.

"Clemency, I'm *already* fucking dead," I replied.

"Still a nasty habit," she sort of tsk-tsked.

I tried to get the conversation back on track. "So, you're implying coincidences ain't actually coincidences."

"*Aren't* actually," she corrected. She did that sometimes, corrected my grammar. Usually, I found it funny, or oddly sweet. "And no," she continued, "I'm only asking questions you haven't asked. Doubt—doubt and curiosity, doubt and suspicion—they may presently be the best allies you have, love. Listen to what they have to tell you. Draw lines, dot to dot. You know how that works, Quinn. Correlate what you know with what you *don't* know."

"And just how am I supposed to correlate what I don't know."

"There's a choke leash around your throat," she said, sounding as sad as I ever heard her sound. "Might as well be a spiked collar. I'd take it off if only I knew how. Might be my loss, doing so, but you're a good kid. You deserve better than what's coming your way."

And before I could ask what the fuck she meant by all that, she turned and kissed me. I've had my fair share of kisses, but never anything came close to that. It was the Olympic gold medal of kisses, right? It was the finest wine, and all I'd ever tasted was Budweiser. Maybe it was even better than smack and the instant my teeth tear into someone's carotid artery. It seemed to go on just about forever. Her tongue slid across mine, then grew longer and encircled it. Maybe, one day, I might forget the alien beauty of Clemency Hate-evill, but no way I'm ever gonna forget that kiss. Or the way she tasted: frankincense, a hint of what might have been charcoal, dried roses, cardamom, chocolate, and the sea.

When she broke the kiss, the whole world seemed to shatter, sure as that hand mirror I'd dropped in Nordstrom's.

"You could always stay with me, Quinn," she said. "Might buy you some time. Might even change the path you're on."

"Don't tempt me," I muttered, and that made her smile.

That was the last time I saw Clemency smile. That was the last time I saw her period. Reluctantly, and with a grand air of resignation, she led me back down the stairs, we said our good-byes, and I was ushered to the rear entrance.

The very last thing she said to me was "Ask those scary questions."

I tried to call her a few days later, and was informed by another girl, informed very matter-of-factly, that she was dead. When I asked how it had happened, I was told there had been an argument with one of her regular johns. This unfamiliar whore, she kept talking at me, how a void dissipation spell had been involved, how Clemency probably never knew what hit her, but by then I wasn't really listening anymore. Before I hung up, I caught one last thing, though. The voice on the other end wanted to know if I was Siobhan Quinn. I didn't answer her; I figured the demon already knew the answer.

I sat on my crummy fucking mattress in my crummy fucking apartment, half starved, and I cried for the first time since the night in the warehouse when I "killed" the ghoul. I cried until I finally couldn't cry anymore, and fell asleep. I dreamed of Lily and Clemency and a friend from elementary school, along with a stingy handful of other precious things I'd known and lost. When I woke, it was a little after midnight, and there was bright moonlight streaming in the window.

Hey, bummer, I know. But comedy and horror, they dance that wicked *danse macabre.* So, it can't *all* be shits and giggles, right? Feel free to stop reading at any time. I won't be insulted.

CHAPTER FIVE

THE BLUNDERBUSS, BOSTON HARRY, AND THE BEAST

I've never much cared for dream sequences in books. Well, to be fair, speaking of those books I've read that have included dream sequences, I've never cared for them. For the dream sequences. Not even sure I can explain why. Mostly, if I set my mind to it, I suspect I dislike dream sequences, as portrayed in books, because I don't think they resemble *actual* dreams. Dream sequences in books have always seemed to me like pointing to one of those little green plastic Monopoly houses and hoping people will mistake it for the Taj Mahal. And maybe there are some people who'd accept the one for the other. Just don't number me among them. Anyway, this is my long-ass winded way of saying that a couple of days after learning of Clemency's death (or whatever), I had a dream. And I suppose it was portentous, and I could pause to read all manner of things into it. Maybe the Bride's hoodoo had left me a dash of the second sight, or maybe it was a parting gift from a demon whore, slipped into me on a kiss. I didn't know then, and I don't know now.

I dreamed of Mr. B sitting there in his booth at Babe's on the Sunnyside, with this row of dominoes lined up on the table in front of him. Hector was there, and the other guys from my street. Mr. B knocked over one domino, and watched as the others dutifully fell, one after the next.

Pretty lousy dream, yeah.

When I woke from the dream, it was late in the day, only a couple of hours until sunset. I sat in my bedroom awhile, smoking and staring at the wall and listening to WRIU on the radio. Then I wandered into the front room and peered out through the curtains. The boys were playing dominoes on the sidewalk, just like usual (loop back to the dream, so I stared at them a moment). And then I noticed what was parked by the curb. My fucking car was parked there, the Honda I hadn't seen since that night out at the Reservoir, that night I had my run-in with Grumet and the Bride. Someone had even gone to the trouble of having it washed (though, frankly, that only made it look that much dingier).

Could've been Mr. B, that was my first thought. But that didn't make much sense, not really, and so my second thought, returning the car, that must have been Mercy Brown's doing. Who the hell else was there left to suspect? Sure, I reasoned, Mercy Brown, she must have minions of her own. Alice Cregan couldn't have been the long and short of it. No doubt, there was a whole clique of little shits who did her bidding, and one of them had been told to bring the car back to me. As to the why, I hadn't the foggiest idea.

I found the Ray-Bans and slipped them on. I wasn't in the mood to bother with the contacts (or the makeup, for that matter). I'd just have to take my chances. I stepped out into the too, too bright day. I asked the boys if any of them had seen who'd left the Honda, and none of them knew shit. I'd sort of suspected they wouldn't.

"Car was there when we set up," said Hector (or Hugo or . . . I'm never gonna figure that out, so let's just stick with Hector). "But it's your ride, yeah, *chica*?"

"I thought it was lost," I replied.

He looked at it and spat tobacco juice on the sidewalk. "Looks like someone found it."

The doors weren't locked, and the keys were in the ignition. In that neighborhood, it was a miracle no one had appropriated my p.o.s. Honda for their own purposes. Oh, and when I started it, I discovered the gas tank was full. And the broken speedometer was working again, and the left headlight had been replaced, the one that had only worked when it felt like it. So, whoever left the car, they'd gone to the trouble to have it cleaned and seen to a bit of fix-up beforehand. Regardless, at least there'd be no more taxis and buses. I went back and locked my front door, and then I drove. I wasn't sure where I was driving at first, just driving so I wouldn't be sitting on that filthy mattress waiting until I was too hungry not to murder the first poor, dumb schmuck who crossed my path.

I drove beneath Aloysius' bridge, and then took the entrance onto I-195, and realized that I was driving to Cranston. I realized I was on my way to find Bobby Ng, even if I wasn't exactly sure why.

Here's another news flash, darling. The grapevine leads one to believe Mr. Bobby Ng isn't long for the world.

Who the hell would bother killing Ng?

Delivers pizzas on the side. Didn't that used to be your neck of the woods, Cranston?

She was mine. They promised. She was supposed to be mine. You fucking cheated, Quinn.

They promised.

Dot to dot.

Ask those scary questions.

They promised.

And I exited onto I-95, heading south, and I started thinking about Humphrey Bogart in *The Big Sleep*, Sam Spade in *The Maltese Falcon*. They sure as hell wouldn't lounge around their shitty apartment waiting for the other shoe to drop. Or the next domino to fall, if you'd rather I not go mixing my metaphors.

I left I-95 and followed Doric to Park Ave. Must be ten, fifteen pizza joints in Cranston, right? And, naturally, I hadn't a fucking clue which one Bobby Ng was working for. But I knew he drove an ancient AMC Gremlin the color of an overripe avocado and even more banged up than my Honda. I knew there was a bumper sticker on the hatchback window, "I Want to Believe." You know, like Fox Mulder. Pure Bobby, through and through. Anyway, I drove. It's not like I was in a hurry, was it? Hell, I could spend hours and hours driving around Cranston looking for the avocado Gremlin. Well, at least until the rumbling in my belly got too loud to ignore. Every now and then I tried to call B, even though I knew it was futile.

But luck be a lady and all that, right? Fourth pizza place I passed, there was Bobby's green-black Gremlin parked right out front. Looked like someone had rear-ended him since the last time I'd seen the car, and the back fender was held on with two bungee cords. Guess delivering pies and chasing nasties wasn't quite lucrative enough to pay the bill from a body shop, or maybe, like me, he just didn't give a damn what the car looked like, as long as it ran. I pulled up across the street from the place, lit a Camel, and tried to figure out what to do next.

Had I come to warn him, because of what Clemency had said? Had I maybe come hoping he knew something I didn't about all this crazy shit? Was I just looking to rid myself of a few drams of frustration by kicking his ass in a convenient alleyway? Or, was I just desperate for a familiar face, even if it was Bobby fucking Ng, demon hunter?

That dream about Mean Mr. B and his dominoes, there was more. I suppose my inherent dislike for dream sequences led to me skimming past those parts. Not like I could *trust* my memory of the dream, right? Anyway, he wasn't alone in that booth at the back of Babe's. The

Bride, she was there, too, all china-doll pale and wispy silken hair. She sat watching the tumbling dominoes, and the way she watched them made me think of a cat stalking a bird. Just crouching for the pounce. And there was a bullet hole right between Mr. B's eyes. His brains stained the wall behind him. Right, right; helluva lot to leave out, sure. But there you go, take it or leave it.

If there are sketchier pizza joints in Cranston, I've never seen them. I figured, right off, the place had to be a front for something. Money laundering, dealing dope, take your pick. Not my business, but I did wonder how much someone was slipping the health inspector to keep the doors open. Or maybe he wasn't on the take. Maybe threats from certain quarters were enough to score a clean bill of health. Place like that, Uncle Paulie's Original Pizza, I couldn't help but think cockroaches and flies had a place of honor on the menu, along with the pepperoni and Spanish olives.

I sat there listening to the radio for, I don't know, however long it takes to hear one song by Echo and the Bunnymen, a song by the Cars, another by 'Til Tuesday, and a few I can't remember. Truthfully, no, I don't recall *any* of the songs. I'm guessing and writing stuff down because it sounds better. But it was an eighties nostalgia show, I'm sure of that much, and those are all bands I happen to like. I sat there across from the banged-up Gremlin and tried to figure out what I was going to do when Bobby Ng stepped out onto the sidewalk. Would I follow him? Would I open the door and maybe shout something like, "Hey, dick cheese!" There weren't all that many options open to me, and I knew he'd bolt the second he saw who I was. Especially if he saw what I'd *become*. Fuck those business cards of his. Talk is cheap. Embossed business cards are probably even cheaper.

Anyway, yeah, I decided to follow him and hope that when he delivered someone's extra large with all the toppings that there'd be someplace a little less public to have a chat with him.

Let's cut to the chase. (By the way, I got curious and just looked up the origin of that phrase. Thought it would lead me back to *Starsky and Hutch* or *Adam-12* or some shit. Nope. Turns out, the phrase "cut to the chase" first appears in 1929 as a line of direction in a script adapted from Joseph Patrick McEvoy's novel, *Hollywood Girl*. No, I've never heard of McEvoy, either, and you gotta figure, he probably didn't invent the phrase, and so it's likely older than 1929. But . . . it occurs to me that it's pretty stupid to say "cut to the chase" and then embark upon a goddamn eighty-five word exposition on the etymology. . . .)

Cut to the chase.

Though it wasn't actually a bona fide chase. It was more like a *crawl*. So, cut to the crawl. Bobby Ng drives like an old woman, but then maybe the Gremlin won't go any faster than fifteen miles per hour. Either way, gotta figure Uncle Paulie gets a buttload of complaints about cold pizzas and calzones. But, as I was saying, Ng was creeping along Park Avenue in his skeezy old car, finally turned left onto Roslyn. Then he proceeded to creep along another, I don't know, but let's say another two or three hundred yards. He finally pulled over in front of a house and made the delivery. I was guessing there must have been a bag of weed or coke inside the box, but, like I said, that's none of my business. What happens at Uncle Paulie's stays at Uncle Paulie's. I pulled in close behind him, and it wasn't until he was back behind the wheel that he realized I was sitting in the passenger seat.

I said, "You really do need to start locking this door, Bobby. All sorts of bad guys sneaking about. Never know."

He made this sort of squawking noise and tried to get out again, but by then I had a good grip on his right shoulder, and we both knew he wasn't going anywhere.

"I didn't come here to kill you," I said, though I'm absolutely sure he didn't believe me. "But it would increase your chances of survival, and decrease the chances of me changing my mind, if you started the car and drove."

"Where?" he all but whispered. "Where is it you want me to drive?"

"I have in mind something scenic. But we'll figure that out as we go," I replied, though I was already thinking about the Pocasset Cemetery, just above Print Works Pond. Lots of privacy up that way.

"You look like shit," he said and turned the key in the ignition. A blue-gray puff of smoke leaked out from under the hood, and he had to try a couple more times before the car started.

"Feel even worse," I told him.

"You know . . . I still have a limp from when you shot me with that arrow. Probably always will."

"I didn't shoot you with an arrow. I shot you with a bolt. It was a crossbow, and crossbows use bolts, not arrows."

"Same goddamn difference," he said, did a three-point turn around, and the avocado Gremlin chugged back towards Park Avenue. "I still got the limp."

"Yeah, well. Poor fucking you. My heart cries crimson piss. I got lots worse than a limp cause of that night, but you've already noticed that, haven't you?"

"Didn't want to come right out and say a thing like that, Quinn."

"Is that some sort of demon hunter etiquette?" I asked.

"No. Just common courtesy. How's it gonna sound, you come right out and ask someone if she's a vampire?"

I gave his shoulder a firm squeeze, sort of like Spock on *Star Trek*, right? He made the chicken noise again, but kept his eyes on the road.

"You're gonna kill me, aren't you?"

"Let's just say it's a fluid situation, Bobby. You play by my rules, maybe I'll just put you in a wheelchair." I didn't mean that, but it sounded good. I watch way too many gangster films. Guy Ritchie. Jason Statham. Quentin Tarantino. Et al.

"So you're dead?"

"*Jesus*, Bobby. Ain't that the way it usually works?"

"Who?"

"Who what?"

"Who did it to you?"

"Mama bear of that nasty I killed back in February. You know, the bitch I took down to save your sorry hide?"

"Yeah, Quinn. Sure. Right before you almost crippled me," he muttered.

I squeezed his shoulder again. Any harder, and I'm pretty sure I'd have broken his collarbone.

"Fuck!" he yelped and almost ran a stop sign. He stomped the brakes so hard I slid forward and smacked against the dashboard. "Stop *doing* that! You break my arm, I won't be driving anywhere."

Gotta admit, he had a point.

I let go of his shoulder, and turned on the radio. There was nothing anywhere on the dial but static, so I switched it off again.

"Yeah, it's toast," he said, and nodded towards the radio. "Some asshole snapped the antenna off a while ago."

I sat back in what was left of the bucket seat and massaged my right breast, the one I'd mashed against the dashboard. I shut my eyes a moment. "I'm not gonna kill you," I told him. "But I hear someone else has it in their head to do that very thing. So, I figure we should talk. Hang a left."

He took a deep, hitching breath and turned back onto Park. I told him when we reached the intersection with Haven, to take a right. He was a good boy, and did as he was instructed.

"So, who's after me?"

"Well, given you've pissed off just about every preternatural son of a bitch in Rhode Island . . . and sizable chunks of Massachusetts and Connecticut, might be hard to narrow the list down."

I don't think he said anything else until after we'd crossed the Pocasset and turned north onto Dyer Avenue. I think you could probably see the stagnant green water of the pond by then. Both the windows were down—because, of course, the AC didn't work, but also because the window handles didn't work and there was no way to roll them up. I didn't bother to ask what he did when it rained. The breeze through the window did nothing much to cool the stifling air inside the Gremlin.

"Didn't know vamps sweated," he said.

"Well, learn something new every day, don't you?"

"Though, if I ever had stopped to think maybe they did sweat, I'd have guessed maybe they sweated blood, like—"

"Hey, Bobby. You got any idea just *who* that nasty's mama bear *was*?"

"No, not really. I mean, I didn't ask. But the way she changed, the wings and all, made sense had to be something wicked big."

"Ever heard of a vamp calls herself the Bride of Quiet?" I took that whiter shade of pale he turned as a yes.

"*She's* the one wants me dead?"

"I'm just guessing here, but that's where I'd put my money. Offhand, can you think of anyone with a *better* fucking reason? Inconvenienced any archdukes of Hades lately?"

"Oh holy God," Bobby Ng said, and the way he said it, probably the way someone on death row might say the same thing first look he or she gets at the gas chamber or the electric chair. Well, not that Rhode Island has the death penalty, but you know what I mean.

"God? When has *he* ever bothered to lend half a helping hand?" And he told me I shouldn't blaspheme and pointed at the five rosaries and various other religious doodads dangling from his rearview mirror. That's something I haven't mentioned. I've seen altars less decked out with Catholic tchotchkes than the inside of Bobby Ng's Gremlin. There was a plastic Virgin Mary glued to the dashboard, along with a pair of those disembodied praying hands that have always given me the willies.

"I'm a vampire, Bobby. Even if I believed in all this Jesus shit—and I don't—wouldn't you think the big guy in the sky has already written me off his holy guest list?"

"Maybe not."

"Turn here," I told him, jabbing a thumb at a bridge leading into the cemetery. The bridge was shaded by a grove of trees, and I almost told Bobby to stop right there. I had that tingling on the back of my neck, and maybe vamps don't combust by light of day, but they sure as fuck get hot. I looked down at the river and imagined how cool the water would feel flowing over me.

"You made me drive to a cemetery, Quinn?"

"Come on now," I said, my throat suddenly gone so dry it was getting hard to talk. "Don't tell me the great and infamous Bobby Ng, Demon Slayer, is afraid of a graveyard. After all, I only *thought* about shooting you in the balls that night at Swan Point. With a *bolt*. So, you gotta be packing something in your tighty whities."

"I only wear boxers," he said.

"Of course you do, Bobby. Of course you do," and I told him to shut up and drive. A few seconds rushed by, and we'd left the shady trees behind.

I had Bobby drive his junk heap all the way to the western edge of the cemetery, and then park on a low weedy bluff overlooking the river. The cemetery occupies a sharp kink in the Pocasset, so there's water on three sides: east, north, and west. Oh, and I forgot to mention, back where we crossed the bridge, there's another myth you can wrap in yesterday's news and leave out with the recycling; vamps have no trouble whatsoever crossing running water. Not sure where that one came from. Anyway, I told him to cut the engine, and he did. I told him to get out of the car, and that he'd better not even think twice about running (suspecting the notion had already crossed his mind at least once). He complied, and I climbed out and stood there by the open passenger door a moment, gazing up at the summer sun. Blinding bright bastard, like the goddamn eye of Polyphemus, or the eye of that sadistic, fickle God I have no intention of ever granting admission to my view of this shit-ugly world.

"What now?" Bobby asked, and I blinked a few times, rubbed at my eyes, then stared at him across the hood. Orange afterimages danced in front of my eyes.

"What now is you answer a few questions, and if I like what I hear, you get to go back to delivering pizzas and dope for Uncle Paulie."

"How'd you know about the . . ." he started, but then trailed off.

"What sort of questions?" he asked instead.

"The sort I need answers to," I replied, and stepped around to his side of the Gremlin.

He opened his mouth, then shut it again. Wise fucking move, Mr. Ng.

There was dandruff on his shoulders, a scatter of flakes that stood out like snow against his black T-shirt (which, by the way—and, as always, constant reader, I shit you not), featured Count Chocula and a cocoa-flavored bowl of cereal. I brushed the dandruff away, then gently placed a hand against the base of his skull, slipping my fingers beneath his lank black hair. He flinched. I had no intention of hurting him, but how the hell could he know that, right?

"You gonna get me fired, Quinn, if you don't let me get back to work soon."

"Then I suggest you tell me what I want to hear, and we'll be on the road again in no time at all. Now, first question, that night at Swan Point, you said 'they' promised you the Alice Cregan kill. I need to know who promised you, Bobby. Who hired you for that hit?"

"I wasn't hired," he said. "I was glad to have the chance to do her for free."

"Well, aren't you a charitable soul. But that doesn't answer my question, does it?"

"Quinn, I tell you that, I'm a dead man."

"Didn't I already inform you I heard there's a price on your head?"

"Yeah, you did," and right *here* he made the mistake of smiling, of believing maybe he had me over a barrel. "But if that's true, what do I have to lose by not telling you shit about who it was?"

"Wrong answer," I said, and gripped the back of his skull, slamming his face smartly into the scalding hood of the car. I gotta admit, he bled a lot more than I'd expected, and Jesus but that blood smelled sweet. I held Bobby's face against the hood until he'd stopped calling me names, then I let him stand up straight again, but I didn't release my hold on him.

"Damn, Bobby. That hurt? That *looked* like it hurt. Now, you want to try again?"

"I think you broke my fucking nose," he sputtered through the blood streaming out of his nostrils and into his mouth.

"Not yet I haven't. But you can be sure I will, you keep that crap up. Was it B? Was it Mr. B hired . . . I mean, was it him granted you the *honor* of taking out Cregan?"

"No," he said very, very quickly, still sputtering. He wiped at his mouth and spat on the asphalt. "It wasn't him. I *never* talk to that asshole." I'm not sure if what I felt was relief at hearing that, or if it was a sudden knot in my stomach, considering everyone else who might be behind this clusterfuck.

"Fine. So, it wasn't B," I said. "Tell me who it was."

"What, you think he's your friend? You think just because it—"

I smacked his head against the hood again, and this time there was a faint, but nonetheless audible, *crack* as his nose did, in fact, break. And suddenly, it seemed to me there was blood spraying just about everywhere. A veritable rain of blood. Bobby Ng howled, and I pushed my knees into the back of his, so that he lost his footing and dropped fast and hard, smacking his chin on the edge of the car as he fell. More blood. And a tooth popped out from between his lips and lay glinting on the ground like an oddly shaped pearl.

This scene was getting a whole lot uglier a whole lot faster than I'd ever intended, and I looked about to be sure there were no witnesses but the dead and their headstones. There weren't. But still, I quickly pulled my hand away from Bobby's head and took a step or two back from him. I drew a deep, deep breath, wishing I could stop smelling all that goddamn blood. Sure, I'd come to suss out whatever Bobby knew, right? But I honestly hadn't gone to Cranston that day to murder the guy in a graveyard.

"Fuh you!" he grunted and spat again, leaving another incisor on the tar and gravel. "Uh duhn't *knuh* 'oo highed muh, 'kay?"

With the broken nose, Bobby's voice was coming out in breathless puffs, like some weird, aspirant version of a Cockney accent. To my credit, I managed not to laugh. But that might only have been the hunger having its way with me, all the world suddenly shrinking down to a pinprick of smell and taste, the promise of the pungent and the piquant.

"Fuh yuh," he said again. "Ah was gunnah tell yuh—"

"Tell me what, Bobby?" I asked, my own voice all at once sounding small and very, very fucking far away. "What were you going to tell me?"

"—uf yuh'd gibbed meh uh *chunce*."

"I'm giving you the *chunce* now. Might be the last time. You might not want to waste it."

I saw there was a small dent in the hood of the Gremlin that hadn't been there before, and I wondered if I'd given the creep a concussion. And I heard Mean Mr. B inside my head then, his purling, slick intonation where my own thought voice should be.

Real clever move, Siobhan. Real shrewd. Keep on

beating him, he'll tell you anything you want to hear. Kill him, he won't tell you a thing, now will he?

"Fuck off," I muttered.

"Fahk yuh, batch!" Bobby squawked loud as he was able through the pain and the blood and what I'd done to his nose and mouth.

"I wasn't talking to you, Bobby," I told him. "Will you just tell me what I need to know. You might think I'm full of shit, but I'd really prefer not to hurt you any more."

"Ah cunt hahly eben *tahk*," he said and coughed.

"I'm sort of almost sorry for that, okay? But you're gonna have to try. Hell, answer the question and I'll even drive you to the ER."

Bobby leaned forward so his forehead was resting against the left front wheel well. Blood ran down the side of the car, dripped onto the balding tires, and spattered the asphalt and the knees of his jeans. I was never before in my life so aware of anything as I was, in that instant, aware of every drop of Bobby Ng's spilled blood.

"Duhn't knah, uhkay? Duh'nt knah huh. Jahst ah phun cull. Nuhber wuhs bocked. Duh'nt knah huh."

"Jesus, Bobby, I can hardly understand a word you're saying." Which was true, but not so much because of his broken nose. More because my heart was starting to sound (and feel) like a kettledrum.

"Huhz faht id dat?"

"Mine," I admitted. "So, it was a blocked number, and you have no idea who called you. Man or woman?"

"Mahn," he murmured. "Huh suhnt meh tuh Bahstun Hahey fuht duh guhn."

"Gun?" I asked, but right then I remembered the ridiculous blunderbuss Bobby was carrying that night at Swan Point, like a movie prop or something maybe he'd stolen from a museum somewhere. The sort of gun John Paul Jones and George Washington and all those other Revolutionary War motherfuckers must have carried.

"You mean Boston Harry?" I asked, leaning closer again, trying to make out the mangled words.

"Whut ah jut *sat*. Bahstun fuckin' Hahey."

Everyone who's anyone wicked, they all know who Boston Harry is, and it was a name you didn't use in polite company, as some are wont to say. A name you don't just toss about willy-nilly, not unless you want to wind up lots worse off than that dumb jerk kneeling there by his car.

"Fuck me," I said, and that's about the time I realized Bobby was crying. "Christ," I sighed. "Will you please not do that?"

"Uht huts."

"It wasn't just any gun was it? There was something special about it, something that would have stopped Alice Cregan."

If he weren't such an incompetent cocksucker, Mr. B said inside my head.

Bobby nodded, but didn't try to say anything else, and I was sort of grateful for that. Besides, I was too busy trying to ignore the smell of blood, *and* come up with a plan for finding Boston Harry that wasn't suicidal to make sense of Bobby's muttering. That's exactly what I was doing when I felt a sort of pain I'd never felt before. Imagine your ribcage being turned inside out after having been doused with gasoline and set on fire . . . and you're halfway there. I saw my fingernails darken and start to curl, and then I didn't see anything else at all until I came to in the stinking marshes at the edge of Dyer Pond. I like to think Bobby Ng never knew what hit him.

So, yeah. I came to in the mud and the cattails, sometime after midnight. I'd figure that out later, the time. I lay there for a moment, listening to the frogs and the sounds of cars in the distance, smelling the ever-present odor of decay one smells in a marsh. It seemed fitting, given my situation. Lying there, my mind, at first only confused and unable to take in more than those smells and sounds, began to puzzle out just what my situation *was.* I was naked, shivering, and the moon was watching me as surely as the sun had. I thought—and I recall this quite distinctly—*So, the God I don't believe in has two eyes.*

I rolled over onto my back (I'd come awake on my left side). My mouth tasted like mud and blood and bile. Mostly mud. I had mosquito bites; lots of mosquito bites. I wondered if maybe there was now a swarm of hairy vampire mosquitoes. My stomach hurt like hell. There was something crawling across my belly. I never did figure out what it was, but I brushed it away into the darkness between the reeds, and stared back at the ogling moon, the nighttime voyeur eye of Jehovah, if it suits your fancy. I lifted my arm to give it the middle finger, a good "fuck off," and that's when I realized just how much every single muscle in my fucking body ached. I turned my head to one side, pressing my cheek deeply into the muck again, and there, only a few feet from me, was a sizable pile of puke, explaining the throw-up taste in my mouth. There were sizable chunks of bone.

I'd turned loup, and I'd killed, and then eaten, Bobby Ng.

I said something appropriate, like "Fucking, fucking fuck all," and tried to get to my feet. It took me several tries. My legs were weak and the mud was deep. The first few steps, I sank in up to my knees. By the time I reached more solid ground, I was out of breath and had to lie down in the grass and rest awhile before going any farther. By the light of that waning last quarter moon (I've learned a lot about the phases of the moon since that night; you live this life, the moon takes on all sorts of importance), I saw that hardly an inch of me wasn't smeared with mud and gore. There were various unrecognizable bits of plant matter plastered to my sticky skin. When I was strong enough to walk again, I did the best I could to get my bearings. I stumbled along eastward until I came to a narrow stream, where I did the best I could to wash. Considering the stream was pretty mucky its own self, the results were so-so. I washed out my mouth, which seemed more important than getting my body clean. There was a cemetery just across the stream, and, if I hadn't gone far during my time as a loup, I guessed it was either Pocasset or Saint Anne's. Turned out it was, in fact, the latter. Saint Anne's is newer and the rows of dead more neatly laid out, like those dominoes from my dream. Anyway, I was walking a little better by then, and it wasn't far north to Pocasset. With any luck, no one had found whatever I'd left of Bobby—assuming I'd left anything—or his car. His car was the most important part. I wasn't about to go waltzing out into the bright streetlights of Cranston bare as the day I was born. If I were lucky, the car would be there, and I'd only have to worry about someone—hopefully not a cop—noticing a naked, muddy woman behind the wheel.

I was lucky. And how often does *that* happen?

And yeah, there was *some* of Bobby Ng left beside the car. Mostly bones, and mostly bones from the waist down. His jeans and those fabled boxer shorts were gone, too. Only his tennis shoes and tube socks remained. Staring at what remained of the corpse, I decided I must have torn the poor bastard in two. Maybe I'd dragged the upper half away into the marshes. Maybe it was tucked not-so-neatly behind one of the nearby tombstones. More likely, I'd eaten most of it, which would explain the vomit and the cramps. I'd soon learn what sits perfectly well in the belly of a loup in loup form rarely ever agrees with a loup in human form. But I wasn't craving blood any longer, so at least Bobby had multitasked in death, which I sort of doubt he'd ever managed to do in life. Unless being an idiot and an asshole at the same time counts.

The Gremlin's doors were still open, and I wondered about security. But maybe Pocasset Cemetery didn't have any. I stepped over the half corpse—legs and intestines and spine and whatever—and slipped in behind the steering wheel. I reached over and pulled the passenger door shut. The keys were still in the ignition. I'd have been screwed if Bobby had taken them out and put them in his jeans pocket. I started the car, then waited to see if the noise would attract the attention of any rent-a-cops who might not have noticed the messily bisected dead guy and his abandoned car, but whose attention might be drawn to the noise of the sputtering engine.

I swore to the ghost of Bobby Ng that I was *not* driving that rust-bucket all the way home. I put the Gremlin into reverse . . .

Cut to the crawl. I drove the Gremlin back to the spot where I'd parked on Roslyn Avenue. I had spare clothes in my trunk (because we learn our lessons), tucked into a canvas bag I'd bought a few months before at the Army Navy surplus place on Thayer. Wait, I already mentioned that bag, didn't I? I managed to change without anyone noticing the nude woman standing in the street. Or if anyone did notice, they kept their mouths shut and their doors closed.

Oh, yeah. I was a lucky little nasty that evening.

Hell must have taken pity on me, or maybe it was just a kindly reward for a job well done.

Down here, down where all us monsters make our homes, the sarcasm and the cynicism is second nature.

The clock on my Honda's dash claimed it was 2:38, but it usually ran about ten minutes fast. I drove home, taking the back roads, avoiding the interstate, and keeping below the speed limit (but not *too* far below). One quick glance in the rearview mirror had assured me I wasn't about to pass for human. I'd lost the Ray-Bans, so there were my eyes, and my skin so waxy white it almost glowed (but did *not* fucking sparkle). There was still so much mud caked in my hair, it was dreadlocked by default. By the time I got back to Gano and East Transit, it was after three, and I was relieved to find Hector and his buddies had either called it an early night or were busy somewhere else.

As I was unlocking the front door, a wave of nausea seized me, and I barely made it to the toilet. I heaved until my throat was raw, and my abdomen felt like I'd taken one hell of a beating. Like maybe someone had gotten me down, and then landed a few good kicks to the ribs from a pair of steel-toed boots. Doc Martens. Okay, maybe it wasn't *that* bad, but it was bad enough.

When it was finally over—the puking—I leaned back against the tub and peered into the toilet bowl. Wish I could say I hadn't, but I did (and, anyway, I've seen way worse since that night). The sight that greeted me was pretty much what I'd expected: shards of bone and shreds of undigested meat, mostly organ meat. I made out parts of the heart and liver, and, in the center of it all—the pearl perched atop a steaming mound of manure—was a gold class ring, set with a green stone. I fished it out, then I flushed the rest away. I had to flush three times before the water was clear again. Not a very Christian burial for Bobby, first victim of my lycanthropic antics, but I wasn't a Christian, and I really didn't give two shits. If he'd never gotten mixed up with the nasties, it never would have happened. Bobby Ng had been the master of his own destiny, right? Then again, like me, maybe he *hadn't* had a choice. Maybe there was some secret in his past, some skeleton from a closet, that had compelled him and driven him to such an ignoble death. But if anyone knows *his* origin story, I've never learned it. Not that I've ever asked. I reached up and put the class ring on the rim of the sink.

What next, Siobhan? Mean Mr. B purred behind my eyes. "Now I'm taking a fucking shower," I replied to the part of me that only sounded like him. "Now I'm scrubbing off every last bit of filth."

Which is what I did. I scrubbed until my skin was close to raw. I washed my hair twice with the bar of Ivory soap, and the drain would have clogged from all the grit if I hadn't kept clearing it with my toes. When I'd shut off the water, the bathroom was thick with steam, and I brushed my teeth twice (yeah, I wasn't such a slob I didn't have a toothbrush). I wished there was a bottle of Listerine, but I settled for a glass of water from the kitchen sink.

I stood there sipping at the water, trying to calm my stomach and peering into that gaping hole in the linoleum. Like Nietzsche said, maybe it peered into me, as well. I was beyond caring. When I finished the water, I went to bed, and wrapped my nude and aching body in dirty sheets. I must have fallen asleep immediately. There were dreams. Bright dreams of running on four legs as the moon cheered me on. The sort of dreams that would become familiar companions in the years to come. By the time I woke, another day had passed, and the sun was setting all over again.

Here's what you need to know about Boston Harry. That is, the *main* thing you need to know if you're to grasp the even tighter spot I found myself in the day after I ate Bobby Ng.

Boston Harry—and if he had any other name, it remains unknown to me—was a sort of transplanar fence, an illicit Walmart for just about any piece of eldritch junk you could ever need. If it existed, anywhere or anywhen, he could get his mitts on it. Fuckin' A. Boston Harry, he was the go-to guy—the "man" who could resolve just about any problem or situation a nasty or those who run with nasties . . . or even those who hunt and kill nasties . . . might conceivably face. An all-purpose conduit for mystical and infernal goods *and* services. He was, in short, The Man.

And if Mean Mr. B is a bastard and a son of a bitch (and he surely is), then maybe the word hasn't been invented for what you'd call Boston Harry. You didn't fuck with him. Not ever and not no how. You make an appointment, you better know *what* you want—exactly—and *when* you want it, and you sure as hell better have the cash (or whatever) on hand. Those who made the mistake of uttering "credit" in his presence didn't live so long, or, if they did, they quickly wished they hadn't.

Also, for a dude looking to make as much money as inhumanly possible, he was never precisely easy to find. There was a protocol. At least, that's what B always called it. I called it a fucking inconvenience, a hurdle that only existed because Boston Harry loved to watch people jump through hoops, like lions or trained poodles at the circus. And because being hard to find was part of his mystique.

Normally, if I'd have need to track him down, I'd have gone to B. Not that I'd ever had any such need. But B was, as the blue-haired boy had said, presently incommunicado. And I had a feeling that whatever these scary questions were I'd been told to ask myself, there wasn't time to set them aside until Mr. B resurfaced. And speaking of Clemency, she *might* have been able to help me track down Boston Harry just a tad faster than the usual rigmarole, but she, of course, was dead (or whatever). So, I was left with dick, except what I knew, what B and others had told me about this purveyor of all things unsavory.

Here's how it went:

Harry had set up different ways of being contacted in different cities. In Providence, it was the old granite drinking fountain on Benefit Street, right out in front of the Athenaeum. It's been there since 1873, and once upon a time, it actually *was* a drinking fountain, the water coming directly from the Pawtuxet River. Chiseled into the stone is the invitation "Come here everyone that thirsteth." Nowadays, it doesn't actually work, and the catch basin is usually filled with trash and dead leaves. Even if it *did* work, knowing the state of the river, drinking from it would likely land you in the hospital. But I digress. If you were in Providence and wanted to find Boston Harry, you went to the fountain and left a drop of blood on the granite. Didn't matter where, so long as the blood was actually *on* the fountain. Then, sooner or later, you'd get a message where he could be found.

So, the night after I killed Bobby Ng, I went to Benefit Street. The RISD students were still on break, so the street was pretty much deserted. Just the streetlight pools illuminating the ancient trees and colonial houses (each graced with its own historical marker, mind you) and the uneven brick sidewalk. I felt like a stroll, hoping it might clear my head, so I parked a couple of blocks from the library and went the rest of the way on foot. There's a pleasant sort of eeriness to Benefit Street after sundown, and maybe it didn't clear my head, but it did put me a little more at ease. It was something familiar, there in the vast wasteland of the unfamiliar in which I found myself. I made a point of breathing, just so I could take in all those comfortable odors, rendered LOUD by my new vamp senses. It was some heady fucking shit, almost as sweet as the best weed I'd ever gotten my hands on.

So, I went to the fountain, pricked my thumb with one of those piranha teeth Mercy Brown had bestowed upon me, and smeared a drop, just below the *e* in *thirsteth*. I don't know; I guess it seemed somehow appropriate.

Then I sat down on the steps of the library and lit a Camel. Thank dog bloodsuckers can still smoke. I listened to night birds and the breeze flowing through the various sorts of leaves. Every now and then, a car passed by. I kept expecting the cops to pull up and ask what the hell I was doing, hanging out in front of the Athenaeum at two o'clock in the ayem, but they never did. I didn't think for a second I was going to hear from Harry right off; I figured it would be at least a week or so, and had resigned myself to that fact. Hence, when the talking seagull fluttered noisily down and landed a few steps below me, well . . . I was unprepared, to say the least. It was just a herring gull, and a pretty ragged one, at that. Now, you buy into all that Edgar Allan Poe crap, maybe you're surprised it wasn't a raven, or at least a crow. But no, it was this ratty gull staring at me with its beady black eyes. It shifted from one yellow webbed foot to the other, and ruffled its feathers.

"You wanna see Harry," it squawked.

"Jesus, you're a fucking seagull," I said, or something equally obvious.

The bird cocked its head to one side, blinked, and asked, "Is that a yes, or is that a no. Because, if that's a no . . ."

"It's not a no," I replied. "I just didn't expect a fucking seagull, that's all, okay?"

"Well, you know," said the gull, "God moves in a mysterious way, His wonders to perform."

"I sure as hell didn't expect a seagull who quotes scripture."

"Ain't scripture, lady. Just a hymn by William Cowper, 1731 to 1800. Fella went crazy as a fruitcake, thought he was condemned to Hell, and that divine voices were urging him to commit suicide. Total kook. Still and all, pretty good quote."

"Seagulls believe in God?" And, by the way, that's got to be one of the strangest things I've ever uttered.

"Hell no!" the bird squawked. "Well, I can't rightly speak for the lot of us, but this one don't."

"I call for Boston Harry, and he sends unto me an atheist seagull."

The bird looked offended. "Would you have preferred something fancier, maybe? Something not so drab and ordinary. How's about a puffin or an osprey or a great big—"

"I'm just surprised, okay?" I interrupted. "Nothing personal." But the herring gull's expression didn't change. "You gonna tell me how to find Boston Harry or not?" I asked.

"Sure, lady. Easy as pie. Just shut your eyes, count to ten, then open them again."

I did exactly as the bird said. But when I opened my eyes, I was still sitting on the Athenaeum steps, with that big damn talking gull glaring at me.

"I do *not* believe you fell for that," it said.

"Asshole," I replied, then flicked my cigarette butt at its head, but missed.

"Now, now, Miss Siobhan Quinn, let's not go losing our temper. I might just fly away. I might just tell Harry how you went and changed your mind, got cold feet and, therefore, wasted his precious time and all. I might just do that very thing, you don't behave yourself. Mind your Ps and Qs and whatnot."

I wanted to throw something else at the creep, but there was nothing handy. I settled on giving him the finger (yeah, I do that a lot; I find that gesture worth a thousand words, as they say; plus, in this instance, the irony of giving a bird the bird . . . well, you get it).

"See now, that's just what I've been talking about. Rude little girls and boys and monsters, they don't get to meet with Boston Harry."

"You gonna tell me how this works or not?"

Ever seen a seagull grin? Well, whether you have or not, this one grinned at me.

"Let me guess," I said, "I just close my eyes, click my heels together, think of Auntie Em and Kansas—"

"Nope," the bird smirked. "It's lots easier than that. Know what a psychopomp is?"

"I'm not a total idiot," I replied (all evidence thus far essentially to the contrary). "Is that what you're supposed to be? My escort?"

"Bingo, vampire-werewolf lady."

"Is it that obvious?"

"Hey, right now, you're the talk of the town. You're a goddamn celebrity. Now, we're wasting time, and the Boss Man, he hates that."

The bird shook itself, and a single feather came free and wafted onto the granite step below it. I noted that it moved against the wind, that the breeze should have carried it in exactly the opposite direction.

"Pick that up," said the seagull.

I did as I was told. The feather felt slightly oily, and I wondered if that was how seagull feathers were supposed to feel, or if it was a trait peculiar to those in the employ of "men" like Boston Harry.

"What now?"

"What now is you think of a song. Think of the lyrics of a song that means a lot to you, and put the feather in your mouth."

I glared at the gull.

"I am not putting this nasty-ass feather in my mouth."

"Then you am not gonna see the Boss Man, and he am gonna be pretty pissed at the way you've wasted his time."

"Did I mention you're an asshole?" I muttered and slipped the feather across my lips. It tasted faintly of dusty sardines.

"You might have. Now, the song. Quick, before the window of opportunity closes again."

I did not think of Patti Smith. I almost thought of Bob Dylan's "All Along the Watchtower," but settled on something by Elliott Smith instead.

"Good choice," the bird said. "You hold tight to that.

Don't dare let it go. Oh, and try not to toss your cookies. Happens almost every time."

Ever ridden one of those Tilt-A-Whirl things? There used to be one down at Rocky Point, before the amusement park shut down. Anyway, there's an accurate description of what I felt for the next minute or two minutes. The world went about a thousand shades of foggy gray, and I rode an invisible, incorporeal Tilt-A-Whirl down to the lair of Mr. Boston Harry. I managed not to toss my cookies, so score one for the "it girl," so good on me.

The tilting, whirling sensation ceased as abruptly as it had begun, but the foggy grayness, that dissipated slowly, by minute degrees, gradually granting entrance to other colors. As it did, I became aware of voices and smells. I became aware of the stink of wet fur, and mold, and a kind of humid closeness. I grew scared, and if I wasn't dead, I'm sure my heart would have raced. I very much wanted, suddenly, to go back to Benefit Street and the steps of the Athenaeum.

"Well, well, well," he said—Boston Harry, I mean—"I must admit, I gave the tales little credence. But here you are, and it's plain as day. The girl who's both. The unfortunate and double-damned who's undead *and* who bears the curse of the moon."

I squinted and tried to blink away the last of the smothering gray. I realized it was sticky, that fog, and I thought maybe bits of it would cling to me forever. I squinted, and my vision cleared. I had the impression I was inside an enormous wooden shipping crate. The wooden slats that were the walls were dark with mildew, and, here and there, water dripped from the ceiling. There were actually great clumps of excelsior and sawdust scattered about. There was a flickering orange light, like candlelight, though there weren't any candles. At least, none that I could see. And maybe ten feet away—perched on a wooden stool that listed because one leg was shorter than the others—was the man himself, Boston Harry.

Only, he wasn't a man. He was . . . something else. Maybe a variety of bogie or goblin or something like that. Maybe he'd *been* a man, once upon a time. More than anything else, he reminded me of a rat trying its damnedest to *look* human and failing miserably. The seagull was standing on an upended aluminum pail to Boston Harry's left. There was an identical pail to the right of the stool, but it was vacant and half lost in tufts of excelsior.

"I admit, it's a mighty sight, what you are, Miss Quinn. What you've been made. A mighty sight, indeed. And you're a looker, in the bargain. Quite an impressive package."

His voice was high and tinny, and scratchy in a way that reminded me of vinyl LPs that had seen better days.

"Glad to meet you, too," I said, and he waved a gnarled paw in my direction and chuckled.

"No, no, no. The pleasure is all mine, Miss Quinn. I'm honored, as a matter of fact."

"Then maybe you won't mind answering a couple or three questions I have."

"Not at all," he said, and smiled an almost absurdly unctuous smile. "If I can be of service, of service I shall certainly be. Ask away."

I wiped sweat from my forehead, only just then realizing I was sweating. I said, "I almost thought you might know without my having to put them into words." Probably not the sort of thing I should have said, but I was disoriented, and nauseous, and I said it anyway.

"As a matter of fact, it happens that I do. Every vowel and intonation. But where's the fun in skipping half the transaction? Which brings me to the admittedly indelicate, or let us say *gauche*, matter of what you intend to offer in the way of remuneration for my services. Do you have anything of value, Miss Quinn?"

"Not much," I admitted.

"Well, I hope you'll understand how that poses a problem, yes?" And he sort of wrinkled his rattish snout, and I got a peek at teeth that were surely as sharp as my own. "A body goes giving out his stock and trade for free, what manner of business acumen is that?"

"Just being honest," I said. "Me being the 'it girl' and all, I was hoping there might be a discount or an exception or something of the sort."

"Very sorry to disappoint, my love," he replied, curling back his black lips in just such a way that he was smirking *and* making a grand show of graciousness.

I held up my left hand, and I wiggled my pinkie finger for him. The seagull looked confused, but Boston Harry, it was clear I'd gotten his attention.

"A souvenir?" he asked.

"A souvenir," I said.

"Oh, oh, that would be most acceptable. That would, I daresay, be both sufficient and generous. You're a woman of integrity, you are."

"One finger, two questions."

"Terms I find entirely within reason," he assured me

again. "But, I do hope you'll understand I'll have to ask for payment up front. Nothing personal. Company policy and all. These days, you can never be too careful, can you?"

"Absolutely not."

What happened next, well, there was a sharp pain that began in my hand and ran all the way to my shoulder. I wanted like hell to scream, and I bit my lip hard enough it bled (not so difficult with these choppers). And then the little rat man was holding my pinkie finger, and the pain was gone. There wasn't any gore, no torn flesh or protruding bone. He'd collected his fee so cleanly you'd think I'd been born without the finger. He cupped it lovingly in his paws and crouched over it and crooned. Like, he was in love with my fucking finger. Somehow, that was way worse than having given it up for whatever he had to say—which I knew, of course, might be as useless as Aloysius' riddle had been. We call this gambling, right? And desperate times call for desperate wagers, and you don't waste time quibbling over the stakes.

"Oh," he trilled. "It is so, so beautiful. I've held few things of such exquisite loveliness and remarkable symmetry. You truly *are* a woman of integrity, Miss Quinn."

"Anything to please," I muttered. Boston Harry, too busy admiring his prize, he didn't seem to hear me, but the gull glared daggers.

"My turn?" I wanted to know, and "Of course," the rat thing replied, nodding his head and looking up, closing a grubby paw tightly around my amputated pinkie. It looked sort of like a pinkish-white grub.

"Why did you sell Bobby Ng that gun?"

Boston Harry closed one eye, opened it, then closed the other. He nibbled at his nails, and flipped his tail back and forth a few times. He furrowed his brow, then laid his ears back flat against his narrow skull. He did not look like an especially happy rat thing.

"You *do* know who Bobby Ng is?" I asked, trying not to sound impatient.

"Of *course* I know who he is," Harry shot back, and opened the closed eyes. Oh, I've neglected to mention that his eyes reminded me of pieces of candy corn. "Rather, I know who he *was*. Monsieur Robert Ng—nom de guerre, *naturellement*—incurably inadequate wannabe, sad-sack postulant to the role of inquisitor and executioner, and, as it happens, *your* first meal as a loup. By the way, you ever hear about the Samhain he was up at Marblehead—or maybe it was Salem—and the silly bastard went and tried—"

"Yeah," I answered. "I have." (Even though I hadn't. But I hadn't given up a finger to stand around swapping Bobby Ng anecdotes with Templeton the Rat.) "So, why did you sell him that blunderbuss?"

Clearly annoyed at my not wanting to hear about whatever antics Bobby Ng had committed in Salem or Marblehead or where the hell ever, he scowled and sniffed the musty air. "I didn't," he told me. "I never sold a thing to that *figlio di puttana*. I have a reputation to worry about, you know? You start doing business with scum like that, potential buyers and sellers gonna think twice, and maybe cast an eye towards the competition. Which we—we being me—do not want."

"But you sold it to *someone*."

"That your second question, my love?" Boston Harry asked and cocked an eager, hopeful eyebrow.

"No. It isn't. It was just an observation."

"Regardless, I prefer not to go blabbing about my clients—past, present, or future. Cuts down on repeat customers, you know what I mean."

"I gave you a finger," I said.

"And you still have nine more. And ten toes. And I'm sure each and every one is as precious as the last. If you'd like to renegotiate the terms of our deal . . ."

Which is when I wondered why the hell I hadn't offered him a little toe instead of a pinkie. Then again, this whole bargaining-with-body-parts enterprise was new to me, and a girl makes mistakes. A shame the rat wasn't in it for booze, porn, and 3 Musketeers bars.

"What's so special about the gun, Ng thought it would take out a vamp like Cregan? *That's* my second question."

"Poor choice," he said and spat into the excelsior and Styrofoam peanuts. "How's it gonna help your case, muffin, learning what the gun can and can't do, when what you *need* to know is who's the dearest bodily part in back of the dead undead lady's assassination, right? The who it is, however indirectly, got you involved in this affair. But, like I said, we can still remedy that."

The seagull, perched on its aluminum pail, made the odd giggling sound that seagulls sometimes make. Boston Harry seemed to be considering his long yellow toenails with the greatest of interest.

"Second toe off your left foot, that'll buy you two whole extra questions. You think about that, Miss Quinn. A little flesh and bone goes a long way."

"How about, first, you answer the question I've already asked?" Oh, I knew he was right, sure as shit, but like I said, I wasn't yet wise in the ways of swapping digits for intel. "How about that?"

Boston Harry snorted in a vexed or disappointed or merely amused sort of way, then turned one candy-corn eye back towards me; the other continued staring at his feet.

"April 19, 1775. Carried by Samuel Prescott, Battle of Lexington, though fat lot of good it did him. Might have popped a few redcoats, but General Gage, he still won the lottery and got the city of Boston. But that's not the important part. The important part about how that blunderbuss got to *be* that blunderbuss, possessed of all its demon-smiting abilities, that happens later on, when Mr. Meriwether Lewis carried it off on his and Mr. Clark's expedition to find the Northwest Passage."

I wanted to ask him if possibly there was an answer available that *didn't* involve a history lesson, but I knew I'd already shown more disrespect towards the rat thing than it was rumored to tolerate. One dilemma to find yourself on thin ice, and another to take the opportunity to dance a fucking jig, right?

So, I stood still, and kept my trap shut, and I listened. And listened. Eventually, ten or fifteen minutes later, the gun made its way to the twenty-first century.

". . . and by then, well, by then the old flintlock had absorbed enough spooky juju and bad vibes even Jesus Harold Christ himself might think twice before looking funny at the damned thing. But, I ask you, how was I gonna pass up a steal like that? A hot piece of merchandise, to be certain, and not without attendant risks. And yet, a discerning purveyor like myself knows there's *always* a buyer, and sometimes there's no such beast as a price too steep."

While the rat had yammered, I'd had time to think it through, and figured losing the toe wasn't going to be much of a handicap.

"Frankly," said Boston Harry, "I'd like to know what became of the gun after that night in the cemetery. Which is to say, I'd like to reacquire said instrument, if the opportunity should ever arise."

"Reacquire it from the person you actually *sold* it to," I said. "The person whose name is all hush-hush and who shall remain nameless unless . . ."

"Unless," he said, and wiggled a crooked index finger at my left foot. "After all, it wasn't I who failed to ask the more pertinent and efficacious question."

"But I only need one more question answered, not two."

"So, you can use the other later. A woman . . . or beast . . . of integrity . . . such as yourself, she, or it, is bound to find herself in need of my aid again at some point or another along the line. I'll simply consider half the toe on account. Charitable terms, yes?"

"You're just as sweet as pumpkin pie," I said, playing the game because it was the only game in town.

"Why, considerate of you to say so. I do like to keep the customer satisfied."

No need to dwell on the details of what happened next. Nothing new, only that quick and searing subtracting pain, same as before—wham, bam, thank you, ma'am.

I didn't have to unlace my shoe to know I was minus three phalanges. Harry was holding the toe up to that unseen light source, examining it the way a jeweler might examine an especially choice ruby or sapphire. Not a drop of blood anywhere.

"This time, you choose with care," he grinned, and the seagull giggled. And I did. I selected each word the way a condemned man might order his last meal.

"To whom did you sell the blunderbuss?"

"I shouldn't tell you," he sighed. "Well and true, I shouldn't. I *do* have my scruples, whatever folks might think of me."

I repeated the question, more slowly this time, pushing the anger down as best I could.

"Very well. A deal's a deal. That was back in January. Impressively shady fellow downtown. Downtown Providence, that is. Dressed like an investment banker, but came across like a pimp. Paid a handsome sum, though. I expect you'll be wanting a name, eh?"

"I expect I will," I replied.

Boston Harry pocketed my toe (forgot to mention he was wearing a claret silk waistcoat that had seen better days).

"Jack."

"Jack," I repeated. "Jack in downtown Providence. I don't suppose he came with a last name?"

"You ask a lot, my love. But, now that you mention it, yeah. Jack Doyle. Butterscotch hair, green eyes, and I think he has his eyebrows waxed."

"So, we're done here?"

"Looks like. Unless, of course, you'd wish to ask that

one remaining question now. Lest the Bride of Quiet finishes you off before we chance to meet again. Would be a terrible waste, should events take that turn."

"I'll take my chances." Me, I was already looking about the huge crate of a chamber, trying to locate anything that might serve as an exit. Right then, all I wanted was to put as much space between me and Boston "the rat thing" Harry as quickly as possible. I take that back. I also wanted another shower to wash away the scent of that place, that and the way I felt after being subjected to his magic and those candy-corn eyes. "Wanna have your bird show me the way back to Benefit Street?"

"That would be the second—or rather, the fourth—question, wouldn't it?"

And I never had a chance to answer, because right about then's when I felt what I'd felt before the blackout back in Pocasset Cemetery, standing next to Bobby Ng's green Gremlin. I heard bones snapping, folding into new configurations. I smelled dog. And this time when I came to, it was broad fucking daylight, and I was curled up amid the garbage cans and recycling bins behind my apartment. When I could stand, I found the spare key I kept under an empty flower pot and let myself inside. If I've ever awakened with a worse taste in my mouth, mercifully, the memory is lost to me.

CHAPTER SIX

A RUDE AWAKENING, A NEW TROLL, AND JACK DOYLE

Well, the good news—if you want to look at it that way—is that I didn't puke up Boston Harry. Or the seagull. Yeah, I assume I ate them both, even if I can't prove that I did. So, that's the silver lining, if you've got a genuinely twisted sense of what constitutes good news. And two years after these events, I admit that I do.

The bad news? Hang on. That's coming.

It was long after dark when I woke and lay staring at the bedroom ceiling. My mouth tasted even worse than when I'd awakened behind the garbage cans, and I lay there, staring at peeling paint and cracked plaster, wishing like hell I'd had the good sense to buy a bottle of Listerine after this whole werevamp thing started. But, it's not like I had to worry about cavities anymore (and, truth be told, after all those years on the street, dental hygiene hadn't been a priority to start with). I lay there staring at the ceiling, letting myself remember the business with the rat thing, the questions I'd asked and the answers it had given. I held up my left hand, and, sure enough, I hadn't dreamed giving him that finger. I made a fist and it felt odd, but I couldn't imagine missing one pinkie was going to impair my manual dexterity (I'm a righty, anyhow). Oh, I checked my left foot, too. Ditto on the proffered toe. I wasn't going to cry over spilled milk. You start offering body parts to . . . whatever Boston Harry had been . . . you deserve whatever you get for your troubles.

I lay there, gazing at the four remaining fingers on my left hand, thinking about the stinking wooden-crate place that I suspected had been no place at all. I could hear cars out on the street, and the domino guys talking, their Mexpop, an airplane passing overhead, cockroaches all around me, mice in the walls, the slow reproduction and growth of fungal spores . . . you get the picture. I'd already learned how to parse that flood of sensory info, the Flood, as I'd begun to think of it. The LOUD FLOOD. It no longer overwhelmed me. I lay there and wondered if my car was still parked on Benefit, or if it had been towed, or if there was a third option. I lay there and wondered where in the name of fuck all Mean Mr. B was holed up, sitting out whatever topsy-turvy hell was unfolding around me.

I wasn't hungry, so I assumed that *whatever* the wolfish half of me had snacked upon in Crate Land, it must have at least sated the bloodsucker half of me. I was filthy, but that probably goes without saying. My skin was smeared with blood and dirt and . . . worse things. My hair was matted and sticky. I wanted a cigarette, but I knew there were none in the house. I thought about taking a shower, and somehow summoned the requisite motivation to do just that. Afterwards, I pulled on one of my two pairs of jeans (at least they'd been washed a couple of days earlier) and a halfway clean T-shirt. I can recall that shirt with perfect clarity, even if it wouldn't survive the next hour: the old Soviet flag, red with the golden hammer and sickle, the golden star, and CCCP printed underneath. I'd found it in a Dumpster somewhere. I liked that shirt.

Of course, there was no sign of my shoes.

Barefoot, I walked to the kitchen and ran a glass of water. It tasted like crap, but I kept it down. I ran another glassful and pretended it was mouthwash, though it hardly helped at all.

And then . . .

"You're her," a gravelly male voice said behind me, the sort of voice that commanded your attention, that wields authority. He hadn't asked a question. He was merely stating the obvious. "The Bride's whelp."

"Fucking unbelievable," announced a second voice, this one female and languid. Mellifluous. She had an accent, but I couldn't make it out. Standing there, I thought about how that would have been the last thing lots of people had heard, and how it could be worse. Her voice was making me horny, no matter how much shit I was in.

"Don't look like so much to me," added a third voice, another dude. I'd already figured out he was back there. Maybe I'd been too busy trying to get the taste of Boston Harry (and who knows what else) out of my mouth to hear this trio of observant douche bags break in, but now I was all ears, and I'd heard . . . never mind. No point trying to explain what I'd heard, but it had been the *sound* of him. Even dead things made a racket, if other dead things are listening in.

"Do I turn around?" I asked. "Or maybe that's not part of your plan." Yeah, I assumed they'd come to do me harm. Seemed astronomically unlikely this was a social call.

"I don't kill anything that's got its back to me," the gravelly voiced man said. I didn't have to look to know he was big, at least six five, maybe two hundred and fifty pounds.

"We ain't cowards," the girl with the honeyed accent (never placed it) all but sneered. Even sneering, that voice made me want to fuck her. I guessed she was no more than five six, a hundred twenty, a hundred twenty-five pounds tops.

"We don't need filthy loup blood in our veins to get the job done," said Mr. Number Three.

So, I was the job. I gripped the edge of the sink and the glass, and felt myself tensing.

"Never heard of such a mutt. An insult, that's what you are, but that'll be over in a jiffy." Just a guess, dude was on the short side. Not much bigger than the chick.

"In a jiffy?" I laughed, and turned, pegging the son of a bitch between the eyes with the glass. He howled and stumbled backwards.

"You cunt!" the girl screamed, but I dodged, and the stake she'd aimed at my chest buried itself in a cabinet door instead.

"What, you thought maybe I *wasn't* gonna fight back?"

There was a very short pause here, and maybe the Three Caballeros really hadn't expected I'd be that much of a challenge. Maybe these creeps were that full of themselves. I stared at her, then at the big guy, then at the guy I'd pegged with the glass. He was rubbing his forehead. Me, I was waiting for the change, the bone-cracking, flesh-burning agony that announced the coming of the wolf. After all, I had every reason to believe that's the way it worked. I get pissed enough—maybe even just a little pissed—and here comes the beast.

"You take this however it pleases you," the big dude muttered. He sort of looked like Ron Perlman with a bad haircut. "You wanna put up a struggle, it'll only make this more satisfying."

"Your call," I said. "Your funeral."

Tough talk, that's one thing, but I've always hated drawn out action scenes in books. Fight choreography can work great in a film (I love kung fu flicks. Oh, and *anything* with Jason Statham), but it usually comes off like a pile of bricks on the printed page. Case in point, just about any of the Harry Potter books. So, like I said before, let's cut to the chase.

No wolf. Just me.

The fellow I'd hit with the glass, I took him out with the stake the girl had thrown at me. The big guy, he proved the most trouble, the bitch of the bunch (no surprise). We rolled around breaking shit, upending the table, etc., you know—until he went down that hole in the kitchen floor. I caught him by the ears as he fell and let him dangle several seconds, kicking and screaming, before I pulled upwards with enough force that his head and neck parted company. By then, Little Miss Honey Voice was on me, one arm tight around my throat, the other poised to skip the staking business and yank the dead, unbeating heart out of my chest with her bare hand. I flipped her, easy as pie, and she went skidding towards the back door. I was on her almost immediately. I pinned her and, I *will* give her this, those black eyes of hers, those empty pools of nothingness, they managed to radiate so much hate, so much spite, I still wish I knew her backstory. My knees were enough to hold her, and I put a hand on either side of her head, tangling all nine of my remaining fingers in her auburn hair.

I stared back at her, but didn't even try to match the loathing in her eyes.

She cursed, and she hissed, and she spat in my face. She made noises I'm not sure there are words for. And then she grew quiet, and I only had to deal with the eyes.

"You finished?" I asked her. She told me to go fuck myself with a lawn dart (I swear that's what she said).

"I'd rather have a roll with you," I replied, then spat back at her. "But I'm thinking we're probably way past a good and mutually pleasurable fuck. Which is really a wicked shame."

"Not if you were the last gash on the face of the earth," she growled.

"Thought so. That settled, I'm gonna ask you a question. You tell me what I need to hear, you won't go the way of Moe and Curly. Capiche?"

"Fuck you," she said again, like it was going to carry more weight the second time around.

"One question, and you get to crawl out of here. Just give me the name of the cocksucker sent you, and you're a free woman."

I could see she was considering the offer. Not long, but she did think it over for the briefest moment.

"I'd rather die now, and get it over and done with."

You saw that coming, didn't you? Kneeling atop her on my kitchen floor, I sure as shit did.

"Probably a wise move," I told her, then broke her neck with a quick twist to the right. The way her cervical vertebrae popped made me a little queasy.

And here's the kicker. I found a yellow Post-it note in a pocket of her jeans. Just two letters and a phone number. The letters were J. D. and I'm pretty sure that didn't stand for Jack Daniels. No, it was that other Jack, the one Boston Harry had given up for one of my toes.

Time to go forth and meet Mr. Doyle.

By the by, I would like to pause to mention that—unlike you see in so many horror films and those paperback vamp potboilers, the ones you see in grocery store racks—my being rendered dead and fangulous did *not* bestow upon me kung fu action grip. Believe me, I was shocked I took out those three who invaded my kitchen. When it was over, I sat and stared at the corpses, scared shitless, confused, and thinking how much trouble it would be to get rid of the bodies. Easier with my car . . . coming to that in a moment. All I could figure was, becoming the "daughter" of Mercy Brown, the daughter of such an old bloodsucker, had come with an edge. Like, older vamps make way for stronger baby vamps. And the three were obviously very young, possibly four or five years since their hearts stopped beating and they cut their piranha teeth, but no older than that.

Still, I couldn't stop thinking, I should be dead, really, truly, once and for all dead.

And, where was the beast? Why the hell didn't it make an appearance this time?

Just like Clemency Hate-evill had said, *Ask the scary questions.*

In case you're wondering, if the domino guys heard the scuffle in the kitchen, they minded their own business. They're good at that. Tit for tat, you know? I washed up a bit, found an older and more ragged pair of Converse high-tops, and left the apartment via the front door. I'd pushed the three corpses down the hole in the kitchen floor. It would just have to do until I had time to deal with them properly. I did take time to bother with the makeup and the contact lenses, even though time was beginning to feel like a precious commodity, and I wasn't in a wasteful state of mind.

Mr. Jack Doyle gave me a little help in that department. I found his address and phone number in the phone book (I had one AT&T had left on my doorstep, I'd been using it as a doorstop).

I stepped out the front door, and there was my fucking Honda, sitting in the driveway. I stared at the boys a moment, then I stared at the boys again.

"You guys happen to see who left this?" I asked.

One of them—I think his name was Carlos, but they called him Popsicle, and don't ask me why—said, "Yeah. Tall white dude. Didn't say a word to nobody. Just parked it here about two hours ago. Was already dark. And I was like, 'Yo. *¿Ves aquel hombre? Mira a ese bicho raro,*' but he didn't say nothin'. Left the car and walked off." Popsicle pointed north, then went back to the game.

"*Fistro*, he acted like we wasn't even sitting here," Hector added, then laid down a domino.

"Did you happen to see those three come in my place?" I asked. "Two guys, a girl. Probably weirder looking than whoever left the car?"

"Oh, yeah. Figured they were friends. Had a key and all. Figured they were cool, *la banda*. They give you any shit, *chica*?"

"No, no . . ." I told him. "It's fine. Just wondered."

Hector shrugged.

I found my keys tucked into the driver's-side sun visor. My keys on my key ring.

And, in the passenger seat, the rind of a blood orange. But things are not always what they seem. I know that. And I didn't jump to the conclusion that my car coming home to me had anything to do with Mr. B, though, clearly, someone wanted me to *think* it had.

Before I went to find Doyle, I needed to clear my head. Talk to someone familiar, someone at least remotely friendly, so I headed for Aloysius' underpass. Sure, I felt strongly that time was not a luxury I had an overabundance of, but even us nasties get freaked out by late-night attempts on our lives, mysterious strangers returning our automobiles, and a cryptic citrus peel. Sure, I knew I was on the outs with the troll, and I didn't have any goodies to try and mollify him, but I went, anyway.

Under the highway, I shouted his name. It echoed, and for a moment I thought maybe I wasn't gonna see those special shadows, that he'd simply written me off as too tainted to hang with. But then, then the shadows came. The shadows and something by the Beastie Boys blaring at full volume. The troll that shuffled out of the blackness wasn't Aloysius. He wasn't anyone I'd ever seen. He was fatter, had skin like one of those weird albino pumpkins, and only a few piercings in his drooping ears. He was carrying a pink and white Hello Kitty boom box. You think shit can't get any stranger, but you're always wrong.

"Where's Aloysius?" I asked. Sometimes, it's best to get straight to the point.

The troll scrunched up his warty face and gave me the hairy eyeball. "Ain't his bridge anymore," the white troll said, then set Hello Kitty on the dusty ground. "I'm Otis, and it's *my* bridge. Don't you think no other way."

"So where is he?"

"Aloysius ain't nowhere no more. Took three arrows in the head last night. Cold-iron bolts, from a crossbow."

I suppose you would say my heart sank. I suppose you might even say I was sad. I never cried for Aloysius, but I've felt bad about it ever since that night.

"Fuck," I whispered.

"My bridge now. Finders keepers."

"No idea who killed him?"

Otis blinked a few times. Then the troll said, "Was thinking about you on that account, Siobhan Twice-Damned. Heard you pack a crossbow. Heard you bargained with him for a dicey sort of riddle not so long ago."

"Well, I didn't fucking kill him. He was my friend. Almost. Maybe." I wanted to tell Otis to turn off the Beastie Boys, but I didn't.

"Yeah, sure," he said. "Maybe that's true. Probably it ain't. Either way, got orders from on high, direct from the Night Court."

"Orders," I said, echoing Otis as the hollow space below the bridge had echoed me.

"We don't talk to you, all dead and wolfish. We don't talk to Siobhan Quinn, who might have done murder against poor Aloysius of the Unseelie. Heard you did in Mr. Boston Harry, too."

"Harry was one of yours?"

"Near enough. Anyway, talk of payback. You best keep a watch out for the Wild Hunt or worse."

"Jesus, I *didn't* fucking kill Aloysius. I liked the son of a bitch. Boston Harry, sure. That one's mine and I'll own up, but I'm pretty sure he had it coming."

"Maybe that's true. Probably it ain't," Otis said again, so there's another echo for the list.

"Fine. Whatever. Let your Court think what they want. Right now, truth be told, I might welcome that hunt with open arms. Get in line." That wasn't a lie. This whole situation—having become what I was, Mr. B leaving me to fend for myself, killing Bobby, eating the nasty-ass rat thing (and probably a seagull), then the assassination attempt by parties as yet unknown—I've been a whole lot more interested in staying alive (undead, dead, whatever adjective applies) than I was that night.

The white troll snorted. "Don't you go calling 'em out. Not the Wild Hunt. Ain't too many worse ways to go. Wouldn't be quick. Wouldn't be clean."

"Fuck yourself, Otis. He was my friend."

"So you said."

I didn't argue. I didn't wait for Otis the Troll to do his disappearing act. I got back in the car, turned around, and headed back up Gano. If the fay blamed me for Aloysius and truly had it in for me, I was determined to settle a few more scores before I went.

Quick interlude.

When all this was over and done, the metric shit-ton that the Bride had dropped on me, the next year I went back to the underpass, just after sunset on Beltane, and made a little shrine in memory of Aloysius. Yeah, I know. The sentimental monster, that's me. I left a bouquet of yellow roses, the sort with red around the edges of the petals. I doubt he could have cared less about flowers, but I did it, anyway. I also left a bunch of 3 Musketeers bars, two bottles of ginger brandy, and a stack of nudie mags. It's the thought that counts, right? And I figure I made some homeless person very happy with all that junk.

I fashioned my shrine (if you can call it that), and sat

in the dirt and cried. I don't think I've cried a single, solitary tear since that evening.

Anyway, easy as pie finding Mr. Jack Doyle. It was a red-brick apartment building on East Angell Street, off Wayland Square. Probably built back in the thirties or forties. Fire escapes for easy access. I figured I could be in and out of the place before dawn, quick as a bunny. Did I forget to mention the thing about Bobby Ng's ring (Class of '85, by the way)? What I did with it, I mean? Well, if perchance I did—right next to the place where Doyle lived there's a little basement junk/thrift/antique store. It's called What Cheer (if you live in Providence, no need to explain that phrase; if you don't, use Google). I had a rosary—black wooden beads, little plastic Jesus—I'd shoplifted there back in my street-kid days. I strung Bobby's ring on the rosary, and I wear it every now and again. Don't know if it counts as a souvenir of my first kill as a loup, or as more sentimentality. Either way, I was wearing it the night I went to find Mr. Doyle.

I parked out in front of a used bookstore and walked to the apartment building. Nice place, but I'd expected nicer. Maybe a pricey loft in some refurbished warehouse that had gone condo. That sort of thing. Nope. Anyway, by the time I got to the building, must have been about two ayem, possibly later. But I guessed I had a couple or three hours before sunrise, regardless. I scaled the fire escape, which was more rickety than it had looked from the ground; I actually almost fell once, when a rusty handrail gave way. Wouldn't have hurt me, but still.

Here's the thing about humans—mortal humans—who go and get themselves mixed up in the affairs of the nasties. They might be book smart. They might even have some sort of mystical talent—telepathy, precognition, clairaudience, all that sixth sense stuff. Maybe they can see ghosts or the fair folk. Might just be they're good with a pack of tarot cards. Doesn't matter. Inevitably, they're not awfully good at protecting themselves, and when you're messing with things that go bump in the night—even if you're "in league" with them, you best have that self-preservation shit down to a science. Virtually none ever do. Makes them easy marks. Some necromancer might be able to make a corpse talk, or maybe there's a witch who can curdle milk. But prudence and caution have an uncanny way of completely eluding these folks. What you have to understand is that a) these are very superstitious people, and b) the nasties have a vested interest in keeping them that way. If they were otherwise, one or two, now and then, might pose an actual threat. Sometimes they prove useful, but you can't risk one of the wannabes, servants, lackeys, and Bobby Ngs of the world, those liminal hangers-on, getting the upper hand. And, despite their inherent limitations, many undertake that exact, fatal, idiotic hustle. Hell, Bad Mr. B's the only one of them I ever met who seems to know the ropes and mind the boundaries, but I half suspect there's a splash of demonic blood in him a generation or two back. Which would make him *not* an exception to the rule.

There were hardly any lights on in the building, and the fire escape was set back a good distance from the nearest streetlight. Doyle's place was on the top floor, the fourth floor. It was nice and dark in there, and I was not the least bit surprised to find his window wasn't even locked. The window that opened onto his bedroom. Utter fucking genius, I know. Not that it would have mattered. Glass breaks lots easier than that vamp bitch's neck had snapped. But here is the funny part: there was a pentagram painted on the window, along with a host of alchemical and voodoo symbols, and a cross. I'm pretty sure the crusty reddish "paint" was dried blood. Probably from a chicken. Or some unfortunate goat. Trust in magic, why bother with locks?

I eased the window open, hoping he was home, and hoping this guy was a light sleeper. I was tired. The last thing I wanted was him putting up a futile and inconvenient struggle. I'd had plenty enough crap for one night, please and thank you very much. There was a dusting of dried herbs on the sill. I leaned over and sniffed, and it was just the usual potpourri of apotropaics. Mistletoe, thyme, mandrake shavings, sawdust from a mountain ash, a dried wild rose, blah, blah, blah. He'd probably soaked the wood in holy water. I brushed the mess away and quietly climbed inside, leaving the window open, because one must never underestimate the value of quick exits.

I stood there by the not so protective window, and it took me about five seconds to realize the bed was empty. The comforter and the sheets were a mess, so I reasoned someone had been in it recently. Unless Jack Doyle never bothered making his bed.

And then someone switched on a lamp.

He might as well have flashed me with a camera an inch from my eyeballs. Then a knife sliced into my right shoulder. I couldn't see shit, just orange-red blobs swimming in the air, but I knew it was a knife. I also knew he aimed for the left, and a little lower down than that soft spot above my clavicle. I ducked and rolled. I hit my head on a bedpost hard enough that a bunch of white stars were added to the swirl of afterimages from the lamp. I sat up, leaned against the wall, and blindly yanked the knife from my shoulder.

"You stop right there," he said. Mr. Doyle's voice quavered like a schoolgirl's.

"You asshole," I growled through clenched teeth, assuming by this time he'd only had the one knife, or I'd be dead already. Dead*er*. Done for. History. You know what I mean. "That fucking hurt."

"Don't move an *inch*," he warned me, and I could tell he was a couple of feet closer than before. I blinked my eyes, and my vision began to clear.

"It *still* fucking hurts." Turned out, it was a huge-ass pigsticker of a knife, something Jim Bowie might have wielded against Santa Anna's troops at the Alamo. And I'd have bet Boston Harry another toe it had been blessed by a priest or smeared with some supposedly magical goop that was supposed to take out nasties.

"What did you expect, sneaking in here like that?"

It was a fair question. Still, the pain had me thinking maybe I should just bury the knife in his skull and look for information elsewhere. Surely there were other breadcrumbs, other trails not quite grown cold.

"I wasn't even planning to kill you, you dumb son of a bitch. Now, I'm seriously rethinking that strategy."

"I've got high friends in low places," he said (truly, he said those very words). "So, maybe you'd better climb out the way you came in and scuttle back to whatever cemetery you call home."

"Maybe *you* should go fuck yourself, Mr. Doyle."

"I'm not messing around here, Miss Quinn."

He knew my name. Of course, he knew my name.

"Second thought, maybe I'll do it for you. Fuck you, I mean. Maybe I'll use this big damn knife of yours. How about that? That work for you, Jack?"

He was quiet for a few seconds. I stabbed the hardwood floor with the knife, sinking the blade in almost to the hilt. Then I covered the bloody slit in my T-shirt and the gash underneath with my left hand. Sure, vamps heal fast. But not fast enough.

"Look," he said. No, he was pretty much whimpering by this point. "They promised none of this could be traced back to me."

"They," I said. "Well, looks like *they* lied. Ain't that odd."

"I was *assured* . . ." Doyle began, but I interrupted him. We'll get to what I *wanted* him to say very shortly, but at the moment he was just pissing me off. And the last thing I wanted was the beast hiding inside me getting triggered before I was done with him.

"Where'd you learn to throw a knife, anyway? The Boy Scouts? You throw like a goddamned girl."

"Who are you?" He'd actually taken a step or two towards me, and I grimaced, raised my head, and he took a step backwards, towards the bedroom door.

"I'm the one whose life you fucked up with your little role in the murder of Alice Cregan," I said.

"*You* killed her."

"Let's table that minor fucking detail just for the moment, why don't we. Now, you sit down, shut up, and don't you even *think* about flinging anything else at me."

He did as I told him, sitting on the foot of the bed farthest from me. Good boy. Maybe he had a few ounces of survival instinct bubbling around in him after all. I took my hand away from the wound in my shoulder and stared at the blood there; it was black, and almost as sticky as hot tar. It was also cold as ice.

"I'm going to ask you questions, and you're going to answer them to the best of your ability. Elsewise, Mr. Doyle, violence *will* ensue, and you *will* be on the losing end of it. You understand what I'm saying?"

He nodded his head, and that's when I realized he was wearing mint-green silk pajamas, which, for some reason, struck me as funny. I put my hand over the wound again, and tried not to think about the frigid goop leaking out of me. I also tried not to think about the pain. There was no space or time here for distractions.

"You bought a gun from Boston Harry, didn't you? An enchanted blunderbuss?"

"I only . . ."

"Answer the question, yes or fucking no. It's just that simple. I don't want to hear any 'yeah buts' out of you. I don't want to hear any qualifiers whatsoever. Did you buy the gun from Boston Harry?"

"You're the one who killed him, aren't you?"

Okay. So maybe he wasn't such a smart boy, after all. I yanked the knife from the floor, and it came free with an awful squealing sound. I held it up, so the lamplight could glint off the blade.

"*I* ask the questions. *You* answer them."

"Sure," he muttered, then glanced at the dark doorway leading out to the hallway.

"Look at *me*, Mr. Doyle. Ain't nothing out there you need to be thinking about just now." And he turned his head back to me. "You bought the gun?" I asked for the third time. He nodded.

"I want words. Say it. Say, 'I bought the blunderbuss from Boston Harry.' "

"Fine. I bought the blunderbuss from Boston Harry." And he stared at his feet instead of at the hallway.

"Must have cost you a pretty penny. That right, Mr. Doyle?"

"Yeah, that's right."

"And you're doing okay, sure. But you're not the sort of man who can afford to pay that kind of money . . . or whatever he asked . . . for an old gun, are you?"

"No," he all but whispered. "I'm not."

"This suggests someone gave you the money, or whatever the rat's asking price was, or am I wrong?"

"You're not wrong."

I took my hand away from the wound again. It had stopped bleeding, and the ache was starting to subside.

"The next question, then, forms part of a logical progression. I'm thinking you could probably even ask it yourself. Wanna try?"

"Not particularly."

"Try anyway," I smiled, showing off my piranha teeth, and I pointed the knife at him.

"Where did I get the asking price?" he whispered.

"Exactly. Hole in one. Where *did* you get the scratch, Mister Doyle?"

He shut his eyes again, then opened them. The guy was *crying*.

"Need a hanky, Mister Doyle? You're getting me all choked up over here."

"I was promised anonymity and protection. I was promised *both*. Nobody was supposed to find out. Nothing like *you* was supposed to come creeping in my window in the middle of the night."

I watched him. If I were someone else, in another life—or another undeath—I might even have felt sorry for this poor, deluded feeb, who clearly had more greed than functional gray matter.

"Or maybe you owed someone on high a debt? Was that the way it went?"

"I was promised. I was given a *guarantee*."

Probably, I actually rolled my eyes.

"Dude, you're working for *monsters*. Likely as not, nasties who make *me* look like a teddy bear. And you're surprised when they don't play fair. Doesn't that staggering level of stupidity embarrass you at all?"

"I don't want to talk about the lying bastards."

"Then please stop bringing them up. Next question, since you're clearly not going to cooperate and cough up the info all on your own, I'm guessing you were a middleman, acting on another's behalf. I know Bobby Ng didn't buy the gun. Not only did the rat tell me so, but he wouldn't have given Ng the time of day, for any price. Plus, you've already copped to that part. I also have a hard time imagining you had some sort of beef with Cregan *or* her porcelain-doll mommy. This leaves me to conclude you were a middleman. But you tell me, is this true or is this false?"

"I answer that question, lady, I'm a dead man."

"You *don't* answer that question, same difference. Only I'm pretty sure I could draw it out at least five or six days before you shuffled off the mortal coil."

That's when I noticed the video camera mounted in one corner of the room. The tiny red LED told me it was recording. I leaned forward and began slicing chunks out of the down comforter.

"You're a paranoid man, Mister Doyle. Must make a lot of enemies, a man of your caliber. Me, for instance."

"It pays to be careful."

"Yeah, sure. But you, you pay for security cameras, but rely on old wives' tales and keep your windows unlocked. You can't even be bothered with a burglar alarm, for Christ's sake. Exactly how does that make sense?"

He didn't reply. I'd cut through to the mattress. It was also filled with feathers, and snow-white tufts spiraled to the floor.

"Then again," I said, "might be that you're not the one taping. It just might be it's someone else, and that someone else just *might* be whoever hired you to buy the gun. Could that be the case?"

"Yeah," he whispered so softly I wouldn't have heard him without my vampire superpowers.

"So, you're the middleman, which is a conclusion I admit was already my working hypothesis, before I came creeping in through your unlocked window. That correct, you're the middleman in this whole mess?"

"Yeah," he replied, even quieter than before. Maybe he was hoping the camera wasn't going to pick up his answers. I didn't really care, so long as I could make out what he was saying. But more jigsaw pieces were falling into place. It was becoming a matter of discovering the pattern printed on the puzzle.

"We're almost done, Jack. In fact, I've only got one more question. Then I leave the way I entered, and you go back to whatever's left of your crappy life."

I didn't even see the pistol until he was holding it, until after he'd flipped off the safety. But . . . I'll give him this much credit. He at least thought he *knew* it would be best to answer me before he squeezed the trigger. He wasn't beyond attempting half a smart move. Right about then, I was wishing more of those myths about bloodsuckers were true. Specifically the one where they can move quick as lightning. You know, like Blade in the comic books. Were that the case, I could have simply plucked the Colt from his hand between his next heartbeat and the one after that.

Instead, I said, as calmly as I could, "You know that won't hurt me, and if it's not meant for me, you know this shit doesn't end with death, not if you've pissed off—"

"Evangelista Penderghast," he said, taking the opportunity to interrupt me. "The Bride and Evangelista had some sort of misunderstanding, back in the twenties."

"You're kidding?" I asked. "You're telling me this is some sort of decades-old vamp catfight?"

And I remembered what B had said that night after I died—The undead, they don't think of time the way you and me think of time. Six months. Six weeks. Not much difference to them. Six months. Six weeks. Nine goddamn decades.

I'll explain about Evangelista Penderghast shortly. Maybe in the next chapter. Right now, let's stay focused on Jack Doyle.

"If you were the middleman, who was on the other side of the deal you made with Evangelista Penderghast? You didn't give the gun to Bobby Ng, did you? You gave it to someone to *hire* Bobby Ng." That part there, sheer fucking intuition. A stunning intellectual leap, if you will. Eureka and all that.

"You said the last question was going to be the last question," Doyle replied, staring very longingly into the barrel of the .45mm. "You lied."

"We covered that part already."

He smiled. He smiled like the proverbial cat that ate the proverbial canary. "Blood oranges," he said, then slipped the barrel into his mouth and pulled the trigger. His skull came apart like . . . never mind. I caught some of the back spatter, but mostly the blood and brains and shards of bone ended up on the bed, the headboard, and the wall behind the bed. He slumped backwards, and his body bounced a time or two when he hit the mattress.

And *then* the pain came.

I woke up naked in an alley in Olneyville, covered with bruises and abrasions—naked, same as the two times before. This time I did vomit, and in amongst what was left of Doyle (and a couple of house cats the beast must have come upon later) were scraps of mint-green silk.

CHAPTER SEVEN

BURNING DOWN THE HOUSE

So, yeah. I woke up in this alley in Olneyville. It was morning, and it was raining, just drizzle, but cold drizzle. But still. The rain made it all just that much worse. The clouds had even more bruises than my body. All evidence of the knife wound in my shoulder was gone.

I shouldn't have been surprised, but right there in the alley off Manton Avenue sat my Honda, waiting for me like the ghetto version of Cinderella's coach. The door was unlocked, and the keys were tucked into the driver's side sun visor. Small miracle no one had boosted it while

I slept off my lycanthropic hangover. Yeah, I know. Repetition. I'm *not* a writer. This is pretty much what happened before, but it's also what happened again. Sue me if it annoys you. There was a plastic bag from Old Navy in the backseat, and I managed to dress without anyone noticing the naked, raggedy-ass white girl standing in the rain by her ugly car (more repetition). There was even a shoebox, from a place on Thayer Street, with a brand-new pair of Converse high-tops still wrapped in tissue paper.

I sat behind the wheel for at least ten minutes—staring at the thing in the rearview mirror. I hadn't bothered with the makeup before visiting Doyle, of course. Neither that, nor the contacts. My benefactor had not seen fit to include those in the bag. Clearly, their generosity had its limits, I knew. I had to be trying someone or something's patience in the worst way. Finally I looked away from the mirror—nothing here to see, move along, move along—and there was a CD in an orange translucent case lying in the passenger seat. I picked it up and saw it was actually a DVD-R. Through the jewel case, I could read "From B" written in what looked like black Sharpie.

"You slimy bastard," I muttered, and then, then I drove back to my dump on Gano Street. The rain had kept the domino guys inside. I slipped in through the front door, and my nostrils were immediately assaulted by the smell of the three dead vampires decomposing beneath my kitchen. If the stink of the place had been bad before . . . well, let's just say I have no idea why no one in the building had called the cops. I tossed my keys and the disc on what passed for my sofa, and stood over the hole in the kitchen floor, over the bodies, for a bit, considering my options. The usual routine—filling the torso with something heavy prior to consigning it to the murky, conspiring depths of a river or bay or reservoir—that was out. No way I was hacking those three up, stashing the parts in plastic bags, and hauling them all the way to Fox Point or the Seekonk. But there was another option. That hole in my floor. Fuck, Ron Perlman with a bad haircut, all but his head was already down there.

I reapplied the MAC and the hazel-green contacts, slipped on the Wayfarers, left again, and drove to Wickenden Street. There's a hardware store there. I bought a shovel and a bag of lime. Probably looked suspicious as hell, but I was past caring. You get indifferent, you get sloppy. Maybe that was the deal with Jack Doyle. Maybe he'd gone so far in hock to the nasties that he'd just stopped caring.

Back home, at least I had the forethought to change out of the new clothes first. I didn't have any other jeans, so I settled for a pair of boxers and a Ramones T-shirt. Yeah, punk-rock grave digger. I decapitated the two vamps that still had their heads, cut out the hearts, and buried the whole mess below the floor. There wasn't a basement. There was hardly enough space to stand upright, and by the time I'd finished, twilight was coming on. I pulled myself out of the hole, cleaned the kitchen floor best I could, and by then I was filthy as a pig, right? I resolved to take time for a shower before having a look at the DVD.

Oh, I didn't bury the hearts, by the way. You have to be careful with those. Not gonna get into the whys of that. Lots of eerie mumbo jumbo. I tossed them in the freezer, to be dealt with at some later date. I did wonder about the mess in Doyle's apartment, and what his neighbors might have heard (and/or seen), and what the police would make of it all. But fuck it. I was done burying dead and mutilated sons of bitches (and bitches) for one day.

After the long, long and very hot shower, and after I'd brushed my teeth, and put the Old Navy stuff on again, I slid the DVD into the player and sat down on the floor in front of the television. I must have sat there watching the screen for ten minutes before I finally had the nerve to pick up the remote and press PLAY.

There was a noisy burst of static, but that ended so fast I didn't have time to lower the volume.

And then, in grainy black and white, a view of Doyle sitting on the foot of his bed, gun already in hand. I was sitting against the wall, at the left side of the screen. The sound quality wasn't so great, but the dialog was audible.

HIM: You said the last question was going to be the last question. You lied.

That .45mm automatic looked huge in his hands.

ME: We covered that part already.

HIM: Blood oranges.

The gun . . . well, I'll spare you a few tiresome adjectives. It made the sound that a Colt .45mm does when it blows off the back of some dude's head. There was a dull thunk as it fell from his dead hands and hit the floor.

What happened next . . . you'd think that after almost two years, it wouldn't bother me writing it down. All the horrors and carnage and crazy goings-on I've seen since that day, sitting there in front of the TV, you'd think

I'd have grown . . . what's the right word? *Just* the right word? *Blasé*? *Jaded*? No . . . so maybe there isn't a word for what I should have become by now. But you get the picture. Or you don't. Either way.

Like I said way back in the beginning, whoever started calling loups werewolves might have done better. I watched my body shift, skin and bone, muscle, metamorphosing organs emerging, then vanishing decently inside again. I saw it all, happening to me. And what was left, there wasn't much of me that resembled me . . . and what was there instead didn't precisely bring anything canine to mind. The sort of abomination that might result from the half-starved pairing of a mangy grizzly bear, a tarantula, and a pig. That's as close as I can come; like I said, I'm no writer. No author. But, that thing, me, also looked like it *hurt*. Like it was in fucking *agony*. And here I am saying *it* instead of *I*. All this time later, I'm still trying to distance myself from that broken thing on the television screen. I watched myself rip Doyle's corpse apart, and I watched myself eat quite a bit of him. I heard people shouting in the distance, from other apartments, maybe from the hallway. I heard a siren.

And then the beast that *was* me turned away from the bed and departed the same way I'd come in. Exit stage left. There's the sound of glass shattering and rusted steel straining under more weight than it was ever meant to bear. The camera recorded an instant of stillness before a second burst of static erupted from the DVD.

Then the picture was in color, and Mean Mr. B was inside that magic television box manufactured in Japan or South Korea or where the hell ever, inside and smiling at me from the other side of the glass. He briefly spoke to someone off screen, then he winked at me.

"Pretty, pretty pictures, Siobhan? Or don't you agree?" he smirked. I was still holding the remote, and I almost pressed OFF. *No*, my mind whispered to itself—that voice that had once been mine, and was now mostly his. *This is something important. This is something you have to hear. This is where those scary questions have led.*

And I suppose I owed it to Clemency and Aloysius, if there was an iota of decency left anywhere inside me.

"Outside looking in," he said, "and all that silly rot. Found art. *Cinéma vérité*, my dear."

It was impossible to tell where he'd been when the tape was being shot. There was nothing in the background but yellow wallpaper, peeling away in long strips. Some safe house he'd set up long ago against this very sort of calamity. A squalid, unknown sanctuary. He was wearing one of his tailored pinstripe suits. His hair was shiny with pomade, and he was smoking a baby-blue Gitane.

"But let's get down to business, because as you may have guessed, the clock is ticking, and there's not so much time remaining as you may *think* there is. The wolves are at the door." And then he paused to let the pun sink in, to be sure I'd gotten it.

"You've done well. I never imagined you'd get half this close to the truth. If I had, well . . . I'd have taken care of you myself that very first night. But no use crying over spilt milk, water under the bridge, opportunities come and gone and never to come again."

Then he proceeded to tell me things I'd already figured out for myself.

"You know, my dear, or you strongly suspect, that you're being used. What was it the Bride of Quiet, the venerable fucking Mercy Brown, said to you? 'You'll be my pet'? Was that it? And, too, that she was making a weapon of you? Yes, those are the things she said. By now you've begun to correlate the available data, as they say."

"A pet *and* a weapon," I said.

Right then, I'd never hated anyone as much as I hated Mean Mr. B. Not even Jack Grumet when he bit me in the ass, or the Bride when she had her way with me.

"A *puppet*, and she pulls the string, yes? Isn't that the way you have it reckoned?"

I muttered something. Maybe it was "You set me up, you motherfucker." I don't exactly remember what I said.

"But just in case you're not as bright as I think you are, my sweet, a quick recap. Oh, I'll freely implicate myself. We've gone too far for masquerades, I think. Doyle, he gave up Penderghast. I've just refreshed your memory on that count. Sometimes the transmogrification suffered by lycanthropes can cause a partial, though temporary, specie of amnesia. But if that were the case, now we're on the same page. So, you know Penderghast hired the late and unlamented Mr. Doyle to buy the blunderbuss. There was a middleman betwixt her and him, but isn't there always. There was a middleman between *him* and *me*. Can't be too cautious, Siobhan. Oh, no. A gent can never, ever be too cautious."

"Cut the crap and get to the point," I hissed between my sharp, triangular teeth. Though I suspect I was already hot on the trail of the point.

"Yes, I was hired in January to get rid of Alice Cregan.

Simple as that. Don't know all the specifics, but Evangelista Penderghast, undying firebug that she is, recalled some slight or another, and finally saw fit to ignite a squabble of old. She wanted the Bride hurt, and hurt badly, yes? So, she took out a contract on Miss Cregan. It was an awful lot of money. How was I supposed to say no? You are well enough aware of my various, unfortunate, and occasionally profitable weaknesses."

I stood up and began pacing the filthy living room.

"Way I had it figured, I hand it down to Ng, and with the right instrument, an instrument that could almost do the job on its own, well, even the supremely incompetent Bobby Ng wasn't going to botch the hit. But . . . I'm only human, alas. Well, mostly. I underestimated him."

Personally, I sort of doubt Bobby could have taken out Cregan even if he'd had a hydrogen bomb at his disposal. I would have thought B would have expected no more of him. Clearly, I was wrong, with a side of toast. And, by the by, I think this is what authors pejoratively call an "infodump." Be that as it may, I'm only parroting what was on that DVD, or close enough. No need to draw it out, or reorder events to contrive a more suspenseful tale.

"Your turning up at Swan Point that night in February," he said. "That was sheer happenstance, Siobhan."

"Stop calling me that," I muttered and paced some more.

"It's your name, dear," he said and winked again. "We ought never be ashamed of—or careless with—our *Christian* names."

Never mind what he said, or if he could hear me, or if

this was an oh-so-clever dash of bewitchment he'd added to the disc. It put to rest the mystery of his ever-shifting name. Whatever B's *Christian* name had been, he'd likely bargained even the memory of it away long ago, names being of such value among the nasties. So, he was just using whatever came along, but probably the terms of the deal prevented him from using any particular name for very long. I digress.

"Call it kismet, fate, coincidence . . . whatever floats your boat, darling. You were there when he screwed the pooch, and it was you, my remarkable enfant terrible, who got the job done, who saved my derrière. Even with the turn events have taken, don't think I'm not grateful."

I grabbed a cut-glass ashtray, scattering ash and butts; somehow, I managed not to hurl it at the screen. I dropped it, and it lay there on the carpet. A sorry symbol of my unspent rage.

"No," said B, "this might sound like a happy ending. After all, I got the job done, through the agency of someone in my employ."

"The druggie in your back pocket," I replied.

"Touché." B smiled his smug smile. "Regardless, Cregan was dead, I'd fulfilled the terms of my contract, and Penderghast was happy. I supposed all was right with the world. Who'd have reckoned the demon child, that Bride of Quiet, would notice her daughter's absence that soon. I thought it would take so many decades I'd surely have since perished of old age before she noticed. Must be they were closer than I believed. I'll take full fucking credit for that faux pas.

"And yet, she did notice, pronto and forthwith. On

the ball, that old cunt, isn't she? And she sent a message . . . to me, of course. As if Penderghast had not been in back of the proceedings, as if it were me, myself, and I had it out for her precious baby. Hardly fair, you ask me."

"I didn't."

"Fair enough," he said, and I glanced at the ashtray again. I imagined the satisfying collision of glass on glass, his unctuous visage dissolving in a burst of smoke and sparks. "So, *this* part you may or may not have worked out. Don't be insulted if you have, and I'm being presumptuous. The Bride, she sends me a message: I've got to square things with her, and right quick unless I want to go the way of Alice Cregan . . . or worse. With her sort, 'or worse' is always an option, as you well know."

"Get to the point."

"As you wish, kitten. An eye for an eye. Seemed straightforward enough. I'd cost her a lover, so she takes one of my lot. I happily offered up any number of my mollies. But, alas, she'd have none of them. She dismissed them, one and all. But finally, a few weeks back, she made up her mind." Here he stopped and pretended to frown. You've heard of crocodile tears? This was a crocodile frown.

"I wish it were not so," he said.

"I wish I had your balls in a blender, but ain't life a bitch."

"But it *was* so, and nothing I could say or do would assuage her decision. She knows how valuable you are to me, and, besides, you were the one who offed Cregan. That it was unintentionally you made no matter.

"Here we come to the heart of it. I arranged for Grumet to show up at the reservoir. And getting you to go after him, that was a piece of cake. You'd downed Cregan. I mistakenly thought one loup would be a breeze. Oh, I knew Mercy planned to intercept, but I hadn't counted on your being infected. Please, even in your present loathing and despair, kindly grant me that much credit. Of course, the rest is history. The Bride must have decided why simply take her prize in retribution when she could turn, instead, that prize against all involved . . ."

". . . in the killing," I finished, and he winked at me again. It wasn't as bad as the fake frown had been.

"The bitch made of you her weapon, her forbidden pet, and she proceeded to set you on everyone who'd played a role in Cregan's death, down to the last mother's son. She put an invisible choke collar around your neck, and fastened a leash to the collar. Don't know the exact spell, but we're coming to that. You have to admire her elegance. Circumventing the usual loup triggers, the moon and anger and what have you, *she* controlled your changes. You get near a target—Ng, Boston Harry, Doyle—and she gives that leash a fierce tug, and *voila*. Revenge. Brilliant. I'm half ashamed I didn't think of it first."

"Where's this headed?" I asked.

"Isn't it obvious? She's working her way along the food chain. Albeit somewhat haphazardly, but still."

"Which leads to you, doesn't it?"

He made a kind of disappointed face, like he'd expected better of me, and I took some small measure in his apparent disappointment, whether it was genuine or not.

"I think you'd find me terribly greasy, worse than last

night's duckling. Maybe not as foul as Boston Harry, but . . . and pay close attention . . . I think there may be an alternative. A way to cheat the Bride, if you will. My apologies for having taken so long to devise it."

"Oh, like you give a shit."

"You wound me, truly."

"Will you *please* stop doing that, talking back. It's freaking me out."

"As you wish, cupcake."

"What do I do?" I asked, and fuck what I'd just said about having a conversation with my television.

"You go to Penderghast, and she'll tell you the rest. She's asked for the honor herself, and who am I to argue? She desires to meet the infamous Siobhan Quinn, enemy of her enemy, the girl who nailed the spawn of her nemesis. She won't be so hard to find as you might think. She'll almost come to you."

"No way," I growled, whirling towards the face on the TV screen. "You're crazy. No fucking way am I going anywhere near that . . ."

". . . terrible, terrible woman?" he finished for me. "I'm afraid we've been left no option. Now, I haven't time to argue. Give Miss Penderghast my regards, and I hope you'll thank me again for having found such a convenient solution to our dilemma. Ta."

And then he was gone. The DVD player switched itself off. I sat down, and lit a cigarette, and listened to the night outside my apartment. Belatedly, it occurred to me I hadn't asked the bastard who'd sent the three goons after me, the same three who'd probably killed Aloysius. But, honestly, it hardly seemed to matter anymore.

* * *

Back at the start of this mess, I sat down to write a story, knowing parts of it would be true and other parts of it would surely be bullshit. Some would be actual recollection, and some would be me making up whatever was required to fill in the gaps in my memory. Frankly, I thought I'd get bored after a few pages and set it aside, a moment's diversion forgotten (and likely for the best). Vamps have notoriously short attention spans, unless the subject at hand is them. Anyway, I didn't set it aside, this *thing* of pages and pages and pages. Instead, the few pages have become . . . *this*. Whatever *this* is. It feels more and more like a confession. Or a row of milk bottles at a county fair, waiting to be knocked over with a good forkball or slider. What the hell was *that*? I've never even *been* to a county fair. And I don't watch baseball. But vampires are also cultural sponges. Helps with the necessary camouflage. Anyway, yeah. A confession of my crimes and acts of criminal stupidity, and of my arrogance.

Also, it's become, I see, a peculiar sort of rogue's gallery (thank you, Mr. Pinkerton), my setting forth of the dramatis personae of the fiasco of that August. All the wicked, ridiculous, men, women, and what have you merely players, and me recounting their various exits and their entrances: Mean Mr. B (yes, it's a Beatles' reference, you dullard), the Bride, Monsieur Grumet, unfortunate Bobby Ng, the more unfortunate Aloysius and Clemency Hate-evill, Alice Cregan, then Boston Harry, Jack Doyle, and, finally—here—the vampire named Evangelista Julia Penderghast.

Which means we're coming to the end of this story, and, perhaps, to the beginning of some other.

Looking back, I see I've said plenty of shit about just what a hard-ass son of a bitch Mr. B is, and how you didn't dare fuck around with the likes of Boston Harry. I've painted my grim portrait of Mercy Brown. I've hinted at the majestic horrors and fucked-up beauty of beings like Clemency and Alice. I've exaggerated and understated. Usually I've ladled it on thick as molasses, just how bad the bad can be. And so I can't fault anyone who approaches the following with a grain of salt. "Oh, here Quinn goes again. Yet another nasty, even nastier than the last. Yeah . . . right."

But . . .

Evangelista Penderghast. Words are never going to do her justice. At some point *evil* ceases to be a useful adjective (and concept), and *sadistic* or *depraved* fail, losing all descriptive value in the face of that which has transcended mere human concepts. And that's what you are, however I may feel about the lot of you. You're humans, and your minds would mercifully shatter before a creature like Penderghast. That summer two years back, I had no such blessing in store. Oh, sure. The damned can be blessed. Happens lots . . . but best if we leave that for some other time. It's complicated.

Even the nasties have their boogeymen, and Penderghast, she's one of those. As vamps go, she's old. If you believe all the hype, she's beaten the odds, dodged the expiration date, and has been lurking around the world since sometime in the fifteenth century. Maybe that's true, and maybe that's not. There are questions you don't ask, 'cause there isn't any point in asking, since no one has an answer, and if they do, you'll never learn it. But here's some of what I know about her. Some of it I knew that summer, and some, gratefully, I've only learned since then.

There are rumors out the wazoo. Like, she's Joan of Arc, who actually escaped her execution in the Vieux-Marché in Rouen. There are those who want to cast her as a bride of Vlad III, Prince of Wallachia—Stoker's Dracula. Dozens of romantic, craptacular, nonsensical tales. But all the truth you *need* to know is that she's been keeping court in a labyrinth of catacombs below Brooklyn since at least the early 1800s, when she left the Old World for the New. And that nothing on this continent has ever dared to stand against her. And that if she loves anything, she loves fire. The sight of it. The sound and smell of it. The spark that gives birth to inferno. The charred stench that follows. These are her glimpses of the Outer Ring of the Seventh Circle of Dante's Hell, of the river Phlegethon, all fire and boiling blood. I imagine she longs for the day she'll take her place between its banks, if you buy into that sort of thing.

Evangelista is said to have been sighted at many of the world's most terrible fires. The first and second great fires of Amsterdam (1421, 1452), the burning of Moscow in 1571, ringside seats for the Great Fire of London in September 1666. And a hundred and ten years later, at the burning of Manhattan in 1776 (this one, of course, contradicts reports that she didn't reach America until the early nineteenth century). Then the Second Great Fire of New York City, in 1835. She likely watched Sherman's troops raze Atlanta in 1864, and must have been disappointed that the general permitted citizens to evacuate beforehand. Sort of like great sex with no orgasm, right? Right. Oh, and what a fucking rush the first week of October 1871 must have been for this bitch. That triangle of fire that reached from Port Huron to Marinette, Wisconsin and south to Chicago. That unspeakable tornado of fire then erased the town of Peshtigo, and left more than two thousand dead, many simply incinerated, reduced to handfuls of ash. Perhaps the second worst natural disaster in American history. There's a photograph of her among the ruins. There are also photos I've seen that place her at the firestorm following the San Francisco earthquake in 1906, and she was a regular at testing sites for the Manhattan Project, beginning with Trinity in 1945. *Ad infinitum, ad* fucking *nauseam, ad conflagrationem.* Surely you get the picture. If the child vamp Mercy Brown styled herself the Bride of Quiet, then Evangelista Penderghast might style herself the Bride of Holocaust.

No one ever claimed she started any of the fires, but you really gotta wonder on that particular account.

Fuck, but there's a lot of fire in this story.

Now, maybe you see why B's instructions left me truly afraid for the first time since I'd been taken in the arms of my "blood mother" (near as I can tell, that asinine phrase was borrowed from a role-playing game, *Vampire: The Masquerade*, all the rage with goth nerds back when). He was sending me into the belly of the beast, off to meet the devil on earth, and, somehow, this undead pyromaniac was going to be our salvation—mine *and* his—from my lycanthropic curse that, again somehow, that alabaster she-goat had found a way to manipulate to her own ends in order to exact revenge for everyone responsible for Cregan's death. Right on up to Penderghast, and, gotta admit, that took some balls. Great big brass ones. Like a fucking flea getting the notion it could lay waste to a Great Dane.

Okay, that's enough of the historical sidebar, setup for the next scene's spectacle. We now return you to our story, already in progress. . . .

I've always hated road movies. Not sure why, just always have. *Bonnie and Clyde*, *The Badlands*, *Easy Rider*, *Thelma and Louise*, all those Bob Hope, Dorothy Lamour, and Bing Crosby comedies, *My Own Private Idaho*, *Grapes of* fucking *Wrath*. All of them. Oh, and I have a special hatred for that one example (of which I am aware) of the *vampire* road movie, *Near Dark*. I'm even capable of recognizing some of these are great flicks, but I hate them anyway, and no, I've no idea why. They bore me or something. No accounting for taste, right?

I suppose that's what you call prefacing remarks, or a prolegomenon—though you'd think my long-winded introduction to Dame Penderghast would have been enough. Only, *this* introduction, it's my way of avoiding all the pages recounting my drive from Providence to Brooklyn. It was not an uneventful drive. I'm just not in the mood. I almost took the train or the bus, then realized what a boneheaded move *that* would have been. Don't look now, old lady busy with your knitting or frat boy looking at porn on your fancy new iPad, but there's a dead girl sitting next to you.

After I watched the DVD, I touched up my makeup, and I said good-bye to Hector and the domino guys (who were out again, their Mexpop blaring louder than usual). I was fairly certain—however this went down—that I wasn't coming back. I figured this was Penderghast reeling in the threat (that could not possibly have ever been a threat to a nasty of her caliber, but surely I'd become an inconvenience, and, besides, she couldn't allow the Bride to continue to have the upper hand). Reeling in the embarrassment. I did think about running. I freely admit that. But it would have been futile, at best. You can't run from this shit. You might elude your just or unjust comeuppance for a few days, a week, a month, but sooner or later, and most likely sooner, you're tracked down. Trust me, running only makes it worse. I've had to track runners before, and the end of the road, for them and for me, is always much uglier than if they'd just faced up to their fate straightaway.

I'll say it was wicked hot that night. How appropriate is that? Fucking punch line, that was, right? Sure it was.

On the way out of Providence, I stopped at a Shaw's and bought five gallon jugs of water ("from the White Mountains of Vermont").

It was almost midnight by the time I exited I-278 onto the Prospect Expressway, and took . . . well, I parked the Honda on Fort Hamilton Avenue near the Green-Wood Cemetery. I poured three of the jugs of water over my head, and tossed the other two over the ornate wrought-iron fence before scaling it. It's a wonder they didn't burst, the water bottles. But I can't say I was thinking clearly by that point. A girl doesn't stroll into Hades every goddamn night. I moved through the labyrinth of headstones and obelisks, marble and granite and Bellville brownstone. Over grave-studded hill and dale, and the night was filled with the songs of night birds and the distant noise of cars. There were a couple of close calls with security as I neared Battle Hill. That's the highest point in Brooklyn, by the way, rising some two hundred feet above sea level, part of an ancient glacial moraine. And maybe that's why Penderghast chose it for her catacombs, to stay high and dry. But me, I suspect it was the fact that about three hundred victims of the 1876 Brooklyn Theater Fire are buried there, all those unrecognizable corpses consigned to a common grave. For her, that's probably as irresistible as horseshit is to flies. She must have been standing across from the theater that long ago evening, watching the festivities.

Anyway, yeah. Oodles of history attached to this vast boneyard, sprawling across the manicured landscape like a Disneyland for the dear departed, but I wasn't there to sightsee. I moved as quickly as possible, lugging those twin gallons of water, towards the mausoleum—guarded by twin marble lions—that led down to Evangelista's halls.

There was a massive lock on the mausoleum door, meant for some huge antique key, but that's only for historians and caretakers. For the mortals who come here. All I needed were a few choice words of Latin (they'd been written in B's hand on a slip of paper tucked inside the DVD's jewel case, thoughtful bastard), and the door didn't so much open as melt away. I stepped inside, and in place of the musty smell I'd expected, I was greeted by the acrid reek of sulfur and gasoline and everything that could ever be made to burn. Which, when you pause to consider, *is* pretty much everything. The arched passageway with stairs that led down and down, spiraling steeply round and round, each round wider than the last. Imagine descending the inside of a seashell's whorl, from top to bottom. The deeper I went, the greater the heat, until I might as well have been standing before a blast furnace. I stopped long enough to open the two remaining bottles of pure Vermont water and soak my hair and skin and clothes. And yeah, fire and vamps are a bad mix, even if the sun's not an issue. But, like I said, at the right temperature, *everything* burns. Humans, vamps, steel, rock, whatever. But Penderghast, she'd spent centuries learning to cheat the laws of nature and supernature. She'd become a pyromancer of the first order. Fire was her lover, and she'd made damn sure it'd never bite back.

I walked, and the water on my skin began to turn to steam. So much for precautions. The walls were increasingly illuminated by an orange-red glow, as though I was making my way into the belly of a volcano, towards the hearth of Pele. Maybe that's purple prose, or maybe you just had to be there to appreciate how well that melodramatic simile manages to go about the cutting of the mustard.

Eventually after I have no idea how long, the spiral ended in a wide platform or ledge, and suddenly the firelight was so bright the Wayfarers were useless and I had to cover my eyes. Again, my expository powers are not even half equal to the task at hand, at any attempt to even half describe the pit stretched out below and before me. Maybe Dante could have come close, but I kinda doubt it. Just think of a cavern that seems to run on forever in all directions, infinitely so far as I could tell, and think of an equally infinite churning molten sea beneath, and, hey, just maybe you're a millionth of the way there. Just maybe. Thousands of chains dangled from the cavern's roof, each ending in a meat hook, and almost every hook was buried in charcoal that had once been some manner of living thing. The rest of them held creatures that hadn't yet died, beasts and men and women whose agonies Evangelista might protract for quite a bit longer. The air broiled.

I wanted to turn and . . . but I've already mentioned what happens to the runners, haven't I?

A rusty iron cage slid towards me, sort of like a cable ferry above the molten sea. No, *cable ferry* isn't right. I'm not a damn engineer. It was a *cage*, all right? A cage suspended from a chain by loops of cable, and there was a wheel that let it roll to and fro along the cable. You've seen a ski lift, right? It wasn't like that, but that's as near as I can come. The cage's door swung open, and no one had to tell me I was meant to step inside. It wasn't an invitation, it was a command. Already, I'd begun to feel a bubble of cooler air surrounding me—by the grace of Penderghast, who couldn't have me combusting prematurely, after all. Not until my usefulness was over and done with. I stepped into the cage, it clanged shut again, and then began to creak along the cable, a hundred feet above that sea of fire. I hadn't even been asked to pay the fucking ferryman, and I wondered if the ride back would also be free. That is, assuming there would *be* a ride back. I was doing my best to hang on to those few, stingy shreds of half-hearted optimism I'd ever been able to call my own.

The door opened, and what crouched on the sizzling dais before me put the pathetic, pale grotesquerie that was Mercy Brown all the way to shame and back again. In some ways, it was almost her polar opposite; the Bride, she was an Antarctic world that had never known the sun, and Evangelista, she was the fusion-reactor *heart* of the sun, the very act of hydrogen flashing to helium, that hellish proton–proton chain reaction (yeah, I read a book about stars once upon a fucking time, okay?). But, even so, there was no valid point of comparison. Oh, if the televangelists and "lake of fire and brimstone as an eternal punishment" crowd could have gotten a peek at her, I think they'd begin to consider the merits of giving the whole matter of damnation a second, third, and fourth thought.

"How sweet," she said. No, screw *she*. Let's dispense with any pretense at gender and/or sex. You remember what I said at the start about a vamp's nethers withering away after such and such amount of time? Yeah, well. Whatever had once been female about this monster, those attributes had long since packed their bags and fled the scene. *Its* flesh—if that was flesh—was ebony shot through with shimmering, spiderweb cracks. The crusty black scum that floats along on lava. Its eyes were bluish, ultraviolet holes punched into the fabric of space.

Now there's a sentence even Lovecraft would have been proud of. But I'm not gonna take it back. That's what I saw, until I had the good sense to look away. That's what I still see sometimes when I close my eyes. That's what watched me from a glistening obsidian face.

"She actually came, and I thought for sure she wouldn't. I thought she didn't have the nerve for this rendezvous."

"She wasn't left with much choice," I said. "And can we stop speaking of her in third person, please. She's standing right here, and she has a name."

"That you do," said Evangelista Penderghast. "I thought, *Quinn*, I might be doing you some kindly service, not speaking it aloud."

It wasn't wrong on that score. No matter how bad the blazing sapphire eyes had been, my name dripping off that tongue, that was way worse.

"He sent you, good boy that he is, and now you'll want to know why? No, you already know the why. You'll want to know *how*."

"I never meant to kill the bitch's daughter."

"Which is neither here nor there, Quinn." And, seriously, liquid steel pouring out of an electric-arc furnace, but something that pure rendered irredeemably filthy, that was its voice.

"We can switch back to third person," I whispered. "Really. She won't mind at all."

It might have laughed then. If that wasn't laughter, I don't know what else you'd call the sound she made.

"As she wishes. I wouldn't have it any other way, not a scion of the Bride of Quiet."

"Don't think I had anything to do with that, either. Or the shit with the werewolf."

"He told me," it sighed, and I know, the moment

that breath touched me, I'd have been gone in a puff of smoke if not for my magical, insulating bubble. "I know how her wretched, woebegone circumstances have come to pass. I don't care, but don't suppose that means I don't know."

I thought about apologizing. Fortunately, it didn't give me a chance.

"The Bride is entirely insane. It's proof enough this . . . this . . . repulsive half-caste amalgam was forged in the belief such was sufficient to end me."

"You'll get no argument there. I mean, her being insane and all. At least a few fries shy of a Happy Meal."

I felt its eyes on me, and time passed before it spoke again. I don't know how much time.

"She thinks I care about her opinion, the scion of the Bride? She thinks maybe her idiot contemplations have some bearing on what's to come?"

"Sorry. She'll keep her idiot contemplations to herself from here on. She has absolutely no problem at all with that."

"No, no. Oh, no. I'm not offended. Rather, she *amuses* me with these recitations of the obvious. She'll not stand silent before me. I'll not have that."

"Fine," I whispered (actually, pretty much everything I said, there below Green-Wood Cemetery, was hardly spoken louder than a whisper).

"Fine," Evangelista echoed. "Yes, fine. She is a prize. I'll grant her that. I'd almost keep her here with me, time and pressure to make a diamond, a fractured jewel among my jewels to look upon from time to time, only my hatred, it would never allow such a concession. Such an indulgence of my own meager desires when I have been so insulted by little more than a worm."

By this point, my mind was casting about for anything to keep myself sane as that voice seeped all around me. And I realized something about this fiend reminded me of the Red Queen, the Queen of Hearts, in *Alice In Wonderland*. Maybe it would have a change of heart, and shout "Off with her head!" and that would be that. It would have been a kindness. I was no longer afraid for my existence. More like, I was terrified of what my existence could become, if it should suddenly suit Evangelista's scalding fancy. I stared at the basalt (at least I think it was basalt) between my shoes. There was that cacophony again, the one that might have been laughter.

" 'That's right,' shouted the Queen. 'Can you play croquet?' " quoted Evangelista Penderghast.

So I started thinking about a Johnny Cash song instead. Maybe it didn't know about Johnny Cash.

"Fine then, here's the how. She best listen close, because I'll not say it but the once."

"Don't worry. She's paying attention," I said.

There were words, precise instructions, though they sunk at once into some subconscious cranny of my mind, and I've never been able to recall them. And in my right hand I held a black dagger, a dagger black enough to consume planets. Around my throat there was a brass locket on a brass chain. The dagger and the locket were both warm, but not uncomfortably so. My left hand went immediately to the little locket.

"There," it said. "There's more, but I know she'll improvise, being clever and resourceful. Now, we have concluded our dealings, and she'll not ever have cause to come back to me again, if she is a most fortuitous beast. She'll go now, the same way she came. She'll go, and won't dare look back."

I did as I was told. I knew the story of Eurydice and Orpheus. On the other side of the chasm, the cooling bubble popped, and I found myself racing up those spiraling stairs. I didn't stop until I was outside the mausoleum and had once again passed between those silent stone lions. Then—fuck it, tell the truth, and ego be damned—I collapsed on the cool, dew-dappled grass and gasped against the pain that seared the back of my neck, my shoulders, my calves. When I reached the car, I'd discover that patches of my hair were scorched. Later, after I'd returned to Providence and my apartment, I'd find the complex network of keloid scars that snaked from the base of my skull to my heels. Like Boston Harry, she'd left me with a souvenir, as good as her signature. My hair would grow back, but the scars, those I still have.

Patience, constant reader. It's almost over.

CHAPTER EIGHT

AND THE WORLD FALLS DOWN

Remember way back in Chapter One when I noted how readers complain about the way characters do stupid things in horror films and protest that no one's *that* stupid? Remember that? And how I said, from a monster's point of view, how very surprised you'd be at the stupid shit people do that gets them killed? Right. Well, anyway, even us creatures of the night aren't immune to that kind of imbecilic behavior, and you'd think we'd know better.

Case in point (as dear ol' Rod Serling used to say): When I got back to Providence, and realized that somewhere during all these jolly misadventures I'd lost my cell phone, I should have snagged a new one. There's a RadioShack on North Main, or I could have grabbed one of those prepaid pieces of crap at a Walgreens. Easy as pie. But no. That's not what I did. I did the stupid thing instead. I went to the troll bridge below I-195, the late, lamented Aloysius' former digs. I went there, called for Otis, and asked him if he had Aloysius' things. Because, as has been mentioned, by this time I was jake with the Unseelie.

It was maybe an hour past dawn.

He sauntered out from those special shadows, the boom box around his neck like a gigantic pendant. At least this time he wasn't listening to the Beastie Boys. He was listening to the Ramones. Yeah, I get the punk-rock troll. He closed one eye, and squinted at me with the other.

"You still walking around in one piece?" he inquired, sounding more than a tiny bit surprised.

"Looks like," I replied.

"The wheels turn slow sometimes. Time below the hills ain't like time above."

I could have told him he was wasting *his* time trying to scare me. I could have told him about what I'd just met lurking below that hill in a Brooklyn cemetery, but I didn't.

"I'm sure they'll run me down as soon as they get around to it. In the meanwhile, do you have his stuff or not?" I asked again.

Otis scratched at one albino armpit. "Let's just say I do, twice-dead Quinn, twice-cursed daughter of Eve. Why would I tell you?"

Good damn question. We return to the issue of stupidity in these sorts of tales.

"I was his friend," I said, 'cause, you know, I already knew he wasn't buying *that*.

"What got him killed."

"Hey, dude. A simple yes or no would be wicked useful at this juncture."

"Wicked," he growled, a soft, soft growl, like faraway thunder. "Yes, you are. You are wicked, indeed."

"That's not what I meant."

"I Don't Care" blared from the boom box.

Otis closed his left eye again, and the right rolled about in its socket like whatever muscles and nerves hold eyeballs in place had suddenly failed him.

"Please," I said. "I'll be in your debt."

Stupid, stupid, stupid. Hell, you might just as well decide I'm making this up to create a more suspenseful scene, like where, in *The Stand*, Stephen King has Larry Underwood leave New York via the Lincoln Tunnel instead of, say, the George Washington Bridge, just because it would make a way scarier scene, having him down there in the dark. Oh, and having Larry forget to even take along a flashlight, and . . . never mind. Point is, rule of thumb, never tell any sort of fairy you'll be in its fucking debt. Not ever. Same with demons. And angels, I imagine, if they actually exist (which I tend to doubt).

"All I want is his phone. He had a cell phone. I know, because he was using it to harass Mr. B, right? That's all I want, I swear."

"My debt?" Otis asked, and cocked a scabby eyebrow. "Mayhap, if you elaborate. Mayhap, then, a bargain could be struck. What about that, for instance?" And he pointed at the golden locket Evangelista Penderghast had given me.

"Not a chance," I told him.

"Strikes me beggars can't be choosers."

I closed my own eyes a moment. I was getting awfully tired of deals and bargains, promises and broken promises. Right then, I wished I had anything at all forged from cold steel. Hell, a chunk of raw hematite would have done just fine. I spoke without opening my eyes.

"What do you want, Otis?"

"I want that shiny bauble hanging 'bout your throat."

"Well, you're not getting it, so try again."

"Stingy ape," he said. "Stingy, ungrateful ape. But very well. Still, I should think about this, long and hard I should think about this, twice-cursed. Has to be dear to you. Has to be precious—like that shiny bauble."

I opened my eyes, and maybe I have a friend below, because only a few feet away, I spotted a rusty stainless-steel hubcap someone had lost and not noticed they'd lost, or just not bothered to retrieve. I reached for it, and Otis made a panicked expression, and I saw the special shadows sliding across the ground towards him.

"You even think about making a break for it, I'll nail you with this so hard you'll think I was on the Olympic discus team. And we both know how that'll go."

The shadows melted away, and the troll the color of those whitish pumpkins pouted and lowered his head. "I Don't Care" segued into "Sheena Is a Punk Rocker."

"Don't think I *won't* use it," I warned him.

And then a burlap sack appeared at my feet. I reached

down and opened it; there was porn inside, and half a quart of ginger brandy, several mouthfuls of human molars, an assortment of chess pieces, bottle caps, a dead, desiccated crow, and a cell phone.

"This isn't going to turn into a handful of gravel or a rotten mouse as soon as you leave?"

"No," he said sullenly.

I had no reason on earth to believe him, but, still, I said, "Fine. Now get the hell out of my face. I'm tired of looking at you." No, I didn't have to be such an asshole. But I was tired, and the vamp hunger was taking hold, and I was pissed as pissed could be. But still, I felt like a jerk, pulling the iron trump card on him like that.

"Hey, wait," I shouted as the shadows began to wrap themselves about him. "You smoke?"

"Time and again," he mumbled.

I reached into my jeans pocket and pulled out a crumpled half-full pack of Camel Wides and tossed them to him. He caught them in an enormous paw and stared at the cigarettes a moment.

"No hard feelings, okay?"

But then he was gone, and I was left alone below the underpass, the morning sun making my exhausted eyes ache. I dropped the hubcap back into the dust and stomped through the weeds to my Honda, Aloysius' sad bag of goodies in my hand.

Of course, I didn't for an instant believe that it was going to be so simple a matter as me picking up Aloysius' phone and speed-dialing Mean Mr. B. But I could be a resourceful beast when the situation demanded that I be (nothing's changed in the last two years, not in that respect). I knew the names of a few of his boys. Not their various aliases and drag-queen names. I had two or three of their actual names, and Nancy boys are susceptible to threats, couched just so. I'd not done this sooner because I hadn't wanted things to come to that. It would only piss B off that much more, and, besides, none of this mess was their fault. They're just a bunch of kids B drags into his various dramas, not so different from me (except, I've never had to take it up the ass so he can get his ya-ya's off). But here I was, freshly returned from Evangelista's inferno, this locket about my neck, this dagger in my hand, and my head full of stuff I could not consciously recall.

I phoned the kid named West, B's most recent acquisition and his current favorite. West almost hung up on me, before I began describing in detail the many means of castration I could devise using nothing more elaborate than a Taco Bell spork.

"I don't know where he is," West said, the tone of his voice filled to overflowing with a curious mixture of nervousness and "Oh, I am so put upon."

"Then you'd better find out," I replied, "because I know how to find *you*." (That part was sort of a lie. I didn't know, not right off. But I'm fairly sure it wouldn't have been too hard, here in the age of the internet.)

"You're not going to hurt me," West said, attempting to come across all defiant and shit. "You harm one hair on my head, he'll make you wish you were never born."

"Too late for that, Sunshine. Someone already beat him to the punch. Just make sure he calls me before lunch."

"Or?"

"The spork," I reminded him, and then he did hang up.

I was sitting in my only kitchen chair, listening to the married couple upstairs fight. The guy, he was a drunk, and sometimes he showed up, any hour of the day or night, and they went at it like cats and dogs. I knew he hit her. I'd seen the bruises on her face to prove it. So, I was sitting there, listening, and beginning to feel the starvation, the hunger pangs, emptiness, the ache, that overwhelming ravenousness—call it what you will. I hadn't had anything since Doyle, and I was thinking on that when I heard two dull smacks overhead. I might have missed it, if not for my fancy new vamp ears that made everything so LOUD. One was that drunken fuck hitting his wife. The other, I knew, was her colliding with a wall or a piece of furniture. Sappy as it might sound, I thought of dear old Mom and Dad. I thought about her, the stink of rye on his breath, him beating her with a bar of soap wrapped in a dish towel. I thought of me hiding until the ambulance came, then running away. Maybe it was just some fucked-up PTSD kicking in, but I dislike all those psychobabble acronyms. Let's just say I was starving, and he was a convenient asshole that the world could do without. Yeah, that works for me.

I took the stairs two at a time and had to bang on the door repeatedly before anyone came. It was her, trying to hide a bloody nose with that dish towel all spattered red.

"You'll want to step aside," I said.

"Did you call the cops?" she asked. "It's nothing. I bumped into a doorframe, that's all."

"You'll want to step aside *now*," I said, lowering my

voice, almost growling the words, becoming that avenging bullshit bloodsucker so popular with the women who read the silly ParaRom pulp I mentioned earlier. The woman with the busted nose promptly stepped aside.

"Now, go downstairs," I said, and she did that, too.

The husband was standing on the other side of the room. He was three sheets to the wind, and put me in mind of a mentally deficient gorilla.

"What the fuck *you* want, bitch?" he sneered. "This ain't your business."

"No, it's not," I agreed. "But I'm hungry, and here you are. You need a punching bag, have a go at me before you die. I won't hold it against you." I showed him the mouthful of piranha teeth and—I swear to dog—the son of a bitch pissed himself. But not even that dark stain spreading across the crotch of his knee-length camo cargo shorts made him look any less tasty.

He had just enough time to mumble, "What in hell—" before I was on him. I admit that I was deeply gratified at the way he screamed. My teeth parted skin, fascia, muscle, and sliced through his carotid. Some of those fictions, they make it sound pleasurable for the victim. Feeding, I mean. Right. Well, it ain't. Trust me. He made a lot of noise, and none of it was the sort people make when people feel good. How you think it would feel, having your throat chewed, then the better measure of your blood slowly sipped out through a loop-the-loop crazy straw? Really romantic, yeah. Gets me wet, just thinking about it.

Anyway, when it was finally over, I left him crumpled in a corner, and went back downstairs to wash up. The wife was standing outside talking to Hector and the gang.

I rinsed my mouth from the tap, watching the reddish water swirl down the bathroom sink. I put on a not-clean T-shirt (but at least there were no bloodstains). My cell rang—the one I'd bought for Aloysius—and I answered it. It was B. The squeaky, scary wheel, grease, and all that happy crappy, right?

"Siobhan, love," he purred.

"You," I said.

"Not very nice of you, threatening poor West like that. He was all but hysterical."

"And I care why?"

There was a moment's silence before he asked, "So, you've been to Brooklyn, I trust? You've had your tête-à-tête with the hellion?"

"Yeah, I did that. And I have the scars to show for my trouble. And a few other trinkets. Not that I know what to *do* with any of this junk."

"Oh, you know, my precious. You just don't remember you *know* you know."

"And you're not about to meet with me, you being on the Bride's hit list and all."

"Actually," he said, and I could hear his smirk through the phone, "the situation has changed, thanks to Lady Penderghast's generosity. I trust she gave you the locket, the one on the brass chain."

"Yeah, she did."

"It cancels out the effects of the Bride's collar. Now you're just a regular old wolfy. Well, except for the also being a vampire part."

My fingers went to the locket. I hadn't yet tried to open it, and had a feeling it was best I didn't.

"Oh, by the way, don't open the locket," he said, and I almost laughed. "That would break the charm."

"She could have told me that."

"That's not her way."

"And the dagger? You gonna bother telling me exactly what sorta voodoo it do?"

"It'll put down Miss Mercy Brown like the rabid dog she is," he replied, "thus ending this whole absurd affair."

"Not for me. Would it work on me?"

"Love, plain old wood would work on you. But I don't think that's what you really want."

I stared up at the ceiling. I could still taste the drunken bastard.

"You might be interested to know I just ate my upstairs neighbor. But don't worry, it couldn't have happened to a nicer guy."

"That's not very discreet."

"You got a cleanup crew on hand," I said, "You might want to send it over, on the quick."

He didn't say anything else for a moment. Then he sighed and said, "Consider it done, love. Only for you."

"What next?"

"Well, don't hang around your apartment, if, indeed, that's where you're calling from. Leaving the scene of the crime, that's a good place to start. You want my advice."

"Where to?" I asked. "I mean, how's this all supposed to play out?"

"The knife is also a compass needle. Isn't that clever? Lay it on consecrated ground. Any church, synagogue, mosque, or cemetery will do. Set it down, it'll point straight towards the Bride, be she east, west, north, or south."

"That's pretty fucking vague," I said.

"Don't worry. Once the knife spins, once you see, you'll know exactly where to find her."

"Jesus, why didn't she just tell me? Oh, let me hazard a guess. It's not her way."

"You're no prat. I'll give you that. But I do wish you'd quit leaving these discommodious messes."

"I don't even know what that means, *discommodious.*"

"Buy a dictionary, treacle-tart."

I hate it when B starts in with the Cockney rhyming slang. I don't get half of it, and he's not even Cockney.

"Whatever. There's a wife. He beat her. Don't you *dare* lay a goddamn finger on her, hear me."

"Loud and clear. And my, oh my, haven't we grown all chivalrous." I ignored the jibe.

"So, simple as that? I go forth and slay the nasty who made *me* a nasty, and who has it out for us all?"

"Simple as that."

I pushed back the drapes, glancing out at the sidewalk. It was a scalding day out there, and none of the domino boys were wearing shirts. The woman was talking to them, and now and then she'd look up, towards her apartment.

"Nothing is ever simple as that," I told B.

"Just do as I say. Then we'll have a long sit-down at Babe's, just like old times. You have a very bright and profitable future ahead of you."

The wife saw me watching her, and I let the drapes swing shut again.

"You set me up," I said.

"We've been over that, love. I did what I had to do. The greater good and all."

"You're an asshole."

"That I am. Now, run along before someone calls the coppers, and you have to try to explain things that can't be explained without recourse to fairy tales."

He hung up. I hadn't even gotten around to telling him about the three vamps buried beneath the kitchen.

I grabbed my car keys and sunglasses. The dagger was tucked into the waistband of my jeans, in back, hidden beneath the T-shirt. Out on the sidewalk, the wife with the bloody nose asked me what had happened. Hector and company looked pretty damned curious, as well.

"He won't ever hurt you again," I said, and then I got in my car and drove away towards the intersection of Benefit and Wickenden, to Our Lady of the Rosary. Mostly Portuguese, not Irish Catholic. But what the hey. I spared a single peek at the rearview, and the wife hadn't moved.

The business at the church went smooth as smooth can go. The sanctuary doors were unlocked, which surprised me. I thought everyone locked everything these days, but maybe the righteous are less cautious than the rest of us, or simply more concerned with saving souls than with material possessions. Anyway, I admit that I lingered a moment at the threshold after pushing open the heavy wooden door. How could I not? Lots of people buy into all those timeworn, treasured chestnuts about interactions between the Old Man in the Sky and us walking-dead types. Those empty superstitions to make them feel just a wee bit safer in the night. Say your prayers, go to confession, drop a buck in the collection plate, whatever, and the nasties won't get you, and you won't go to the Bad Place, and you'll even be forgiven for cheating on your income taxes. See, you hear that shit repeated all your life, you have it drilled into you as a kid, and some of it sticks, and it really doesn't matter if you realize it's all a crock later on.

But I only lingered a moment.

I stepped into the sanctuary, and nothing happened. Nothing whatsoever. The air in there was heavy with the odors of dust and aging hymnals and Murphy's Oil Soap, felt and polished wood, plaster dust, sacramental wine, candle wax, the bodies of a thousand different men and women and children . . . and no, you probably wouldn't have smelled all this stuff (or it might have struck you as a *single* complex scent), but I did. The door creaked shut behind me, and I stood there in the silence, as though I'd forgotten why I'd come to this place. It reminded me too much of a childhood I'd done my best to forget, but always wanted to remember. Former homeless, junky runaway *cum* pissed-off and terrified werepire, thy name is contradiction. But if I looked at the pews, there I was with my mom. I shut my eyes, and when I opened them, the phantoms had gone.

I walked a little way down the aisle, kneeled (as Jesus, Mother Mary, and any number of saints watched on) and pulled Evangelista's black dagger from the waistband of my jeans. I laid it on the red carpeting. And, at once, it began spinning like a top, finally coming to rest with the tip of the blade pointing, more or less, southwest.

"Great," I whispered. "So, we could be talking about Connecticut. Or New Orleans. Or Mexico fucking City. Or . . ."

But then I remembered some of what Evangelista had slipped into my head. I saw a tumbledown wreck of a house, and knew the address that went along with it. It was in Exeter, less than twenty miles from where I kneeled there in the sanctuary of Our Lady of the Rosary.

"Tag," I said. "Got you now, bitch."

This was, obviously, a tad premature. I did *not* have her. I only knew where she was, and the one ain't the other. Not even close. But I was tired, the church was creeping me out big-time, and I was getting a headache. Probably, whatever had been coursing through the veins of Mr. White-trash Wife-beater Crack-head wasn't agreeing with my bloodsucker's anti-metabolism (just made that phrase up). Or it was a side effect of the hocus-pocus Penderghast was playing at with my mind. I picked up the dagger, and pulled that heavy door shut behind me as I left. I prayed to nothing at all that it was the last time I'd ever have cause to enter a "house of God." Whether he was there or not, I'd not felt welcome.

What I did next, it sure as hell wasn't on Bad Mr. B's itinerary. It was, in fact, a major deviation from the plan, his and Evangelista's. But I did it, anyway. I didn't do it to spite them—but I also didn't do it *not* to spite them. I was the black knight being sent into Blake's "forest of the night" to slay this "Tyger! Tyger! burning bright." "What dread hand? And what dread feet?" indeed. I was the one who was about to face her fearful symmetry, and, the way I saw it, that gave me a certain degree of latitude as to *how* this endgame was going to play out. And, besides, I was in the mood for a big-ass, fuck-ton of Fourth of July fireworks—the ones that get all the *ooohs* and *ahs*—not a handful of bottle rockets. Maybe this would be my coup de grace, and if that were to be the case, I wanted a blaze of glory that the nasties would be talking about for decades to come.

I knew the late and possibly lamented Jack Grumet, formerly of Woonsocket, had a wife. It had come up in that conversation with B, right after I'd made my first kill. Her name was Hannah. Getting her phone number was easy. A walk in the park, or two for one; choose your favorite idiom. I drove to the parking lot at India Point, there where the polluted waters of the Seekonk and Providence rivers flow into Narragansett Bay. I rolled down the Honda's window and dialed her number on Aloysius' cell, and stared at the late afternoon sun glinting off the calm blue water. It rang six times before anyone answered. Before Hannah Grumet answered.

"I'm Siobhan Quinn," I said. "I was there when your husband died."

There was quiet then. Let's toss in another idiom: you could have heard a pin drop. Well, except for the crows and the catbirds making a racket in the trees.

I heard her draw a deep breath, and the exhalation

seemed to take forever. And then she said, "The bitch-whore that murdered him. That's what you mean."

"Is that the way they're telling the tale up Swamp Yankee way?"

"Don't think this is over," she said. "Don't think I won't have my retribution."

"Re-tri-bu-tion. That's an awfully big word, Hannah. How about you just say you're gonna get even and be done with it? See, that's what I'd have said."

I'd never heard the cold, hard hiss of seething rage, but I heard it in the spaces between her words, the spaces between the syllables.

"We've got a *fine* plan for you, darling," she said.

"That a fact. And don't call me *darling*."

"Can flay a bitch like you at our leisure, keep you alive for days. Throw in a little rock salt—"

"Hey, puppy dog. You wanna hear what I got to say, or you gonna spend this whole conversation barking like a mangy junkyard cur? 'Cause if that's your plan, I'll hang up now, and you loup fucks can get back to your shucking and salting and whatever the hell torture makes inbred shits like you happy. Capiche?"

"Why'd you even call me?" she asked, and, I will admit, I was impressed how she didn't take the bait I'd tangled with all those werewolf-specific insults.

"Shut up half a minute, I'll tell you."

She sighed loudly, but she also shut up.

"Now, I didn't kill your husband. Or your mate. Whatever it is you people call each other. I was *planning* to, won't lie to you about that. But someone beat me to it."

"And who was that?" she sneered, and you've heard

how somebody's voice can "drip with sarcasm," right? Bingo.

"Vamp calls herself Mercy Brown. Or the Bride of Quiet, depending on her mood. She's the one did Jack Grumet, and, while we're at it, she's the one did me, too."

This time the silence on the other end was different. It was a shocked silence.

"You still there, puppy?"

"The Bride? So, you're a vamp?"

"Alas, I am. But it gets better. Your fella, he had just enough time to sink his teeth into my backside before Mercy laid him low. So . . ."

Another surprised silence.

"You're saying . . . ?"

"Smart puppy. That's what I'm saying. And I'm also saying I'm heading down to Exeter this evening, and when I'm done, there isn't going to be any more Bride of Quiet. No more precious little china doll of doom. And seeing how it was *her*—not me—killed Jack . . ."

"So you say."

"So I say. Seeing as how that's what happened that night by the reservoir, how he and me were *both* set up by Mercy and a certain ne'er do well calls himself B . . ."

"I know about him," she said. "You work for him."

"I'm beginning to think that's past tense. I'm beginning to think we ought to say I *worked* for him. But I'm never gonna get to the point, you keep cutting me off like that."

"I'm listening," she said.

"Way I see it, Hannah, you deserve your pound of flesh, same as me. Way I see it, I let you in on putting her in the ground once and for all, that squares us, good and even. No more vendetta. I leave the loups alone, the loups leave me alone."

"You *are* a loup," she said, and there was a note of humor in her voice.

"Again, touché. But let's not get all worried about technicalities. This offer's on the table for about the next sixty seconds. Then I go forth to do the job alone, and later you can send in the pack, and we can play who's the worst nasty in the days and nights to come. Personally, I don't give a shit. Just being polite, and I wouldn't mind the backup. Anyway, take it or leave it."

She took it. I gave her the address, and I gave her a time. I also told her not to make a move until I got there, because I was fairly certain Evangelista Penderghast hadn't put that black dagger in my hand just because I needed a compass. Vamps get that old, old as Mercy, it generally takes special tools to get the job done.

Hannah hung up first, and I sat there in my car awhile. I smoked a couple of Camels and listened to the birds. And I wondered if I was right about B, about him being my former employer and all. Sure, with the Bride out of the way, neither he nor Penderghast would have to worry about me (it was hard to imagine the molten thing below Battle Hill ever had). But B, he wasn't one for loose ends. Maybe he'd keep me around, and maybe he wouldn't. But, no matter what a fine soldier his wolfpire might make, all I could think was, *Better safe than sorry.* I could hear him saying it before putting a hallowed ash bolt or two in my chest.

Better safe than sorry. You bet.

* * *

You will, I'm sure, recall what I said about my dislike for road movies? Those interminable scenes of protagonists driving, driving, driving across some road-scape or another, slithering along highways, interstates, and back roads. Conversations as wheels whir along tarmac. So, let's just say I left Providence and followed Ten Rod Road southwest to Exeter. I've never cared for that part of the state. Something too stark, too wild. Like, maybe some old pagan mind-set still holds sway in those woods and fields, behind the crumbling drystone walls. I get this same vibe from Moosup Valley. Like, you know, those annual corn festivals maybe get all *Harvest Home* or *Wicker Man* or . . . listen to me, will you? Regularly rubbing shoulders with demons and trolls, and then getting all wigged out over the secret habits of rednecks.

But I can be embarrassed, ashamed, perplexed—whatever—by my reactions, but that don't change them, does it? The good folks of Exeter would likely take offense to how their town makes me feel, but that doesn't change nothing, either. There are places that make my skin crawl for no particular reason, and there you are, the long and short of it. Hell, I never have understood why people get freaked over spiders and snakes and the dark. To each his or her own irrational reactions. Which is not to say I have a phobia of Exeter. I don't, it's just that left to my own devices, I'd stay away from the place.

I spotted the sign for my turnoff—Purgatory Road (the Bride, her flair for the cliché and melodramatic seems to know no bounds). And . . . I just kept going. Passed right on by, heading deeper into what Lovecraft might have employed his purple prose to name "dread and shade-haunted Exeter." The afternoon was still so bright. Roll down the window and get a face full of hot air, yeah? Only twenty-five minutes, half an hour ago, I'd been at India Point, talking to that loup bitch, offering her a piece of the action.

But how long would it take the doggies to reach the address I'd given her? No goddamn idea, but I'll tell you *this* for free—right about then I was wishing for the pretty fairy tales spun by the likes of *Buffy the Vampire Slayer*, wishing for the company and backup of my own "Scooby gang." Give me a lesbian witch named Willow, and the bumbling dork who sometimes fucks up and saves the day despite himself, and an ex-vengeance demon, and, *most* of all, please give me Giles—all his wisdom in the ways of the nasties and his grimoires and mannered-bad assery. But that's the shit that can get you killed, wishing for the comfort of fantasies. Wishful thinking. Wind up some poor deluded boob like Bobby Ng. Wind up even worse off than I was that day in Exeter. You go into battle, you stay as sober as sober gets . . . and here, ha, ha, ha, case in point, we've come full circle, me stopping to shoot up by the Scituate Reservoir. Screw this. I'm talking in circles.

I went to the last place I ever thought I'd go that day, the Chestnut Hill Baptist Church and the cemetery out behind it. See, here's the place where that gang of superstitious yahoos I mentioned early on exhumed the body of a twenty-nine-year-old, way back in March of 1892. The Real Mercy Brown. The woman who was *not* a vamp.

I parked in front of the church. The day was so hot and still. I stared at the sky and cursed it for not being decent enough to offer at least a few clouds. My shoes seemed so loud on the sandy road leading into the cemetery, crunch, crunch, crunch, my LOUD vamp senses pumping up the volume. There are times I want to pop my goddamn eardrums, I kid you not. Just take a pencil or a penknife and *pop*, no more LOUD. Unless—and here's an ugly thought—maybe I'd still be able to hear afterwards.

There was a listing, broken-down sign as I entered the graveyard, a stenciled warning—NO PARKING UNLESS VISITING CEMETERY PLOT. The kids like to park out here for necking and third-base action, and I understand the place is a teenage nightmare round about Halloween. Not far beyond the sign, on the left side of the road (my left), stood one of the few trees in the place, the tall cedar that shelters Mercy's grave. The tombstone's nothing fancy, a slab of marble with dates of birth and death, just the usual. Visitors had left a random assortment of tokens lined up along the top of the stone: pennies, small stones, a pewter pin from the Newport Folk Festival. In front of the stone there was no grass at all, just a dirt patch worn smooth by long years of the feet of those who came to see. The letters engraved in the marble had become ever more indistinct as a hundred and sixteen years of rain had eaten at the stone. Another hundred, it'll likely only be an anonymous slab. But maybe I'll still be around, and *I'll* remember.

The stone was securely bolted down with iron bands and concrete to ensure some damned frat boy, goth kid, or eBay huckster wouldn't try to make off with it.

Jesus, what am I on about?

Am I stalling so I won't have to write about the shitstorm that went down outside that old house on Purgatory Road? Yeah, probably. Ask me, I've always been a coward, no matter *how* it might look from the outside.

Maybe here's the point, what I'm trying to get at: even the infamous are washed away, given time. The truly infamous *and* the falsely infamous. So, maybe one day the Bride would be only a legend, and then a whisper, and then . . . well, then nothing at all. That was the curse in my heart. I'd come to kill her, sure. But I'd also come to curse her with utter obliteration from the world. That's the worst fate you can visit upon anything "immortal," seeing how they get it in their head they'll be feared for always and forever. Take that away from them, and *presto*, check fucking mate, dude.

But, I sat down in the shade by Mercy's grave and watched the afternoon slide towards twilight. Towards the *gloaming*. That sounds more appropriate, yeah? I dug a quarter from my pocket and left it atop the stone. No one ain't a nasty deserves to have her body desecrated like she was; no one who ain't deserves that infamy.

I sat there with her, with all the others who'd escaped life the way it was meant to be escaped. Even to my ears, it was halfway quiet. Only the occasional car rushing past on Ten Rod Road, and insects in the trees, and the birds. Finally, pulled out my cell phone and I checked the time. Almost six p.m. That was a bit of a shock. I'd let much more time slide by than I'd intended. Maybe the loups had already descended on the Bride, and I'd missed the show. I half hoped that, but I was also half scared I'd missed my chance to send her to Hell myself. Anyway, I reminded myself, apparently you needed that dagger Evangelista had given me to end the bitch's misbegotten tenure upon the world. And I had that. All the loups had were jaws, and claws, and anger.

I stood up, dusted off my jeans, said good-bye to Mercy. The *real* Mercy, the actual tragedy. Maybe I'd come back and visit again one day, I told her. And then I retraced my way to the car.

So, I took a left out of the Chestnut Hill Baptist Church parking lot, and the turnoff onto Purgatory Road was so close (on my right) I almost missed it. It's a narrow road, lined with tall hardwoods and white pines that were doing a damn fine job of shutting out whatever remained of that August day. Only splashes of sun dappled the road. I was entering a cool green tunnel of trees, a narrow, winding tunnel, and maybe it would have been just a mile or so of good ol' New England scenery, fit for postcards and Robert Frost poems. Only, I *knew* what waited for me a little farther down that road, coiled like a serpent in some fetid hidey-hole. And knowing that sort of ruined the scene.

It was upon me sooner than I'd expected, that house, that house at the address Evangelista Penderghast had filed away in my head. It had clearly been something fine, before neglect and decay and the Bride had gotten her mitts on it. Before a hard-core case of entropy had taken hold. Must have dated back to the eighteenth century, that farmhouse, which had been painted a sort of cinnamon red the last time anyone had bothered painting it (and I'm guessing that had been decades before). The wide front porch listed drunkenly to one side. But that evening, if ever a house had sagged in upon itself, in every way it's possible for a house to sag in upon itself, that house had turned the trick. It looked fucking exhausted. *Just please, let me lie down and fucking die*, it seemed to sigh from every broken window and missing shingle. It had the cancers of dry rot, mold, termites, and a vampire's filth in its ancient bones, and I imagined that house must dream every night of the kindly, purifying kiss of flames.

But there was something in between me and the house, and it was the first thing that commanded my attention. Before I got a good look at the house itself, I mean. Check this shit out: sort of slewed to one side in *front* of the house, taking up the wide patch of gravel and weeds that separated the house from Purgatory Road, was a battered antique school bus. A *periwinkle* antique school bus (I remember that color from my box of Crayola crayons, not quite pink and not quite violet, but periwinkle). The bus had been gaily decorated with flowers and a rainbow, rendered with all the artistic skill of a kindergartner, and, in among the periwinkle and daisies and that rainbow, in big black blocky letters—WOONSOCKET SACRED HEART PENTECOSTAL CHURCH. The bus was filled with men and women, the scruffy vengeance I'd brought down upon the Bride with my phone call to Hannah Grumet. Most of them could still pass for human, but a few were already going wolfish. They spilled out of that cheerful periwinkle bus from both doors, and, honest injun? I thought maybe I should just keep right on driving, and not look back.

But that's not what I did.

Because, by definition, werewolves are fuckups.

And because I was angry, and because Penderghast had embedded something in this or that part of my brain that demanded I see this farce through to its bitter end.

I pulled up next to the church bus, cut the engine, checked to be sure the dagger was still in the waistband of my jeans, and got out of the Honda. I stared at the bus, and managed not to laugh; I think the sight of it was just too goddamn weird.

Okay, so far, so good, right? Right. Everything according to Hoyle, near as I could tell. Right on schedule, and here we all were, sticking to the plan.

And then . . .

"Hey!" a redheaded woman in a Narragansett Beer T-shirt yelled at me. She was standing near the front fender of the bus. I pointed at myself, and she jabbed a very long black nail at me and yelled again. "Yeah, I mean you, you fucking vamp piece of garbage! You're exactly who the hell I mean!"

Every loup eye turned towards her, and then turned towards me. I didn't have to ask if this was Grumet's widow. Anyway, I was too busy asking myself all sorts of other questions that seemed a whole lot more pressing.

"She's the one," the redheaded woman yelled. No, excuse me. By this time, she was howling, and the words were only *just* intelligible, because she was in the throes of the change. "She's the one helped kill my Jack!"

I looked at the crowd, most gone halfway to full-on

fuzzy in the time it had taken for her to start shouting at me, and every one of them was advancing on me. I knew there was no way I had time to make it back to the car. I thought I might, you know, respond to this predicament by turning wolf myself, but nope. Wasn't happening. All bristling hair, lolling tongues, snapping teeth, and . . . well, you get the picture—all of that was barreling down on me. I had maybe, I don't know, ten seconds before I was as good as undead hamburger.

Now, I know what you're probably expecting right about now. An expertly executed dance of violence, as our plucky heroine, armed only with her fists, well-aimed kicks, and a magical dagger takes down werewolf after werewolf, carving a bloody trail of fur and gristle, bone and sinew, to finally stand triumphant atop a great mound of dead loups. And maybe, if this were a film by Tarantino, or Robert Rodriquez, or maybe, let's say, someone like Zack Snyder, that's what *would* have happened. You could sit back with your overpriced popcorn and soda and enjoy the interplay of fight choreography, CGI entrails, and my body double. A regular summer blockbuster. But this *ain't* no action movie. And that's *not* what happened.

This is what happened (and if it smacks of the convenience of a deus ex machina plot device, and you're disappointed, you can blow me; it's what fucking happened).

The pendant Evangelista had given me, that brass locket on its brass chain, rose suddenly from my chest like it was being tugged at by the grandmother of all magnets. It yanked violently once or twice, seeming to want to tear itself free of the chain. And, yeah, I know brass isn't magnetic, but, magic, right? It was yanked so hard that I almost tumbled forward towards the oncoming wall of loups. But I didn't. I heard a sound that reminded me of thunder, though it was not at all the sound of thunder.

Then the lycanthropic congregation of the Woonsocket Sacred Heart Pentecostal Church, every mother's son and daughter of them, even the kids (there were a few children, pups, yeah), went up in flames. A storm of flames that engulfed them in an instant, flames licking skyward, and I was able to turn away just as the blast wave hit me. I felt myself lifted a few inches off the ground and blown across Purgatory Road, where I tumbled over one of the crumbling fieldstone walls. I lay there, listening to the screams and howls, to the roar of the fire, and, before too much longer, the dull, but almost deafening, *fwump* as the bus' gas tanks exploded. There was a second smaller *fwump*, and I guessed (*correctly*, as it turned out) that was my Honda's tank. The air reeked LOUDLY of burning flesh and hair, and chunks of flaming loup and bus rained down all around me. A damned miracle nothing hit me. My back was awash with searing pain, all that keloid scar tissue Penderghast had blessed me with not the least bit numbed to the heat that had lifted me like a rag doll and tossed me into the woods. I shut my eyes against the pain and the stink and the fading cries of dying monsters, and I felt consciousness slipping away. For a merciful while—not long, but you take what you get, yeah?—everything was dark and cool.

* * *

I didn't come to until after sundown. But it wasn't quite dark. There was still a yellow-orange flicker reflected off the trunks of the birches and maples rising up around me. I was nauseous, and everything from my shoulders on down to my ankles felt thoroughly fucking seared. A lot of my clothing had been burned away, and I stripped off the scraps that remained, and lay naked in the detritus of the forest floor. I wished for the cool soil to please, please, please swallow me up, and let me be a proper dead girl. Let me spend a hundred years with no other company but earthworms, grubs, black beetles, and nematodes. Let these trees drink me up, and wrap me in a burial shroud of roots. But I knew better. It wasn't finished here, and neither my will nor Evangelista's nor B's was gonna let me stop until I was done. That bit with the puppies going up like Roman candles, that had only been a distraction. I lay in that mat of dead leaves, in the lee of a wall built before the American Revolution, until I could lie there no longer. I stood up slowly, hurting too much to move quickly.

The scene before me would have put a big ol' grin on the face of that pyro squatting below Battle Hill. The flames had spread to the porch and roof of the sagging house.

At least, I thought, *something here gets its wish.* I climbed over the wall and stood at the edge of Purgatory Road. In places, the explosions had left the tar shiny, gummy, gone almost back to goo. I pulled off my shoes and socks (nothing looks more idiotic than a vampire crossing the street in only her socks and shoes; trust me on this), and wondered dimly where the hell the Exeter Fire Department was. People must have seen the Big Mystical Mushroom Cloud for miles around. More of Penderghast's voodoo? After all, couldn't have a bunch of hayseed do-gooders getting in the way of this avenging angel, now could you? I walked towards the husks of the Honda and the bus, taking care to avoid the sticky spots in the road. That's really all that remained of the two vehicles, charred and twisted shells. Here and there, small flames still licked from them. What was left of the melted tires was still smoldering. As for Hannah Grumet's swarm of righteous indignant loups—avenging angels in their own right, I suppose—it was no more than ash and a few bits of bone. What sort of heat is needed to reduce a corpse to ash? Fuck if I knew. I know now that crematoriums burn bodies at temps ranging from 1,598° to 1,796° Fahrenheit to get the task done. So, maybe that gives me some idea just how hot the spontaneous conflagration from the locket must have been. I walked naked through the sooty ruin of my fallen enemies, and a breeze made minute tornadoes of the ashes as I went. Whirlwinds to dance circles around me.

Here's a joke, but I won't be offended if you don't laugh. A naked vampire walks into a burning house . . .

Never mind.

That's what I did, and Evangelista Penderghast's sorcery kept the fire from touching me. It parted like the Red Sea is said to have parted for Charlton Heston. There was cool air around me, and I shivered as it caressed my burns. As the sagging house was consumed, not so much as an ember was allowed to fall upon my skin.

I was pretty sure where I'd find the Bride.

I followed what was left of a hallway to what was left of a basement door. The knob should have barbecued my palm, but it could have been ice in my hand. Even through all the smoke, I recognized the mustiness rising up from the basement. It was the place where I'd awakened on that mattress, needing a fix so badly I thought my guts might come crawling out and skip the light fantastic. The place where the china doll who called herself Mercy Brown sat on a stool and taunted me, promised me I'd be her weapon and her pet. The place where she'd taken my blood, and I'd become the creature the trolls called Siobhan Twice-Damned, Double-Cursed, undead *and* roiling with the beast. I descended the wooden stairs. The fire hadn't made it this far yet, but it wouldn't be very much longer. The house was dying all around me, and I was happy for it.

Let's not draw this out.

There she sat on her stool, dressed exactly as she'd been the last time I saw her: so small, the protruding teeth and wisps of gossamer hair, the cyanotic lips, the ancient babe dressed in a white lace pinafore, and barefoot as her executioner to be. Her long toes curled about the rails of the stool, nimble as any bat's. She was slowly clapping her hands, and smiling.

"I'm most wonderfully impressed," she said. "You truly are my child, blood of my blood."

I stared at her for a few seconds, and then I looked down at the glinting dagger of volcanic glass gripped in my hands. I don't even remember how it got there, how it wasn't lost in the explosion or when I pulled off my shredded clothes.

"Then you knew it would go this way?" I asked her.

"Of course I didn't," she replied in the high, sweet voice of the child she'd still been when she died. "I'm not clairvoyant, Siobhan. I had no idea. I only knew it would be a grand game."

"A grand game," I muttered.

"The grandest," she gleamed. Overhead, fire was quickly chewing through the floors.

The Bride sat up straight on her stool.

"And the prize is yours," she said.

"Just like that?"

"Just like that," and so maybe part of her wanted the void as much as the house she'd taken as her own and soured against any cleansing.

"There were five deaths so you could play your game." I said. "Two of my friends died. I killed them." I recall no emotion in my voice, none whatsoever.

"This is the way of our existence," she said. "Life and death, births and murders. Now, you're wasting time," and she glanced up at the glowing timbers overhead. "I think you have me in checkmate, daughter."

"Daughter," I whispered, and without another word I plunged the black dagger into her heart. The Bride of Quiet shattered precisely the way porcelain shatters. She shattered, and shards broke into still smaller shards when they hit the cement floor around the stool.

Where are you going, my pretty fair maid? Where are you going, my honey?

The dagger vanished from my hand.

A shower of flame, engulfing the basement.

I'd walked into the fire, and then I walked back out again. As soon as I was clear, the tunnel of cool air was gone, and the sagging house was permitted, at last, to collapse in upon itself.

I stepped past the shell of the loups' bus, and there was Mean Mr. B, standing by the shell of my Honda. He smiled his oily smile. He bowed a gentlemanly bow.

"What is it tonight?" I asked, raising my voice to be heard over the inferno behind me. "Your name, I mean."

"Why, Quinn, let me think on that," he said and tapped at his left temple. "Tell you what. Tonight, call me Balthazar, like the last king of Babylon."

"Balthazar," I said.

"Yes, as I have seen the writing on the wall, love, and damn if I can make heads or tails of it. She dead?"

The best I could do was nod. All at once, every inch of my body was swept with a degree of weariness I'd never even imagined. The locket and brass chain around my neck abruptly changed to quicksilver and trickled down my exposed chest and belly.

Balthazar frowned and asked, "Whatever happened to your clothes?"

I opened my mouth, but realized I didn't have the energy to explain.

"Well, I think I heard sirens," he said. "The enchantment's gone. Let's not stick around for the after party."

I think I laughed. I know I said, "The party's over."

"Oh, the party's never over, love. There's always a party somewhere." And he led me down the road to an emerald Porsche. One of his boys was behind the wheel. B helped me into the backseat, and I lay down, even though the cool leather started me shivering again. The last thing I remember before sleep overtook me is B telling the boy to head back to Providence. And as dreams of snow and ice flowed over me, I wondered how differently it might all have gone if taking out monsters *did* come with a how-to manual.

AUTHOR'S BIOGRAPHY

Kathleen Rory Tierney, despite her very Irish name, has never once left her home state of Idaho. She is a three-time recipient of the Dewda Yorger Prize in Poetry, and her verse has been collected in two volumes—*Hark! The Yaks Are at the Door Again* and *Reflections on Inevitability and Entropy.* She currently lives in a raccoon-infested house trailer in Deerfield, Illinois, where she spends her spare time collecting bottle caps and antique license plates. *Blood Oranges* is her first novel, and if there is another, no one will be more surprised than she.